FANGS AND FELONIES

K. MALADY

To everyone who thinks there *aren't* enough books with
lawyer main characters written by lawyers.
Because 90% is definitely not too many.

Also, I am a lawyer and no, this is not real lawyering.
Like at all.
Except for the stubbornness and insomnia. Those are legit.

ALSO BY

<u>THE ASCEND TRIALS</u>
YA fantasy romance adventure

<u>THE HARMONY CHRONICLES</u>
NA paranormal romance/contemporary fantasy

<u>THREADS OF FATE</u>
NA/Adult romantic fantasy retellings

<u>KNEELING KINGDOMS</u>
Adult interconnected standalone romantasy

<u>WELCOME TO THE TROPE-ICS</u>
Standalone short romantasies in varying heat levels
Interconnected world, separate stories

Chapter 1

The anticipation builds as the clock ticks closer to announcement time. It feels like I've been waiting for this moment for an eternity. Fourteen years of blood, sweat, and tears—all the late nights, missed dinners and birthdays (including my own)—has led up to this. In ten minutes, I'll finally learn whether my firm was inviting me to the partnership meeting, the last step before they picked which associates would be promoted to law firm partners.

No more grinding away in the trenches, no more worrying about putting my foot in my mouth, no more feeling like a cog in the legal machine. Nope, as a partner, I'll be calling the shots, making the moves. There's security, respect, maybe even a corner office with a view.

My assistant Liz stands in the doorway to my tiny office, looking as polished and put together as ever, a stark contrast to the chaos inside my mind. She was assigned as my assistant six years ago when I first joined Johnson & Marcus, the prestigious international law firm with twenty-six offices and two thousand attorneys scattered across the globe. Even though there's only ten associates in my branch, there are one hundred associates worldwide vying for just seven partnership openings.

"Get the email yet, Emily?" Liz asks, her voice equal parts excitement and anxiety.

"Not yet," I reply, pressing my hands against my eyes in an attempt to clear my thoughts. My fingers spread to reveal an overflowing inbox, cluttered with client emails and snarky demands from opposing counsel, but no sign of the crucial partnership notification. "You need to distract me. I can't work or think of anything else."

Liz saunters into my office and perches on one of the guest chairs reserved for clients—though none ever ventured to see me in my humble abode beside the copy room. They prefer to gather in the fancy conference rooms or the partners' corner offices.

"Well, besides the firm announcements, everyone's buzzing about the upcoming mayoral election. Did you hear one of those pro-paranormal socialists is running to primary Mayor Peterson?" She smoothes an invisible wrinkle on her crisp burgundy sheath dress and shudders delicately.

I bite back the urge to roll my eyes, opting instead to cover them with my hands. Liz might as well have been gossiping about the latest celebrity scandal for all the interest I had in politics. The paranormals are a fact of life now. Paranormals like werewolves, vampires, and ghouls have been living alongside humans since they were exposed during Prohibition in the 1920s and '30s. When the humans turned to speakeasies for their clandestine alcohol, they also discovered a hidden world of supernatural beings, originally cloaked by witches whose spells *apparently* weren't strong enough to overcome the desperation of booze-seeking humans. Since then, some 'sanctuary' cities allowed the paranormals to live in designated areas, like Chicago.

Somehow, society managed to slot the paranormals into it. Come the full moon, werewolves have their own designated safe rooms, with reinforced steel or something. Ghouls, well, they're living it up on pallets of artificial meat, the kind that's probably as close to the real deal as tofu is to steak. And vampires get donor blood from humans who've got a prescription for bloodeez, the blood replenisher. Back in the '80s, some genius cooked up this stuff to limit the need for surgical transfusions, with a nifty side effect in favor of the vamps.

Sure, there were tensions, but paranormals kept to themselves, staying as hidden as ever. It was the humans creating a ruckus, worried the paranormals were murderous boog eymen... assuming boogeymen didn't *also* exist. Honestly, people should be more worried about their own lives than what some paranormals might do. But thoughts like that are still seen as radical.

"Just because she's pro-paranormal doesn't mean she's a socialist," I say mildly, trying to keep the annoyance out of my voice. "The pro-paranormal stance has some compelling arguments. No one should be driven out of their homes and killed because of something they can't control."

Liz frowns. "I like what Frank Mitchell's saying."

I scrounge my memory to remember who that is, the synapses in my brain more focused on *my* life than the lives of random city politicians. Suddenly, Mitchell's smarmy ads run through my head. "The anti-candidate? The one who'd rather paranormals never surfaced than have to share his toys with them?" I ask, the annoyance resurfacing. "Just what we need in this city, more division."

Liz sniffs dismissively, her perfectly manicured nails tapping against the leather guest chair. "Be careful with that talk, Em. We don't want the bigwigs hearing about your bleeding heart for the monsters. We already get enough of that from Mayor Peterson."

Peterson, the master of fence-sitting. He's all about playing both sides, leaning pro-paranormal while keeping the skeptics happy. It's a funny old world we live in, with all this anti-paranormal fervor when we've only seen a handful of paranormals, anyway. Sure, everyone blames gremlin when their computer malfunctions, or succubi for a cheating spouse, but has anyone seen them? No. We're taking the ghouls' word for it, who pointed the finger at other paranormals when the government was worried over a potential zombie-style uprising in the '60s. For all we humans know, there're only three types of paranormal creatures anyway.

"And please tell me you're not recording this conversation," Liz continues. "We don't need *proof* of your radical views."

I drop my hands and confirm that my trusty tape recorder is switched off. Liz might have a point—to the first part, best not to voice my opinions on paranormal rights at work—but I only use the recorder during meetings and brainstorming sessions to ensure I don't miss any important details. Mishearing or misunderstanding an assignment could ruin my reputation at the firm. "We're good. And now we only have five minutes left," I grumble.

"Oh, sweetie. What happened to your mascara?" Liz exclaims. "You should have let me do your makeup," she scolds gently, rushing back to her desk as quickly as her five-inch heels will allow. She meets me at the small mirror behind my door where she expertly fixes the raccoon-like smudges against my pale skin. "You know you're terrible at it, sweets," she teases, reapplying my mascara that I'd donned earlier that morning.

With the looming thought of a virtual party for potential partnership picks hanging over my head, I upped my make-up, going for a 'client meeting' face rather than 'hiding in my office drafting briefs' face. I added mascara to my normal porcelain foundation and slapped on a tinted chapstick to give a subtle touch of color to my pale lips. I even wore my only on-the-rack purchased suit.

"Yes, so you've said," I grumble. "But I had that deadline this morning and couldn't ask you."

She would've tried to style my hair too, but I couldn't spare the extra hours it would take to tame my long black locks. Instead I donned my usual messy bun, what I consider my thinking cap, the ponytail of problem-solving.

As she reapplies the foundation that had worn off throughout the day, Liz's hands hover near the high collar of my turtleneck. I tense at the thought of her revealing the faded mark on my neck, inches above my collarbone. Thankfully, Liz moves on without questioning it and finishes off my face with lip liner and oddly sticky gloss.

"On the plus side," she says, capping the tube of pink lip color. "I've sufficiently distracted you. Want to check your email?"

"No need," says Mark, my direct supervisor, as he leans against the doorway. "Congratulations, Emily. You've been invited to the partnership interviews."

At six p.m., the virtual party dies down, and the staff heads home for the evening. I shut off the video after a measly twenty minutes; I had a mountain of work waiting for me, and doing any more virtual chit chat with my competitors, the only attorneys still online, might kill me.

Liz comes to see me before her husband, who works in payroll, brings their car to the front of the building to drive them to their house in the suburbs.

"Will you celebrate tonight?" she asks as she buttons her white peacoat, which won't do much against the September chill but looks stunning against her honeyed complexion.

I stare down at my phone, feeling the weight of my recent 'break-up.' My not-quite-boyfriend Brett and I called it quits two weeks ago after he met someone else. He told me he wanted commitment, rather than the barely-more-than-friends-with-benefits he had with me, and the new girl could do that. I didn't miss *him,* but the endorphin rush made the stress of work less... stressful.

"I'll do something with friends," I say casually.

Liz purses her lips, the red lipstick still bright. "I hope so. All work and no play makes Emily a dull girl."

"Hilarious," I grumble. "All work and no play makes Emily a partner."

Technically, all work and a *smidge* of play keeps me from having a full-on meltdown, but no one knows about my bi-weekly evening pastime. And without immediate access to sex and the spotlight on me until the partnership interviews, it might become my *daily* escapade.

Liz laughs and blows me a kiss before sashaying off down the hallway.

Liz's words echo in my head as I unlock my phone. Maybe she's right. Once I'm a partner, I'll need a healthier vice than my current choice. Like... drinking?

I find the 'law school classmate' group chat and tap out a message. *"Hey! Anyone free for drinks tonight? I've got work updates that need to be celebrated!"*

The gang all came to Chicago post-law school, and the alumni society reintroduced us when I moved here so I wouldn't be totally friendless in this concrete jungle.

Responses quickly flood in.

"Em! Oh my god are you actually messaging back?" That's from Brian, an environmental lawyer from the East coast who gave up his trust fund for public service. The thought still sometimes irritates me.

"EMMY! UR SUGGESTING DRINKS? IS THE WORLD ENDING?" says Megan, a bubbly private attorney working at a firm that competes with Johnson & Marcus.

Finally, Matty chimes in. *"Hey Emily! Long time no chat! Did you read any of the previous group messages before sending?"*

Twisting my lips, I scroll up-thread. Matty, an uptight Assistant District Attorney, wanted the group to hit up a basketball game tonight, and they snagged tickets weeks ago.

"Looks like I'm too late," I write. Something twists in my gut, but I can't quite pin down if it's disappointment or relief.

"No! We'll make room for you, Em! We're meeting in ten at TapCar, if you want to join before tipoff?" writes Brian.

"That's okay. I've still got work to wrap up tonight. Maybe next time," I type.

"At least tell us what you're celebrating, and we can reschedule something that works for your calendar," Brian adds.

Megan sends seven heart emojis and then writes, *"YES! INQUIRING MINDS NEED TO KNOW!"*

"Next time, we'll plan something with you and Brett," Matty signs off.

I toss the phone to the side of my desk without answering and rest my head in my hands, leaning my elbows against the glass top. The mark on my neck twinges. It's only been two days since my last hit, but I still have some bloodeez the surgeon's office accidentally overprescribed after my appendix burst last year. It's like a blood boost, good for anemics and whatnot. It slashes the need for blood donations because it kicks your system into overproducing your own blood. And is perfect for donating to vampires in need.

I glance at the clock. Sunset's in less than an hour. That's just enough time to pop a tablet and let it work its magic. I don't need to paint the town red with friends to celebrate. The rush I'll get from donating is celebration aplenty.

Unregulated blood donation was outlawed in the '70s after four people died. Now, you have to be on a special list and can only donate every two weeks under the eagle-eyed watch of a nurse who hooks you up to a blood bag and hands the vamp a funnel. No touching allowed, and no risk of overdoing it. Problem is, the vamp misses out on the warm stuff straight from the vein, and you don't get that blissful high either.

There's something in a vampire's teeth that makes you feel like you're floating when they're siphoning off your blood. I've never done drugs, so I can't compare, but the few donors I've met describe it that way. For me—everything slows down. My head gets heavy and my limbs lighter; all the chaos running through my mind suddenly clears. It's like having the best sex without the irritating need for another person.

But here's the catch: if you don't pay attention, that euphoria can turn into a nasty case of anemic shock quicker than you can say "bloodeez." Even with that stuff in your system, the vampire can feed until you're a shell. It takes some serious control from both sides to stop the draw before you die of blood loss. Luckily, I have iron-control and the coven I visit has excellent rules and boundaries to keep the donors safe.

Donating isn't addictive like drugs and alcohol, but people do lose their lives in search of the high. Like my dad, bless his misguided heart.

The first ten years of my life were me and Mom. She'd drag me along to her home health client's houses after school, but it wasn't until years later that I realized she was building her own personal pharmacy while I emptied her client's catheter bags. When she wrapped her car around a tree a week before my twelfth birthday, I got shipped off to Dad's. Dad spent his weekends having donor parties with his friend Kent. (That Kent wasn't *just* a friend was another later in life epiphany, one that made Dad's obsession with keeping Kent happy at his own expense even more tragic.)

Dad rode that high through four jobs and three apartments, Kent right beside him and me trailing behind like those sad cans tied to the bridegroom's car after a wedding. Every dollar went to cover his and Kent's black market bloodeez habit so they could keep donating. If he'd ditched Kent, we might have kept the first apartment, if not the second. And without Kent's constant demand for more donations, Dad wouldn't have hunted for quick cash fixes. He could've stuck with his sales gig instead of calling in sick every other day because Kent knew *someone* who had some scheme for fast cash. They up and vanished in the dead of night a week before I was supposed to start my junior year of high school. Aunt Bea took me in then.

I didn't blame the vampires, or even my dad for chasing that fleeting sensation of peace. The vampires are just trying to survive, and Dad—well, I appreciate the need for vices. But vices can't come at the expense of personal security. If he'd worked harder, if he'd focused on his own needs and not Kent's cravings, then I'd at least understand him. But putting all of his needs behind Kent's? That was his problem.

And Kent? How selfish could he be? If he'd spared a minute considering how to help Dad instead of keeping that tunnel vision on his next hit, maybe they'd have found a happy medium. Instead of orphaning me.

Apparently, I wasn't all that big a loss.

Chapter 2

The neon lights of downtown Chicago pulse in time with my heart. With each step through the city streets, the anticipation coils tighter in my gut, knowing I'm about to get my fix. The vampire quarter is in the Near North Side, and I decided to walk the mile from my office to the rundown park where Lucian's coven hangs out after sunset.

Decades ago, the government handed over Old Town to the existing vampire covens. Vamps *can* go elsewhere at night, but being too far from a safe spot away from the sunrise could be deadly. So, they congregate together in the nearby parks and alleys in the area before absconding inside or underground. Now, those places are their domains, and venturing into them after dark is like stepping into a whole other world.

After five years of navigating the vamp society, I'd picked up a thing or two about their ways. First, they were fiercely loyal to their chosen donors, sticking with them like glue. It had taken me three years to convince Tina to take me on, and now she timed her feeds to my schedule like clockwork. With Brett out of the picture, I'll have to sweet talk Tina into a few extra sessions while I scramble to find a replacement (for him, or a second Tina). Second, vampires lived by a strict code: one of coven hierarchy and rules that they take deadly seriously. Crossing them was like playing with fire, and I'd seen a few donors—and vamps—get burned. Other than that? I haven't quite figured out if *Dracula* is fiction or an instruction manual.

I quicken my pace, my boots clicking against the sidewalk in a steady rhythm. The cool night air feels alive, charged with an anticipation I can almost taste. Crossing into vampire territory is always a thrill, where the lines between safety and danger blurred like shadows in the moonlight.

It might also be the contact nicotine high. Apparently, being immortal means you can smoke all you want and most of them indulge.

As I round the corner into the dimly lit alley beside the park, I catch sight of Lucian leaning against the brick wall like he owns the place. And here, he does. With his back to the wall, he seems both a part of the shadow and separate from it.

His black hair falls in sleek waves, framing a face so chiseled it could rival Michelangelo's finest work. Clean-shaven and with a jawline sharp enough to make diamonds jealous, his skin holds a faint glow, as if he bathed in moonlight itself. But it's his eyes, those piercing gray orbs, that *truly* mesmerize. They're windows to centuries of secrets, depths that promised both danger and desire.

I mentally berate myself for the dramatic thoughts. I need to donate and get my 'orgasm' fix to stop sounding like I'm describing a character in a vampire romance novel.

But Lucian's gorgeousness simply *adds* to his allure. His magnetic presence also speaks volumes, radiating power and authority as the coven's leader. The chance to donate to Lucian would be like hitting the jackpot, but he wasn't one to indulge in public displays. I assume he has a lineup of willing donors in some seedy back room.

"Good evening, Emily," he says, his voice smooth as silk but carrying a weight of authority that makes my skin prickle. It's like he can see right through me, straight to the beating heart beneath my ribs and the extra blood sloshing in my veins.

"Lucian," I reply, my tone mirroring the seriousness of his. He allows donations to curb his vampires' more violent impulses, but he's otherwise not a fan. '*Too likely to bring unwelcome attention to us*,' Tina said when I'd asked. But his dislike means extra precautions, and I'm all for that.

"Careful out there tonight, Emily," he cautions, a ghost of a smile playing on his lips. "The night is young, and so are some of the predators." His gaze shifts pointedly to the shadows behind him, where I know fledgling vampires hungrily seek the opportunity to feed once they gain a modicum of control. Lucian doesn't even need magic to keep them at bay, his authority is that absolute.

I nod, trying to play it cool. "Thanks for the warning."

"Always," he murmurs.

Turning away from Lucian, I scan the park for Tina, but she's nowhere in sight. The paths are overgrown with weeds and littered with fallen branches, creating a maze of tangled greenery that seems to swallow you up as you venture deeper inside. I navigate through the throng of evening revelers, human and vampire alike, looking for a familiar face.

I finally find Stardust, the vampire who introduced me to Tina. He's a vision straight from the '70s, all sharp cheekbones and pale skin, eyes like chips of the night sky. His resemblance to the fantasy character a certain bisexual and stunning rockstar played is uncanny, right down to the mismatched pupils.

"Stardust," I greet, my voice steady despite the tremor of anticipation that dances along my nerves.

"Emily Lane, as I neither live and nor breathe," he croons, his usual smile looking more like a wince. "Girl, there are some things you need to know."

I'm too focused on my fix to waste time on whatever vampire gossip Stardust has. The *last* time he had something I 'needed to know,' it was that one of the abandoned swings had fallen down. Unimportant and not worth delaying my donation. Not when this is supposed to be my gift to myself.

"Where's Ray?" I ask instead, scanning the vicinity for his usual companion. Ray is a regular donor, his blood apparently sweetened by an unwavering loyalty to Stardust's charm. Where goes Ray, follows Stardust *and* Tina.

He blinks like I've surprised him by asking. "...Sleeping it off."

We stand in awkward silence for longer than I'd like, especially since I'm dying to donate. Stardust is giving me an oddly intent look, like I'm missing something. Normally, he says hello and then I leave with Tina.

"...Is Tina here?" I finally ask.

Stardust's tight smile fades into a thin line. "Nope."

The awkwardness returns. I don't know what he wants.

"Look, I need to donate tonight," I blurt with no pretenses. "Would you be willing to help me out, maybe direct me to someone who won't drain me dry since Tina's gone?"

Stardust flicks ash from the end of his cigarette, his gaze never leaving mine. "Tina's gone, is she?"

I swallow hard, feeling like I just walked into a trap. "I mean, you said she wasn't here."

"So, the two years with Tina was nothing doing, eh? Like you're at market and the crisps you like are gone, so you pick another?" He scoffs, tossing the cigarette towards his feet and immediately lighting another. "Why the hell would I help you do that?"

"Because we're... friends, Stardust," I say, hoping that's what he wants to hear. God knows I spend more time around this crowd than anyone else, not including my coworkers.

But instead of softening, Stardust's expression hardens even further. "Friends?" he echoes, his voice dripping with scorn. "You don't know my birthday, princess. Or my favorite song. Hell, you don't even know my real name."

"Stardust—" I start, but falter under his intense stare. Surely after five years, I could pull up his name. The answers must be buried somewhere under layers of client files and court transcripts.

"Don't know, do you?" he presses, the edge in his voice a blade against the softness of the night. "We're replaceable, like dirty needles to you, eh?"

"Don't be like that, Stardust. I..." I've always prided myself on being able to smooth-talk my way out of any situation. I try to guess, unsure why this is so important to him, throwing out names and dates, hoping one would strike true, but with each wrong answer, the tension between us winds tighter.

"Thought so." Disappointment laces his words and he turns away, the conversation clearly over, leaving me standing there with the bitter taste of rejection on my tongue and too much blood in my veins.

I loiter at the park for a minute longer, trying to shake off the sting of rejection. It gnawed at me—his sudden coldness that made no sense. I mean, two nights ago we'd been laughing about God knows what, all relaxing off the high with Tina and Ray.

But there was no time for self-pity, not when there were hungry vampires lurking around every corner. Even with their loyalty to their own donors, surely one of them could go for a feed. Scanning the area, I search out another vampire willing to accept my donation when a soft voice pierces through my concentration.

"Emily, right?" Alice, with her porcelain skin that glows beneath the moonlight and the wide-eyed innocence of a fledgling, appears beside me. Her tone is timid but carries an undercurrent of excitement. "I heard you're looking to donate."

"Hi, Alice," I say, offering a small smile to mask my relief. *Maybe my night isn't a lost cause after all.* "Yes, I am. Are... are you sure you're ready for this?"

"More than ready," she says, her fangs peeking out as she speaks. She's new to this world, her transformation still a topic of hushed conversations among the community. And something I *didn't* learn from Stardust, either. But she wasn't with the fledglings Lucian was watching, so she must be safe.

"Alright, let's find somewhere... private." My voice trembles with anticipation.

We slip into the alley, secluded from prying eyes. Stardust's eyes follow us, his mismatched gaze piercing and unrelenting as he lights yet another cigarette. But soon, the sounds of the city and its vampires fade into a distant echo, replaced by the thrumming of my heartbeat. Alice's gaze fixes on the pulse at my neck, a hunger swirling within her iridescent eyes.

I tilt my head, exposing the vein. "Go ahead."

My breath hitches as her cool lips brush against my skin. The anticipatory sensation is always surreal, a cocktail of fear and exhilaration.

Her teeth sink in gently, and a sigh escapes my lips. That first moment is a pinch, but it quickly dissolves into euphoria. The world lifts away, my body light as air, floating on an ethereal cloud of endorphins. It's a moment of pure, unadulterated bliss. I lean into her embrace, savoring the sensation as she draws more and more of my blood into her mouth. A soft moan escapes me as I drift, all my worries fading into insignificance. For a moment, nothing else matters except the intoxicating rush coursing through me.

But the serenity shatters as Alice's grip tightens, her initial restraint giving way to something sharper, deeper. *This wasn't right.*

My heart races, pounding like a battle drum. "Alice..." Panic surges through me, drowning out the sound of my voice as I struggle to break free from her grasp.

She doesn't respond, doesn't seem to hear me. The draw on my blood grows stronger, greedier, and the edges of my vision begin to blur.

Adrenaline surges, and I summon the strength to push her away from me. "Enough!" I shout.

Alice stumbles back, her features contorting into a snarl, her once-innocent demeanor replaced by something altogether more sinister. Stardust appears beside us, his presence a comforting anchor amid the fear, as he places a hand on Alice's shoulder, halting her advance.

"Watch it, Emily," he hisses.

Another half dozen vampires crowd us in the alley. The fight-or-flight instinct I'd experienced with Alice reappears. But vampires had to control their behavior, especially in public spaces. Too much attention could spell disaster for them. I heave a heavy breath to calm myself down.

"You know the rules," some unknown vampire says. "No scenes or the cops will be swarming this place."

"I know," I snap, my fingers pressing against the puncture wounds at my neck and leaning against the cool brick behind me. "She just got... carried away."

Alice, now a few feet away, looks mortified, her hands trembling as she realizes the gravity of her mistake. The small audience murmurs amongst themselves.

The air crackles with a sudden charge, the tension already high from the near-miss with Alice. Then, like a ripple through the crowd, bodies part and whispers hush to an anticipatory silence. My pulse races, not solely from the blood loss, and I know without looking who has arrived.

"What exactly do you think you're doing, Emily?" Lucian demands, his voice low and dangerous.

I press my back firmer against the brick wall, my hand still covering the tender puncture wounds. The dim streetlight throws shadows across Lucian's face, accentuating the sharpness of his jaw and the unnatural gray of his eyes.

"Lucian," I start, my voice firm despite the situation. "Alice was willing—"

"Of course she was willing!" He cuts me off, stepping closer until he towers over me. "She's a vampire, and you were offering her a tantalizing neck."

His presence is overwhelming, suffocating. But I never let rude opposing counsel intimidate me, and I refuse to let this cocksure vampire do it either. "She seemed capable enough," I retort, though doubt creeps in at the edges of my conviction when I remember his warning from only an hour earlier.

"Capable?" His laugh is devoid of humor. "She's like a child, Emily. A newly turned vampire with barely a grip on her own instincts." He leans in, the scent of ancient earth and power emanating from him. "And you should have known better."

I straighten, pushing away from the wall to stand my ground, nearly brushing my chest against his. "I didn't see any of you stepping in to stop her when she offered."

A muscle ticks in Lucian's jaw, the only sign of his controlled anger. "You've overstepped. This isn't a lark you can partake in at your leisure. It's life—our way of life—and you've put it at risk. Clearly, I have become too lax in my boundaries for allowing donations. That will be rectified immediately."

His announcement ripples through the group, and the other vampires groan. He raises a brow and they fall silent.

"Your reckless disregard for the consequences could have endangered us all," Lucian says, turning back to me with a look that had all the softness of steel. "You are no longer welcome here."

My heart falls into my chest. "What? That's not fair." My voice rises despite my efforts to keep calm. "I stopped her from going too far. Next time, I'll wait for Tina to—"

"Tina is no longer an option." His words snap like a whip.

"Why? Come on, I've been coming here for five years." I'm almost whining, but I have nothing to lose by playing coy now. "It isn't like I'm some—"

"This is not something you can argue your way out of," he continues, his gaze never wavering. "You're not one of us."

Lucian's rebuke slices through me, the bite of his words stinging my chest. I'm not a part of this place, I know that. But I'd proven myself trustworthy as a donor and Alice's mistake shouldn't be my fault. This was my one escape away from the stress of real life.

As if sensing the end of the spectacle, Lucian addresses the others again. "Cut the evening short. You know what that means. I'll be going uptown—to Sara's place."

Sara's place? The name tugs at my thoughts. Sara Harper, the mortician, a human that hangs around Lucian's coven like one of the inner circle.

"Keep out of trouble," Lucian warns the vampires, his tone taking on the timbre of an older brother rather than a ruler. He glances at me briefly before disappearing into the night.

His departure sends a signal, and the vampires disband, melting into the darkness until I stand alone on the concrete. I draw my coat tighter around me, feeling the echo of Alice's fangs and the heat of Lucian's anger. And then I walk the mile back to my car alone.

Chapter 3

The next morning finds me hunched over my desk, knee-deep in papers and surrounded by the chaos of ringing phones and bustling employees. The tip of my pen taps against the legal pad like I'm auditioning for a marching band. On the other side of the wall is the copier, rattling and whining, spewing out reams of paper. My gaze lingers on the open case file before me, but the words blur into obscurity.

Normally, the 'sounds of productivity' wash over me like a white noise machine, but my mind is far from focused today. Lucian's stern words and Stardust's unsettling intensity keep repeating in my brain.

And where was Tina? Her presence would have stopped last night's drama from being even a possibility.

Suddenly, Jeff's voice cuts through the background noise. "Did you hear about Frank Mitchell?" he asks, his tone dripping with the sound of gossip that spreads like wildfire.

I glance up to see him leaning over Sandra's cubicle, sharing the news in hushed tones. Liz is peering over the other side, eyes rapt with interest.

"Murdered," he mock-whispers, voice tinged with a salacious thrill that sets my nerves on edge. "It's not been announced publicly yet, but Sam let it slip when he came home from his shift. It happened last night. They're saying it was brutal."

"Frank Mitchell? The mayoral candidate?" Liz's reply is disbelieving, her hand fluttering to her collarbone in shock.

"Who would want to kill him?" someone else chimes in, their words sparking a volley of theories that bounce off the walls like ping pong balls.

"Anti-paranormal platform," Sandra mutters darkly. "Probably got himself on the wrong side of someone."

"Or some*thing*," Jeff corrects with a knowing look. "Sam said there were puncture wounds on Mitchell's body."

My fingers clench around my pen, the plastic threatening to snap under the pressure. I don't have time for politics, but Liz's constant chatter about local news makes escaping it almost impossible. My mind races with thoughts of the upcoming mayoral election. Mitchell's murder will ignite a firestorm of controversy, especially given his anti-paranormal stance. The city's been buzzing with anti-paranormal rhetoric, and his death will only fan the flames further. Was Mitchell's death the trigger for last night's panic? Did the coven already know about the murder and fear the backlash?

"Emily, you okay?" Sandra's voice breaks through my thoughts, her concern pulling me back to the present.

"Fine," I lie smoothly, pushing back from my desk as I grip the tape recorder that was always at my side—a lifeline in the tumultuous sea of my profession. I press stop, halting the captured cacophony of the office and the fragments of conversation about Frank Mitchell. "Just thinking about what I need to do this afternoon. You can keep talking."

I force my features into a semblance of a smile, but Liz just laughs.

"Sorry, Emily. I'll get the door, so we don't distract you anymore." She closes the door to my office, muffling conversation still happening on the other side of the wall.

I skim through the headlines on my computer screen, a mix of morbid curiosity and a lack of streaming services driving my search. Reality TV has nothing on the drama unfolding in the news, especially when it might shed light on why Lucian showed me the door from his coven. The articles blur together, a mess of political rhetoric and grim speculation, until one headline freezes me in place: "Local Businessman Frank Mitchell Found Dead, Vampire Coven Leader Lucian Belmont Arrested."

The screen shows a midnight image of Lucian, surrounded by cameras and handcuffed. I try to picture him at the scene of the crime, his usually composed demeanor shattered by a moment of primal hunger. Despite his refined façade, he's still a vampire. Memories of our terse exchange last night swirl in my mind, his sharp gray eyes flashing with an intensity that was unsettling, even for a vampire. But the image captured by the flashing cameras reveals not defiance, only resignation.

The website blinks with a pop-up. "LIVE PRESS CONFERENCE ON MITCHELL MURDER" flashes across the screen. I quickly click on it.

Mayor Michael Peterson appears, standing behind a lectern against the backdrop of City Hall. He looks tired, his short black hair unruly as though he hasn't slept all night. A hush falls over the crowd as he clears his throat, his green eyes scanning the gathered reporters.

"Ladies and gentlemen," he begins, "esteemed members of the press, and concerned citizens of our great city, I stand before you today with a heavy heart, mourning the tragic loss of Frank Mitchell, a well-known businessman and candidate for mayor. Though we were opponents, I respected his opinions and platform. These recent events have cast a shadow over our community, and we must come together in solidarity during this difficult time." His voice, tinged with solemnity, booms through the speakers. The camera pans to the side, revealing an older woman in pearls. Two glinting hair pins peek out of her styled hair. She sniffs audibly into a lace handkerchief.

"My deepest sympathies go out to Frank's family and loved ones. Their loss is immeasurable, and our thoughts and prayers are with them during this difficult time. However, let us not turn a blind eye to the broader context in which this tragedy occurred. In recent days, our city has seen a surge in violence, not only against our human citizens but also against the paranormals who live among us."

A murmur ripples through the crowd as his words hang in the air.

"Just two days ago, we witnessed the senseless killing of a vampire, a member of our community, at the hands of misguided protesters. Such acts of violence cannot be tolerated, but neither can the actions of those who provoke them. I hope that with the northside vampire coven's leader behind bars, further violence will not occur."

"Who was killed?" I mutter with raised brows. My fingers hover over the keyboard, poised to switch tabs and do a search. But Peterson's expression shifts, his gaze hardening with resolve, and I stay glued to his screen.

"As your mayor," he continues, "I am committed to ensuring the safety and well-being of all our citizens. Tensions are running high, fueled by fear and uncertainty. However, we must also acknowledge the legitimate concerns of our human population. We cannot allow ourselves to be blinded by political correctness or naïve idealism. We must confront the harsh realities of our society and take decisive action to protect the interests of our citizens.

"In the memory of Frank Mitchell, let us strive to build a city where all can live in safety and security, free from the threat of violence. Let us work together to address the root causes of these issues and to forge a path forward that benefits us all."

Reporters shout questions the moment his voice fades.

"Dammit," I hiss. Who knows what that will mean for the coven now? A voice reminds me that it doesn't matter, because I'm not welcome back. Another voice tells me that I'd tried to call them friends last night, and I should care. A third voice tells me to stop talking to myself.

"Emily? Earth to Emily Lane." Liz's voice cuts through the fog of my thoughts, her tone laced with amusement and a touch of concern. She stands beside my desk, one hand resting on her hip, the other waving in front of my face to snatch back my wandering attention.

Quickly, I close the browser, erasing all evidence of my interest in Frank Mitchell's murder and Lucian's coven. "Sorry, Liz. My mind took a minor detour."

"Clearly," she says, her curly red hair bouncing as she tucks a loose strand behind her ear. "But now that I've reeled you back in, spill the beans—what kind of name is Stardust?"

I blink, caught off guard by the mention of that name. "Stardust?" *As in vampire Stardust? Or did the dearly departed rockstar decide to haunt me?* After last night, I wouldn't mind the impossibility of the latter.

"Some girl said she was a mutual friend of Stardust." Liz leans against my desk with a grin that doesn't quite reach her green eyes. "Says you'd know who she meant and be willing to meet."

"Who is the girl?" I ask, my mind racing with possibilities.

"Sara Harper. I did a quick check on her," she confides, her voice dropping to a conspiratorial whisper. "Turns out she's a mortician who caters to the paranormal crowd. Weird, right?"

I reach for my trusty tape recorder, seeking solace in its familiar presence as my fingers trace its well-worn buttons. "Stardust is the nickname of a friend from law school. He must've given her my name for some legal advice," I lie, hoping to deflect any further probing. "I don't know why, though."

"From law school?" Liz echoes. "I thought it might have been a prank, her trying to get in with any attorney she could. You know how crafty those paranormals and their friends can be."

I inwardly cringe, realizing I missed a golden opportunity to get out of this without suspicion. "Well, she might not end up as a client after all," I say, trying to keep my tone unconcerned.

"Let's hope not," Liz agrees, her delicate shudder a testament to her unease.

"But Stardust is... a friend," I add, emphasizing the word. "Go ahead and schedule the meeting."

"Consider it done. I'll slot her in fifteen minutes before the Jenkins call, so you've got an easy out," Liz promises, shooting me a sly wink before bustling off, her presence fading into the busy hum of the office.

"Thanks, Liz," I call after her, grateful for her quick thinking. But as I reopen the browser to the image of Lucian's arrest, a knot of apprehension forms in my stomach. Meeting with Sara to discuss anything 'paranormal-related' after last night's debacle can't be good for me *or* my partnership chances.

The conference room door clicks shut behind me, sealing me in with a woman wearing a lace black dress fit for a funeral. She's young, with platinum hair cascading around her russet brown face like a veil. Her hazel eyes, lined with heavy black eyeliner, narrow at my appearance.

Once I'm seated, she juts out her hand to shake, revealing muscular forearms. Her skin is soft and cold, like the steel of a mortuary slab. Then her fingers return to the manila envelope she brought with her, fidgeting against the sharp edges.

"Ms. Harper," I say, retrieving my tape recorder and setting it on the table. With a click, I start recording. "How can I help you?"

She shifts in her seat and the faint scent of chemicals wafts towards me. "Ms. Lane," she begins, her voice low and deliberate, "I need your help to clear Lucian's name."

A pang of fear hits my gut. "You know I'm not a criminal lawyer," I say. "I deal with human civil litigation, not even paranormal defense." As far as I know, there isn't any such specialty.

Sara slides the folder across the polished mahogany of the table, her movements precise and deliberate. "Look at this," she insists, her eyes drilling into mine.

Frowning, I crack it open, grateful for the excuse to avoid her intense gaze. Inside are glossy photos and sterile reports that smell faintly of antiseptic and ink. The images are stark, clinical, showing a body ravaged by what appeared to be gruesome puncture wounds. I squint at the notes, the meticulous measurements and diagrams that document each opening with dispassionate detail.

"See here?" Sara jabs a manicured finger at an enlarged photo, where the ragged punctures on Mitchell's neck stand out against now-pale skin. "These aren't Lucian's marks. He's meticulous. All his coven is. Two punctures, clean and precise, not this... butchery."

I lean closer, my recorder forgotten beside me, drawn into the grisly scene. With a fingertip, I trace the outline of the wounds. Sara's right; they're chaotic and messy, overlapping in ways that speak of frenzy rather than the controlled feeding habits of a vampire. My hand involuntarily moves to touch the covered marks on my neck, remnants of the encounter with Alice. Even her ferocity didn't leave behind this level of devastation, just slightly jagged bite marks. Whoever went at Mitchell's neck was violent.

"Could be *another* vampire though," I suggest. "One of his, and he's taking responsibility."

"Mitchell barely lost a drop, only what you see here. He bled out at the scene." She leans closer, conspiratorial now.

"What the hell kind of vampire doesn't suck someone dry? I mean, if they're committed to murder, why not drain the tank?"

I stare back down at the macabre photos. "The books say werewolves, ghouls, gremlins, and even fairies like to bite too," I murmur, more to myself than to her.

"Lycanthropes and ghouls, *maybe*," Sara counters. "But fairies and gremlins wouldn't leave behind this... carnage. But what matters is that vampires, that *Lucian* wouldn't do this," she says, sounding resolute. "You've spoken with him. You've seen how he leads, how he cares for his people. Would he risk exposing them all for... for what? A wasted feed and more paranormal deaths?"

She's not wrong about Lucian's outward persona. Charismatic and brilliant. But beneath the surface, what lay coiled in the ancient depths of his being? I *had* spoken with him, only pleasantries until the argument last night. Had I not been still dazed from donating, I probably would have peed myself in fear when he was towering over me. I swallow hard, tasting the bitter tang of uncertainty.

"Even if I believed you," I say, pushing the folder away with a shaky hand, "taking this case could destroy me. My career, my reputation—it's all on the line."

"Isn't justice worth the risk to your career?" Sara asks, her voice steady even as her eyes burn with emotion.

Not when it's all I have. "Lucian could still be guilty," I say, half to Sara, half to the ghosts of ambition that always haunt my thoughts. "I'm sorry, Sara. I can't do it. I can't take this case."

"Can't or won't?" Her question is sharp.

"Both," I admit reluctantly. "It's not my practice. And even if it was... it's too much of a risk. If I defend Lucian and fail, if he is guilty, it won't just be a case lost. And even if he is innocent, with the politics around paranormals lately... it could destroy everything I've built."

"Everything you've built?" Sara's eyes darken, the hazel irises flickering with a storm of emotions. "What about what Lucian stands to lose? His life, Lane. His existence hinges on your 'reputation.'"

I flinch at the raw edge in her voice, at the accusation clinging to each syllable. "I can find you a list of names of lawyers that practice criminal law and might be willing to represent paranormals."

"Fuck that." She spits the words out like a curse. "You were our best bet since you're the only lawyer that hangs out at the park."

I recoil at the implication, anxiety surging through me. "Please, keep that to yourself. Unless..." The walls feel like they're closing in. "Are you threatening me?"

"Of course not," she snaps. "Because *I* have integrity."

Her words sting, leaving me reeling. But she isn't finished. She leans across the table, her face inches from mine, her voice a venomous whisper. "I thought Stardust had it wrong. But you're a user. Literally."

Then she rises, folder tucked under her arm, her movements fluid and charged with a silent fury. Her hand rests on the handle. "By the way," she calls back to me, sounding casual now. "Not that you ever asked, but the vampire that died two days ago was Tina." And with that parting shot, she storms out of the room.

Chapter 4

The morning sun spills through the vertical blinds, slicing shadows across my desk where a neat stack of documents awaits review.

Today is a big day: Mark invited me to join a meeting with a VIPC, a very important potential client. He didn't tell me who, but being in the room with him doesn't matter who the person is. That's another benefit of partnership: firm clients. I'm not so great at rainmaking business myself. Too blunt, too desperate, too whatever, so I've been told. Being able to cash in on the company cow? Yes, please.

My heels thud softly on the carpet as I walk towards my mirror. A thick layer of foundation attempts to mask the sleepless night's toll on my face. I'd tossed and turned, thoughts swirling about Tina, Stardust, Sara, and Lucian.

Tina's death in particular lingered like a ghost in the room, casting a pall over my nighttime groove. I've known her for years, but our relationship was always rooted in necessity rather than genuine connection. And yet, her absence now leaves a strange void in my routine, my hard-fought connection to the vampires gone. Unless I risk it all for Lucian.

I've spent years busting my butt at work, clawing my way up the ladder. If I stick my neck out for Lucian, my career would be deader than he is. It isn't like I can do something special, I'm just a random lawyer. Any lawyer in Illinois could help if they pushed past the risk to their *own* reputation.

"Emily Lane," I tell the reflection, continuing my usual one-sided conversation with myself since I didn't have other people to talk to. "You made the right choice and today you'll prove it."

A knock interrupts my pep talk. Liz peeks in, cracking the door. "Mark's ready for you in conference room A. I tried to pry the client's name out of Jenny, but she's tight-lipped."

I smooth down the creases in my shirt. "Thanks for trying."

"Oh," she adds, frowning. "Jenny said Mark invited Stuart too."

Stuart is another associate, one who'd been at the firm longer than me, doing estate law. According to Jeff and his gossip network, Stuart's been throwing shade my way, jealous I was picked for the next round of partnership interviews and he wasn't.

"Fantastic," I mutter.

"But you look great," she says, green eyes scanning me up and down. Her lips twitch when her inspection gets to my hair in its usual ponytail. She pats one of my fly-aways down and then bustles me out of my office.

I enter the room after Mark. Stuart's already there, at the head of the table. He shoots me a smug smirk, likely hoping to make me squirm.

Thankfully, we don't have to wait long for our visitor. The door opens, revealing a woman draped in black, her face obscured behind a veil held in place with two ornamental hair pins. She clutches a handkerchief tightly in one sienna hand, knuckles tight against the dark fabric. Even before the receptionist introduces us, I immediately know who she is—Frank's widow, the woman I saw on TV during Peterson's press conference.

"Mrs. Mitchell," Mark says, guiding her to her seat. The chair seems to swallow her whole, dwarfing her compact frame. "I've brought two of our best associates to join the team, assuming you'll have us." He gestures to Stuart. "This is Stuart Walsh, our estate guru."

Stuart stands and shakes hands with Mrs. Mitchell. Now I get why Stuart is here. Mrs. Mitchell likely needs someone to probate Frank's will. But that doesn't explain my presence.

Mark turns to me. "This is Emily Lane, one of our best civil litigators."

"Mrs. Mitchell?" I offer, standing and extending a hand.

"Please, call me Margaret," she says, her voice barely above a whisper, her eyes full of sorrow. "Thank you for agreeing to represent me," she begins, dabbing at the corners of her eyes. I notice the tremble in her fingers, the way she clings to the handkerchief.

"Of course," Mark says, his voice oozing with charm and empathy. "We're terribly sorry for your loss. Please know that we're here to help you in any way that we can."

"Night or day, rain or shine," Stuart adds, slick as an oil spill and just as slimy.

Margaret nods, her voice trembling as she speaks. "Thank you. Frank... he didn't deserve this. He was a good man, a loving husband. We had twenty-five wonderful years together. He was my rock, my confidant. Our marriage was... perfect."

"Now," Mark continues. "I understand you're seeking legal representation for the probate of Mr. Mitchell's estate, as well as potential litigation against the vampires responsible for his death?"

Margaret nods again, her eyes flashing with determination. "Yes. Them and *Peterson*," she spits, "that bleeding heart mayor. I want justice for Frank. Those bloodsuckers took him from me, Peterson helped with his loose paranormal policies, and they all need to pay."

I watch Margaret's face closely, noting the flash of anger that crosses her features. She may have looked grief-stricken a moment ago, but now there's steel in her eyes. As if sensing my scrutiny, she turns towards me, and for a split second, our gazes lock. In that moment, there's a spark of something else entirely, beyond grief or anger—a glint of calculation.

"Of course, that's what we're here for," Mark chimes in. "Emily, what are our options?"

I lean forward, my heart pounding in my chest. If I take this case, I wouldn't just be ignoring Lucian's plight, I'd be adding to it.

"Margaret," I begin, keeping my tone steady even as butterflies perform acrobatics in my gut. "I understand your desire for justice, but we need to be realistic about the situation. The vampires, they... they have limited rights. They're not considered full citizens, and the laws that apply to them are ... complicated." We've never done a paranormal case either, but I'm not about to admit that in front of a potential client.

Stuart scoffs. "Translation: she can't sue them."

If Margaret leaves, at least Stuart will be the one getting blamed for losing the client. I shoot him a glare, my jaw clenched. "That's not entirely accurate, Stuart. It's just... more challenging."

Mrs. Mitchell looks between us, her brow furrowed in confusion. "But... but they killed my husband. There must be something we can do?"

Mark clears his throat, drawing everyone's attention back to him. "There are legal avenues we can explore, Mrs. Mitchell. It won't be easy, but we'll do everything in our power to seek justice for Frank."

"We'll leave no stone unturned," I tell her, eager to make up for my *own* blunder in this meeting. "You have my word on that."

Margaret offers a grateful smile, her shoulders sagging with relief. "Thank you, all of you. I want to make sure Frank didn't die in vain."

"In fact," Mark says, "Emily will start researching the possibility right now. She's the best attorney to have on your side."

I sneak a glance at Mark. I don't want to get kicked out of the meeting once I just got in the room, but he nods encouragingly. Even Stuart looks like he licked a lemon, irritated with the compliment Mark gave me.

I push back from the table, snatching my tape reporter. "I'll get you something concrete by this afternoon," I promise.

I leave the conference room, the door closing behind me with a soft snick.

"This is Frank's will," I hear Margaret say, before I get too far from the door to learn anything else.

I zip through the maze-like hallways of my law firm, itching to dive into my research because I'm not staying late tonight. Instead, I've got plans to make up for the disaster from two nights ago. I set up drinks with the law school gang yesterday, hoping to find a new vice now that Lucian's kicked me out of the park. Though, with his recent arrest, maybe I'll be able to donate again.

I cringe inwardly. Better not stir up *that* hornet's nest after my dealings with Sara yesterday.

Once I'm safely ensconced within the sanctuary of my office walls, I dive into my research.

I wasn't kidding when I told Mrs. Mitchell that the law applied oddly to paranormals. I've never looked into it before, but heard enough at various conferences to give me an idea. There have only been a handful of paranormal-human cases, mostly minor annoyances and nuisance cases. I suppose it makes sense there'd be so few. Paranormals hid from us humans for centuries. They're probably experts at avoiding situations ripe for lawsuits. Lucian ran his coven with the militaristic precision of, well, a military. Special rules to avoid attention, enforcing donor limits, the whole shebang. Which makes him being the one caught up in this extra weird.

The first snag for Mrs. Mitchell is figuring out what yardstick to use to measure them. They're not people, so we can't judge them by human standards for liability. We humans don't let each other get away with hurting one another, but for vampires, it might be in their blood, literally. Instinct they hold back. But here's the real kicker: say you do sue a paranormal and win, how do you collect your damages? None of them have bank accounts. Vampires might have property in their names, but since they're legally dead, how do you prove title?

By the time the afternoon winds down, I've given Mark a few brainstorming ideas on how someone might hold a vampire accountable for wrongful death, and I've got a splitting headache pounding behind my eyes. Ah, the joys of legal research.

I meet up with Megan and Brian at a nearby bar. Megan, the perpetually over-exuberant, greets me with a hug that threatens to crack my ribs, while Brian flashes a weary smile from his place by the door, his auburn hair flashing pink in the bright light.

The place is dimly lit, with a faint smell of stale beer clinging to the air. The jukebox in the corner blares out some classic rock tunes, drowning out our conversation until we settle into a booth in the back.

"Sorry about Matty, Em," Megan says after she's shotgunned her first beer. She lifts a blue fingernail that looks gorgeous against the dark umber of her skin tone, signaling to the bartender for another round.

Matty couldn't come, too last minute. '*Some of us are planners, Emily,*' he'd texted yesterday, '*and can't indulge in whims. But pour one out for me, anyway.*'

'*Live a little,*' I'd texted back, adding a winking emoji he ignored.

I lick a dab of foam from my lips. So far, alcohol is *not* a great replacement for donating blood. "It's cool. It *was* last minute. And I could tell I pissed him off with the thing from a few nights ago."

"O.M.G., you should have been there," Megan chirps. "Matty had to leave in the third quarter because of some emergency. He was going to flip at his meticulously detailed schedule getting derailed."

I huff a laugh. "Why did he leave? Calendar convention get rescheduled?"

Megan leans forward. "So, you know about that Mitchell murder?"

I nod. I can't *escape* the Mitchell murder at this point.

"Matty got called in to get an indictment written *that* night," Brian says after taking a swig of his beer. "The Mayor apparently called his boss and demanded it."

"Matty went with the police to the presiding judge, too," Megan continues, pursing her lips, painted a matte blood-red. "They got the warrant *and* indictment out within an hour of finding Mitchell's body."

"It was a busy evening, that's for sure," Brian adds with a wry grin, his ruddy cheeks dimpling around his freckles. "None of my cases ever start and end that fast. All done by 10:00p.m."

"It's not *finished*," Megan counters. "They still have to actually do the trial."

"Do we give trials to paranormals?" Brian asks, frowning.

But my mind is stuck on what Brian revealed. "Did you say it was all done by 10:00p.m.? That's fast."

Megan tosses her black braids and signals the bartender for another round. "His wife found him when she got home from dinner and the police and DA were called immediately."

My demeanor shifts from casual inquisition to invested intensity. "And they figured out it was L—the vampire that fast too?"

Brian shrugs. "They found a cufflink with his family crest on it. Plus, witnesses saw someone matching his description lurking around the area right before."

Megan nods in agreement. "Yeah, and apparently there were some... other things found at the scene." She discreetly gestures to her teeth and mimes a vampire bite. "Nothing concrete, but enough to build a case."

My mind races, trying to piece together how they could have tied Lucian to the crime scene without DNA or blood evidence. It sounds flimsy, but with what I've learned about paranormal laws, Lucian's as good as fried. Not simply from the sun, that is.

But the timeline didn't make sense. I was with Lucian from 7:30 until at least 9:00 p.m. Unless he murdered Mitchell, left the so-called evidence, was seen by witnesses, and came back all between the sunset at 7:00ish and me seeing him in the alley. If only I'd paid more attention to the file Sara brought me, then I wouldn't have to deal with these doubts.

I run a finger over the rim of my drink, trying to appear casual. "What was the time of death, if they know?"

Brian and Megan exchange a glance. "Matty said it was between 7:45 and 8:00 p.m., based on when the wife found the body and the coroner showed up," Brian answers.

"Why does it matter?" Megan asks, her brows furrowed behind the rims of her thick tortoiseshell glasses.

My stomach drops like a lead weight. Lucian *is* innocent. I was with him then, all the vamps were.

"It doesn't. Just curious," I manage, the words scraping against the dryness in my month. I chug my drink, letting the bitterness coat my throat until I can talk without croaking out in alarm. Now I just need to get through the night without having a panic attack over what I've learned. "Work's been so busy lately and you know I don't have any streaming subscriptions, so this is like my TV."

Brian nods, apparently appeased. "True. You're basically a monk with how you never do anything fun."

I smother a snort. Monks don't donate blood to vampires, but they don't know about my illicit dealings.

"Not a monk," Megan says, elbowing me. "A miser."

"Subscriptions are expensive," I mutter, glad for the conversation switch.

"But you're working for Johnson & Marcus," Brian says teasingly, winking his brown eyes. "Aren't you earth-killers all richies?"

Megan jumps in her seat, grabbing my and Brian's shoulders. "Oh! Em, you were going to tell us your good news at work!"

I take the conversational lifeline, and the night continues. The noise of the bar fades into the background, replaced by the implications of what I've learned.

Chapter 5

I convince the gang I need to head home early to prepare for some partnership things tomorrow morning. Which I *do*, but that isn't why I need to leave.

Instead of hoofing it back to my car, I find my feet taking me towards vamp territory. The shadows swallow me up as I turn towards the park.

With Lucian behind bars, the park feels more desolate than ever. I scan the area, searching for any sign of movement. It says something about his leadership that things aren't running wild with him out of the picture.

I finally spot Stardust draped on a park bench.

"No Ray again?" I ask as I close the distance, working hard to keep my voice level despite the swirling mix of nerves and guilt in my stomach.

He flaps a hand in the air. "No nobody in the quarter. No donors, no music, no fun. Not with Lucian gone." His voice is silk wrapped around steel wool, a casual indifference that doesn't quite reach those sharp eyes. He sits up like he's coming out of a coffin in one of those old-school vampire movies, fixing me with his mismatched gaze. "No Emily Lane, too, if you don't catch my meaning."

"Public park, Stardust," I remind him.

He arches a glittery eyebrow in acknowledgement. "Fine. Why are you here?"

Before I can answer, another vampire melts from the shadows behind him. He's straight out of a Hollywood casting call, all chiseled jaw and muscle, with a blond haircut that probably has its own stylist. Underneath the grouchy scowl appears to be a pretty face.

"You alright, Richard?" he drawls, his eyes locked on me.

Stardust rolls his eyes. "Fine, Severin. This is Tina's old donor. I'm telling her where to go," he says, punctuating his statement with a crude gesture.

Severin nods slowly, his gaze lingering on me like he's sizing me up. "Alright. Finish up. You're on south quadrant watch from 2300 until sunrise."

"Aye aye, Cap," Stardust says.

Severin shoots me one last intense look before disappearing into the shadows like a ghost. Which *don't* exist. Or, at least, they haven't come forward yet.

"Who was that?" I ask, squinting into the darkness where Severin had vanished.

Stardust snorts, his frustration palpable. "Thought you were a friend to the vampires. And you don't even know who Sev is?"

"I said I was your friend," I mutter petulantly. "*Richard.*"

"Listen, I've got another twenty minutes of wallowing in self-pity before I'm roped into Sev's irritating paramilitary game. At least Lucian never made us *guard* the quarter. What've you got to say?" Stardust says, crossing his arms over his chest like a barricade.

I brace myself, ready for the verbal onslaught. "I need to talk to you about Lucian."

"You had your chance to talk about him, when Sara had that harebrained idea after his arrest," he fires back. "You think you can strut in here and expect us to give a damn about what you've got to say?"

"I know I messed up. I'm not here to ask for forgiveness. But here me out. The murder happened while Lucian was here that night, with all of you as witnesses. He's got an alibi."

The brief flicker of interest in his gaze dims almost instantly. He pushes off the bench and stalks towards me, his movements like a predator. My heart starts thumping like a jackrabbit.

"You don't get it, do you?" he growls, his voice low and menacing. "Vamp rights are so limited that we can't be alibi witnesses. We can't sign affidavits or testify in court. We're invisible in the eyes of the law."

Defeat settles over me like a heavy cloak. I hadn't gotten that far in my research today to discover what Stardust revealed. Ironic that this new knowledge would help in any lawsuit Mrs. Mitchell might bring against Lucian. "There has to be something," I say. "He was *literally* not there."

"Emily, darling." He drawls my name like it's fine wine gone sour. "There is something the *human* who was with us could do, giving Lucian a chance in court. But she told us to take a hike yesterday." His tone leaves no room for discussion, his closing argument. "Now, I'll return the favor. Take a hike, Emily." With that, he turns away, back towards his solitary park bench.

"I'm sorry about Tina," I call, but he doesn't so much as acknowledge me.

I pace back and forth in my tiny apartment, trying to puzzle through what I should do. I pride myself on my decision-making skills. I've tackled some tough ones in my day. Go to law school, go to med school? Law school, easy. My bedside manner would fit best in the morgue. Move to Chicago or return to my hometown with Aunt Bea? Sorry Aunt Bea, Chicago's pizza is better. Order takeout for the third night in a row or attempt to cook? My fire extinguisher was expired, so cheap food delivery it was. Splurge on fancy coffee at the cafe down the street or stick to the office's never-ending, but subpar, brew? Quantity over quality, I always say.

Okay yes, those last two make me sound like the miser Megan thinks I am. But they were tough!

Although this decision puts the others to shame. I'm not a monster. (No pun intended.) But can I really risk my entire career for a vampire? A hot, but grouchy, one? The thought alone makes me break out in a cold sweat.

I sink onto the couch. On one hand, helping Lucian could mean the end of everything I'd worked so hard for. But would turning my back on him make me no better than Kent who dragged Dad around?

In the end, I know there's only one choice to make. Whether or not it's career suicide, I can't stand by and watch an innocent man—vampire or otherwise—go down for a crime he didn't commit.

I snatch my phone from my jeans pocket, dialing a number I've never called outside office hours. My eyes close tight as it rings and is answered.

"Hello?"

"Matty," I say with resignation. "We need to meet."

Matty snarls at the other end of the line. "Jesus Christ, Emily? Do you know what time it is? I thought someone had died!"

"Can I buy you coffee tomorrow morning? At that place off Washington that Megan is always talking about? By your office?"

"Fine," he says gruffly. "I'll pencil you in for 6:30 a.m."

I wince. "Great, see you then."

You'd better be worth this, Lucian.

The coffee shop Megan is obsessed with is tucked away around the corner from the District Attorney's office. Inside is a mishmash of mismatched furniture and a hodgepodge of knick-knacks that look like they were rescued from a garage sale. Not somewhere I'd expect the DA or her minions to frequent.

The place is bustling this early, and I try not to imagine what kind of people are 'usuals' before the sun rises. Morning people: yuck. Behind the counter, a tattooed barista with a nose ring and two sleeves of ink pours steaming cups of caffeine like she's conducting a symphony. She flashes me a bright smile as she hands over a cup to a bleary-eyed customer who looks like he hadn't slept in a week. After my nights tossing and turning, it's like looking into a mirror.

A chalkboard behind the counter lists an array of quirky drink specials with names like "Caffeine Kick" and "Espresso Explosion," each one promising to jolt you awake faster than a defibrillator. I pick Espresso Explosion for myself, and order a boring black coffee for Matty. I don't know his order by heart, but it seems to fit.

I huddle in a corner booth, our orders cooling in my hands, watching the clock slowly tick by. Matty lumbers through the door the second the clock hand hits 6:30 a.m. Although he still looks put together and clean-cut as ever, there's a new bleariness in his honey-brown eyes and sleep lines against his olive skin.

"Emily," he says, taking the offered cup and downing more than half of it before he sits down. I smother a smirk that *he's* not much of a morning person either.

"Thanks for seeing me on short notice," I say.

He grunts, still nursing the cup. He finally drains it and eyes my own concoction greedily. Biting back a sigh, I push it towards him with a finger. Once he's finished *my* coffee too, he leans back in his chair and shakes away the few short brown strands of hair that fell over his eyes.

"What's up?" he asks gruffly.

My eyes dart around the shop. "I need to talk to you about the Mitchell murder," I whisper, my voice barely audible over the hum of conversation around us.

Matty's eyes furrow. "What about it?"

"I know the coven leader didn't do it. I... was with him at the time."

Matty's mouth drops open like his jaw broke in half. He tries a few times to say something, but nothing comes out.

I barrel on. "He was in that vamp park, you know, the one with the weird cat statue, from 7:30 until at least 8:30 p.m. or later."

Finally, he finds his voice. "That's where you went when you wouldn't meet us for drinks before the game? What the *hell* were you doing there?" His gaze darts to my still covered neck. Luckily in the odd September cold front, my turtlenecks are both fashion-forward *and* great camouflage.

"Did you..." he starts to ask, but fumbles like he can't even say the words.

I'd practiced this part. No use getting myself locked up in jail with Lucian. "I was looking for a... friend who hangs out around there. I finished work and planned on seeing him since you all were busy, but couldn't find him. Ray. You don't know him. He's not a lawyer."

Matty gives me a long piercing look, like he's looking for the lie written on my forehead. "But the *park*?" he finally says, resigned.

"It's public property," I say primly. "And that's not the point. I saw the coven leader when I arrived, and he was there the entire time I was walking around. He needs to be released."

Matty leans back in his chair, looking like I'd smacked him across the face with a semi truck. Finally, his expression hardens. "It won't change anything. We have the evidence to put him at the scene and Mayor Peterson wants this handled quickly," he says, his voice low but resolute. "You can testify if you want. You'll probably be the only thing the defense will have. But unless there's another murderer that presents himself, Lucian is it."

My heart sinks like a stone in my chest. I figured this would be enough. I'd sign a little affidavit, put a heart over the 'i' in Emily, and then Lucian would walk free. I could explain away the affidavit at work and we'd all go off, separately, into the sunset.

"Look, Emily. I believe you probably saw him," Matty adds. "But the media frenzy surrounding this case is already out of control. We need a target, and Lucian is it. The Mayor is adamant about it. I had to get an indictment at 9:00—"

"Yeah, that same night. Megan said," I say, my thoughts racing. *I suppose I could testify.* "Who are the witnesses that put him at the scene?"

He frowns, from my interruption or the question. "Two of Mitchell's associates. Not the most... trustworthy. Their rap sheet is a mile long, each. If we didn't have a paranormal on the other side, I don't know that I'd risk their testimony."

Which means mine would be as credible as a nun's in comparison.

Matty must sense where my thoughts are heading, because he adds, "But with the cufflink, the wounds, and the new fervor against paranormals, even if you had a timed recording of Lucian with you during those hours, they'd still likely convict."

I huff an irritated laugh, the irony not lost on me. I could have easily recorded our conversation if I had turned on my trusty recorder. *But who in their right mind tapes their own illegal activities?* "My testimony wouldn't help at all?"

He shakes his head, his expression grave. "They'd paint you as the same monster he is, but worse because you're willingly conspiring with paranormals."

Frustration surges through me, and I clench my fists before releasing them on the table with a defeated thud. "That really blows."

"I mean, you tried. That's better than a lot of other people. He likely murdered a man, your alibi notwithstanding. But he's a vampire," Matty says, his tone softening. "If we're wrong about his guilt, if the real murderer is still out there, then... it's not a big loss."

I offer him a tight smile. "Thanks for... letting me know, I guess."

He stands, grabbing our empty cups. "Good to see you, Emily. Next time, give me a little more advance notice and something stronger than coffee." And he leaves.

The coffee shop is even more packed by then. Customers are circling my table like hawks and I gather my things to head to work. It's probably good I'm getting there so early. It will make up for my not being able to stay up late.

Because apparently I now have to solve a freakin' murder.

Chapter 6

Chicago doesn't have *bail* anymore. At least, not like you see on TV. There's no bonding out, no million-dollar cash requirements for murderers. It's up to the judge whether you rot in a cell or stroll out to freedom before your trial. But with a vampire... who knows if a judge would release them when they've got fangs as lethal as loaded guns?

Luckily for Lucian, *paranormals* still have bail. Unluckily for me, because I'm dragging my penny-pinching butt to the jail after a grinding day of work, having spent my lunch break trying to convince my bank that a massive withdrawal was no big deal. I'm probably on some kind of list now.

The lobby of the jail is a cross between a circus and a waiting room in purgatory. The walls are lined with bulletin boards plastered with wanted posters and memos that looked like they hadn't been updated since the Stone Age. I'm in a sorry disguise, sporting a ratty blonde wig and a trench coat, feeling like a reject from Dante's Inferno. A stressed-out receptionist juggles phone calls like flaming torches, while the metal detector is beeping out a techno beat, a symphonic performance for the gaggle of folks stuck in limbo with me. Friday's a busy day for bailouts, I'm told. No one wants to spend the weekend here if they can't help it. Which I understand, I've been here twenty minutes already, but it feels like a year. The sun sets slowly behind me and I hug my bag like it's a lifeline.

Then a grizzled cop storms in, nearly scaring the life out of all of us. "Zelda Nightshade?" he calls out, panting.

Everyone looks around, clueless, and I can feel my cheeks heating. I reluctantly stand, keeping my head low, bail form crumpling in my grip.

"That's me," I say, defeated. *At least only 'Zelda Night-shade' will be on whatever* this *list is.*

The cop gives me a once over, his tag reading MARTIN. "Follow me."

He leads me past reception, down a maze of doors with cops and staff buzzing around in various stages of stress and donut consumption. We end up in a barebones room with a table and two chairs.

"Have a seat, Ms. Nightshade."

I sit as dignified as I can, adjusting my pathetic wig. "What can I do for you, sir?"

Martin slumps backward in his chair, arms crossed and sneering. "You here to bail out the freak?"

"I'm here to bail out Lucian Belmont," I correct, my resolve not wavering even as my jaw clenches. My bag whispers as I fish out my wad of cash and show it to him. I'd have used my credit card, but that's tied to my real name.

"You know him?" Martin eyes me, skepticism etched in every crease of his weathered face.

"I know... someone that knows him." I try for an excuse that's half-rooted in the truth. "My friend... Sara. You can't stop attraction. No matter how I try to talk sense into her, she just..." I trail off, hoping I sound helpless instead of like my pants are on fire.

He frowns. The clock ticks away as he stares at me, and a cold tendril of dread snakes around my spine the longer he stays quiet. My fingers itch for the tape recorder in my bag, to record this meeting in case I'm the next one locked up.

Finally, he cracks a smile. "I get it. Got a son going astray. Tried to bring home a yoga instructor, can you believe it?"

I flash what I hope passes for a sympathetic smile, but probably looks like a grimace.

Another cop peeks in the door. "This the freak fucker?"

The words hit me square in the gut, like a sucker punch I didn't see coming. But I muster up all the grit I've got and keep up my poker face.

"Nah," Martin says. "Just someone stuck in the middle. Was just getting around to telling her." He turns back to me. "You can't release him without signing a bunch of crap and giving over your I.D."

My name in the official records. How likely is it that Johnson & Marcus will check? Or the press finds it? I swallow a gulp. "Is that required for all... paranormal bailouts or only this one?"

"All of them," the cop in the doorway grunts, dripping with disdain. "Gotta keep tabs on vamps and their cheerleaders."

You're an officer for the entire city, I want to say. *Bound to protect everyone, paranormals too.* Instead, I give another tight smile. "Will it be public record?"

Martin's gaze softens. "Only if they specifically request it."

So, yes.

"You don't have to," he adds gently. "Enable her, that is. That's the problem with my boy. Too soft." He frowns, his eyes fixed on the table like he's lost in memories. After a beat, he shakes it off and meets my eyes again. "It'll be no loss to her, anyway."

I take a slow breath. "I'll need another bail form for my legal name, Officer Martin."

Martin looks like he wants to object, but he obediently brings another.

"Sign here," he instructs once we're finished, and he's scanned my I.D.

I scrawl my signature across the bottom, feeling as though I'm signing my own death warrant.

"Payment?" Martin eyes the envelope.

"Here," I say, pushing a hefty chunk of my savings towards him.

"There's a side door you'll have to use. Head down the hall and wait," he says, snatching the envelope and form off the table. "We'll bring him out."

I fix my wig and head toward the back area, where there's a single visitor's chair. I slump into it to wait. Another twenty minutes drag on, the sun completely disappearing behind the horizon. *At least we'll be able to leave immediately.*

"Quite the Good Samaritan, aren't you?" sneers an office worker leaning against the far wall. His voice is dripping with sarcasm, judgment, and something darker, something sinister.

I shift in my seat and ignore him.

"Helping your boyfriend, or just have a thing for weirdos?" another chimes in. Their laughter cuts like broken glass.

"Cut it out," a tanned brunette woman says from behind me. She's in uniform too, her vest tight over what must be a bulletproof vest. A name tag reads "GREENE." She offers me a small smile. "I'll make sure Mr. Belmont's out in a jiffy." With that, she disappears back into the holding area.

"Alright, Lane, he's all yours," another voice finally says, gruff and about as warm as an iceberg. The officer shoots me a final sneer, his arms folded over his hefty chest, staring me down.

I rise as the holding door creaks open. Officer Greene's gently nudging Lucian through. His long black hair's a mess, and his shirt's wrinkled and stained. He stops a few paces from me. The broad-shouldered man who announced him stumbles away as Lucian looks to have planted his feet, his gaze searching mine with an intensity I can almost feel. There's a muzzle strapped to his face and two of the officers are behind him, trying to convince the other to undo it.

I scoff and stalk forward. "I'll do it," I announce, slipping behind him and releasing the straps. Greene smiles again as she releases his handcuffs.

Lucian whirls around to face me. An officer squeaks in terror and two pull out their guns. Greene shouts at them, giving Lucian and me a semblance of privacy.

"Emily?" His voice, usually smooth as butter, carries a note of disbelief.

I clear my throat as what I've done finally sinks in. "Let's talk in the car," I manage.

He gives a curt bow, regal even after a few nights in jail, and gestures to the small back door to the parking garage. "After you."

"Did Sara put you up this?" he asks once we're huddled inside my sedan. The engine sputters in protest, like me being dragged out of bed before dawn, before finally turning over.

My fingers tighten around the wheel as I veer towards the vampire district. "Can't I have thought of it myself?"

"Did you?" His tone's like gravel underfoot.

"Kind of," I say under my breath. "She thought I should be your lawyer." I jab a finger in his direction. "Which is not happening."

"But you'll bond me out instead?" he asks, raising a dark brow.

"Apparently, I'm your only alibi," I retort. "Which is *also* not happening. No way am I getting in front of a jury and having my nighttime activities questioned. I'd lose my job, my reputation. Hell, I could go to jail." I cut myself off, face draining of blood as I realize just how bad an idea it would be.

"So this is my final act of kindness?" He scoffs. "You'll give me a taste of freedom before they come to take me away?"

"No," I say resolutely. "We're going to figure out who really killed Mitchell and get you out of this mess." Get us *both* out of this mess.

He goes quiet, and I sneak a glance at him. His brows knit together, lips pressed tight. Finally, he points ahead. "Take this turn." And deeper we go into vampire turf.

CHAPTER 7

The wrought-iron gate squeaks open with an ominous groan that echoes down the street. Lucian's home looms in front of us, a real life haunted mansion straight out of a gothic novel. Its spires reach for the sky, casting eerie shadows across the cobblestone street. When we parked, he asked me inside, saying he had something for me. Despite my better judgment (or maybe because I was hoping the 'thing' he was giving me was his teeth in my neck), I agreed to follow him inside.

"Your place certainly doesn't scream 'low profile,' does it?" I say, trying to ignore the goosebumps pricking up my arms as I eye him.

He walks beside me, still a vision of centuries-old grace. Even with dirt on his shirt and a rat's nest in his hair, he looks good.

"This has been my home since I moved to Chicago," he says. "In 1850."

I stumble over my own feet at the reminder of his ancient origins juxtaposed with his perpetually youthful appearance. "Is that why this area is the vampire district?" I ask, mid-realization. "You were already here?"

"In part," he admits, leaning in conspiratorially. "Many of my brethren once lived nearby. Convincing the others to relocate proved challenging. Some still linger in the shadows, reluctant to embrace this new locale."

"And the other supernatural types?" I prod, curious about what other paranormals lurked around. I've always wondered what a fairy looks like.

He smiles, though it looks forced. "All around us. Shall we?"

He swings open the fancy door, and we step into his mansion of mystery.

Inside the house is a museum, with tapestries covering the walls and furniture lifted right out of a period movie. Gold accents and velvet upholstery give the room a regal feel. It smells like a library, mixed with the mustiness of a forgotten attic. But underneath it all, there's a hint of the iron rich scent of blood.

"I half-expect a portrait of you in a ruffled collar," I say, scanning the walls for one, only to find modern art mixing with older pieces.

A grand staircase spirals upward, but it's not this architectural marvel that catches my eye. It's the family tree displayed prominently on the wall beside it—a tapestry woven with ancient threads. BELMONT is written in ornate script at the top. Beside it is what must be the family crest, which refocuses me on why I'm here. Even so, curiosity is a lifelong disease and I ask, "Your family, I presume?"

Lucian is inside the library off the foyer, shuffling through papers atop a centuries-old desk. He doesn't even lean out of the doorway to see what I'm talking about, calling out, "Yes, from our arrival in North America."

"Where are you on it?" I ask, trying to make sense of the faded names and dates.

He makes an irritated groan as he stalks back to the foyer and squints up at the faded writing. "Fifth from the top. My sister's line continued, but I lost track several generations ago. The names became too common. Now if you will please give me a moment, then I'll answer whatever questions you desire." He returns to the library.

"Don't tempt me," I mumble as I hop up a few steps to better see the family tree. After giving myself a headache from squinting, I find the faint line of his name, LUCIAN BELMONT. Beside it is a line following from GEORGIANA (BELMONT) HARRIS that trips down to MARK MATTHEWS then finally ends at MICHAEL CARTER (?) in 1910.

"Are you finished snooping?" Lucian's voice calls from the library, snapping me back to the present.

"Almost," I shout back, ignoring his impatience. I'd spent two hours waiting on him at the jail, he could handle a few minutes of my curiosity. There's something magnetic about the tree, a silent testament to survival. I can't help but respect it. And maybe envy it a little. "But it's not snooping if it's literally out for all to see," I remind him.

"Touché," he says dryly when I enter the library. Books are stacked on the desk, alongside yellowing papers and what looks like a map from the 1700s.

"Your home *is* fascinating," I say, taking in the shelves crammed with books that probably predate the printing press. "You could charge admission for historical tours. Or drag out a white sheet and throw some cobwebs around and you've got yourself a haunted house side hustle."

"Shall we get down to business? Or do you have more historic insults to lob my way?" Lucian leans back in his chair, looking every bit the composed aristocrat. Back to the statuesque coven leader who watched over all from his ivory tower.

"Better watch it, or I'll start billing you for this delightful banter," I warn, tapping the recorder in my pocket. Always ready to catch details, even amid this gothic tableau. "But just so you know, I'm full of zingers."

All the better to keep from panicking at the path I've somehow chosen for myself. I'm betting if I'd been calmed from donating blood, I wouldn't be planning to solve a murder with Fitzwilliam Darcy over here.

"Here," Lucian says, drawing me out of my thoughts as he extends a white envelope toward me. "You'll need this."

Inside are hundreds upon hundreds of bills, a mimicry of what I left at the police station an hour ago. I hesitate, the paper crisp and cool under my fingertips. "I was kidding about billing you. I'm not on your retainer."

"It is the repayment of my bond." His voice softens, his gray eyes meeting mine intently.

"Should I be worried about losing my deposit?" I ask cautiously, unsure of what this exchange means for our budding partnership and my reputation. Only if Lucian flees or commits another crime would I surrender the money. Maybe it was naïve of me, but I didn't think those were actual risks.

"The money is not an issue. I have decades worth of savings. Most paranormals do, with our own banking system. But the American judicial system wouldn't recognize it. It needs to be traceable by human standards."

"Inequitable, illogical, and irritating. The 'I' trifecta," I say, shaking my head. "I might have some ideas for you folks to look into." After my Margaret Mitchell research, I've got an entire dossier's worth of things that really should be changed if we want to remain a 'free' country for all. I'm happy to pass it off to the paranormals and their buddies to figure out.

He leans forward, elbows on the desk. "If I need to bond out from another crime, perhaps I'll seek your counsel."

"So," I ask, shooting him a sideways glance, "why couldn't Sara bail you out?"

He frowns, a flicker of confusion passing over his face. "Sara?" He raises an eyebrow, and it's clear he hadn't even considered it. "Morticians aren't exactly known for their overflowing cash reserves. Certainly no one would believe the money came from her."

"The legal limitations for your kind keep adding up," I say, trying to keep things light, but the laughter doesn't reach my eyes. "You all really do need lawyers."

The corners of his mouth twitch upward. "So claims the lawyer."

"Alright, back to business. Let's focus as I'm not planning on solving this thing on my own." I stand, pushing the chair back with a screech that echoes through the library. "Unlike you with your fancy estate and riches to spare, I have to work for a living."

"You needn't bother," Lucian says, rising too. He moves with purpose, a leader rallying after a momentary break. "Sara left a note that she will be bringing the case file she showed you by later tonight."

"You already talked to Sara?" I frown, but I don't know why.

He gives me a sidelong glance. "No. But my departure from the jail would have been reported, given the age of the building."

"What do you mean?" I press, but he dodges the question.

"Come this way. We must speak more privately."

I gesture to the empty library. "More private than here?"

"Follow me," he demands. That intensity appears in his eyes again and I swallow my discomfort, agreeing to leave without further argument. For now.

He leads me through the maze-like corridors of his mansion. The walls are crowded with generations of somber faces peering from oil paintings, their eyes seeming to glare at me as we pass, making my skin crawl.

Finally, he ushers me through an archway into a more intimate sitting room, but my irritation is overflowing. He sits at a plush chair and points me towards the other.

But I plant my feet in the doorway. "Look, I'm in this too. You can't pull the 'I'm the leader, everyone listens to me without question' card with me. I'm not in your coven, I'm not on your payroll. Stop blowing me off and explain when I ask you questions."

His gaze sharpens, and for a moment, I swear I see a hint of crimson. "Fine. Sit down, Emily, and I'll explain."

Still annoyed, I begrudgingly take a seat.

"This is my private domain," he explains, gesturing around the room. "None of my coven or visitors will come to this part of the house. The library is open to all who wish to visit, meaning our entire conversation could be overheard." He flicks his attention to the walls. "I have an agreement with the hobgoblins that they will leave this, and a few other rooms, alone, meaning it is as private as it can be."

"Hobgoblins?" I ask, frowning. "Are those like... gremlins?"

He offers a wry smile. "You're lucky they cannot hear you. No, hobgoblins. And it is the hobgoblins in the jail that would have alerted my allies to my release."

"*In* the jail?"

"In all older buildings," he confirms.

My face drains of color as I think about my own in-home activities. "My building is from the 1800s. Does that mean …"

"That there are hobgoblins there? Likely," he confirms with a smile that's almost too beautiful to bear. "Is there something you did not wish them to see?"

"Of course not," I reply stiffly.

He crosses one leg over the other and leans forward in his chair. "Now, my explaining this was a courtesy to you, as you requested. But I do not need your help in investigating the crime lodged against me."

Immediately, my concerns at an uninvited nocturnal creature in my apartment refocus on *this* nocturnal creature, my hackles raising at his dismissive tone. "I beg your pardon?"

Lucian meets my defiant stare with a firm gaze. "While I appreciate you bailing me out of jail, I do not want you involved any further in this matter."

A wave of righteous annoyance floods through me. Folding my arms across my chest, I lean back in my chair and lock eyes with him. "And who are you to dictate what I can or cannot do? This is a free country."

"For some of us," he replies sharply.

"Which is why I need to be involved," I counter. "I have more access to things than you do. I know how to maneuver the court records, and after touring this place, I highly doubt there are smartphones or laptops anywhere for research. *And* I have a car, which beats taking the Red Line everywhere. Unless…" I eye him suspiciously, "…vampires *can* fly?"

The joke seems to diffuse some of the tension in the room. Lucian shakes his head, looking slightly amused.

"Well, there you go. So, what do you say?" I ask, brows raised and arm outstretched. "Partners?"

Lucian rises from his seat and stalks towards me with a feline grace, his movements fluid yet purposeful. He shakes my hand. "Don't make me regret this, Emily Lane."

"Likewise, Lucian Belmont," I reply, matching his intensity. Lucian's grip is firm and cool, sending a shiver down my spine that has nothing to do with fear.

With our alliance solidified, we reseat ourselves and I launch into the facts I'd been given, about the witnesses and the cufflink.

"Depending on Mr. Mitchell's residence, one of the nearby paranormals could provide some clarity on what occurred," Lucian suggests, staring hard at the table between us in thought.

"Yeah but they can't testify," I point out.

His eyes are sharp. "It doesn't mean the information is any less meaningful."

"You're right." I clear my throat. "About the cufflink, can you think of anyone who would want to frame you using your own family's crest? Did you notice them missing?"

"Let us check," he says, rising with a flourish. Offering his arm to me like we're characters in a Jane Austen novel, he adds, "I wish to take you to my bedroom."

My stomach drops and it feels as though heat rushes to my face and groin. All I can think about is how it's been two-plus weeks since Brett and days since donating blood to vampires, which ended in fear that removed all 'orgasm'-like feeling from the act. "Okay..."

"I wished to advise you so you knew we were still on a *team* and I was not keeping you in the dark. My cufflinks should be in my bedroom," he explains.

"Oh. Got it." My voice is steady but inside I'm kicking myself.

He seems oblivious to my disappointment as he leads me out. I stride alongside him down another long corridor of his ancestral home, our footsteps muffled by the thick, ornate rugs that line the floor.

"Here." His voice breaks the silence, awkward only on my side, opening a door to his personal quarters.

The room is an opulent blend of modern aesthetics and timeless elegance—clearly, this vampire has taste. The walls are a rich cream color, dotted with abstract paintings in gilded frames. His sparse furniture is a mix of deep mahogany and plush velvet in shades of deep blue, with a grand bed covered in silken fabrics. God, I'd love to live there, get tangled in those sheets. And in between his legs. Irritating or not, he's gorgeous and I'm stressed out.

Amidst the luxe furnishings and shelves lined with literature, I spot the cufflinks atop a dark mahogany dresser. They gleam under the soft lighting and smell faintly of lavender.

"These are mine. I have never lost them," Lucian explains, picking up one of the tiny silver shields adorned with the crest. "Whatever was found could not be my family's crest."

My curiosity piques as I inch closer, examining the intricate engravings. It's a miniature replica of the image on the family tree. The crest is a small silver shield, engraved with a tree, branches that reach to the edge of the shield and roots anchoring the bottom. "Are there any copies out there?"

"My father had a similar pair, passed down through generations. They have likely been lost to time," he says with a shrug that doesn't quite reach his eyes. "Or perhaps pilfered. It's not uncommon for family heirlooms to inspire envy."

"Maybe someone found the other pair. Or the crest they found at the scene is a similar style and they took a bad logical leap," I muse aloud, allowing the pieces of the puzzle to shift and settle with my new thoughts. "Has anyone outside your... society seen these?"

"Possibly," he admits. "But someone would need to be incredibly familiar with the design to pinpoint it to me. It certainly narrows the playing field."

"Or widens it," I counter.

"Ever the optimist."

"Realist," I correct him. "I deal in facts, not fantasy."

He hums thoughtfully, placing the cufflinks back on the dresser with a care that borders on reverence.

I glance around, noting the lack of personal touches—a neat bed, no signs of a significant other. No photo frames, no trinkets from a lover or lingering scents. Oddly, the realization that Lucian might be as solitary as me sparks something—a silly thought given our circumstances.

"Something wrong?" Lucian catches my wandering eye, hopefully misinterpreting my sudden flush.

"Nothing at all," I deflect quickly. "Just making mental notes."

"Of course," he nods, though I detect amusement dancing in his eyes. "Shall we reconvene at a later date?"

"Absolutely," I answer, a tad briskly. But there's something about being in his private space that makes the walls around me feel like they're closing in with possibilities. But none I can afford to explore now.

Lucian escorts me to the door, every bit the gentleman, even if he's of the undead variety. The atmosphere shifts, a subtle but unmistakable change that skitters across the back of my neck. Centuries of evolution haven't wiped out the instinct prey have when a predator's lurking nearby. I'm halfway into my coat when the reason for it appears as Severin strides in, accompanied by two vamps I don't recognize. The two unknown men stand tall and imposing, their features sharp and angular like ice sculptures. Their skin is unnaturally pale, almost translucent, and their eyes are a piercing silver, giving off an otherworldly glimmer. Only their hair is distinct: vamp one's is pitch black, vamp two's is flecked with gray. They look like vicious siblings, causing the room to crackle with tension as they enter.

"Severin," Lucian greets, his voice as cool as the marble beneath our feet.

"Lucian," Severin replies, his tone equally icy. "And Miss Lane, what an unexpected delight."

"Is it?" I ask, unable to help myself. Knowing he could have only learned my name from Stardust, my presence here must be about as pleasant as a garlic garland at a vampire ball.

"Enough with the pleasantries," snaps the first unfamiliar vamp, shooting me a glare that could curdle milk. "We've got urgent matters to discuss."

"Indeed," Severin says, eyes narrowing in my direction.

"If haste is necessary, out with it," Lucian says. "I have no concerns with Emily overhearing."

The first vamp trails a dismissive gaze over me. "Tina's former donor," he says, narrowing his eyes. "The one that should get a haircut."

Something like guilt—for forgetting her, for it not affecting me—burbles in my gut. But it's quickly stifled by a swallowed huff.

"I've never heard of her," the second unfamiliar vampire says, scowling.

"Which is exactly why I'm entitled to Tina's estate!" snarls the first.

Lucian shoots me a glance, and I wonder if my face reveals my feelings. "Gentlemen, stop bickering and wasting my time," he says firmly.

The second unfamiliar vamp jumps in again, his eyes ablaze. "It's about Tina's property."

"Go on, Jasper," Lucian urges.

"Tina left several items of both emotional and physical value at her demise. We had been lovers for ten years and I wish to retain this property," Jasper says, fangs bared. "Just as Tina was mine, so too is her legacy."

The other vamp growls, his black hair standing on end like he was electrocuted. "You were nothing but a lark. Tina and I were inseparable for decades, since her conversion in 1935. She was *mine*, body and soul."

"She loved *me*, Alistair," Jasper says, beating his pale hand against his chest.

"She loved your tongue," Alistair shoots back.

Standing like two video game fighters, hands up and ready to pounce, they look even more similar. Like a copy+paste job with limited ink. *Tina had a type*, I think. Maybe I *should* have tried to get to know her better...

Before I can say "catfight" (or... batfight), Jasper lunges at Alistair, ready to turn this place into a vampire brawl. Severin steps in, trying to play peacemaker, hands pressing against each of their chests as they try to fight around him.

Lucian claps his hands, bringing the room to a stand-still. "Enough. Severin, what's this property we're talking about?"

Severin straightens up like a soldier at roll call, listing off Tina's belongings like it was a grocery list, the few things a vampire might try to keep over the years.

Lucian pinches the bridge of his nose with long fingers. "Fine. Jasper, you may have the instruments and her family portraits."

Jasper puffs up like a rooster.

"And Alistair, you may have the clothing and her journals. The books we'll bring here so you both may view them at your leisure."

Alistair frowns. Both he and Jasper exchange wary looks.

"But, sir..." Alistair says, whining. "I want the photos from her conversion, as a reminder of her."

"And I want the journal that depicts our first time making love," adds Jasper.

"Then you shouldn't have demanded my aid," Lucian says sharply.

Alistair and Jasper burst into more complaints as a headache starts forming behind my right eye.

"Seriously? You guys don't have a system for this?" I blurt out, rubbing my temples.

The four vamps stare at me like I'm speaking Martian.

"Like, I get not having laws and doing things the 'vamp way,' but surely this comes up over and over," I say as they keep staring. "Why would you not have figured this out before?"

They all frown, Lucian's the deepest of all. I heave a sigh. This could go on until sunrise unless someone steps in.

"You need funeral rules," I tell them. "You know, like when the family divvies up Aunt Mabel's china after the funeral? You go around in a circle and each take turns picking one thing you want until it's all gone."

"Who goes first?" Jasper asks, sounding intrigued.

"Draw straws, flip a coin, I don't care. Just sort it out like civilized creatures."

They nod like I'm some kind of genius.

"And for Pete's sake, get some wills," I add.

"Those laws don't apply to us," Severin says, crossing his arms.

"It's not for the courts," I explain, fisting my hands on my hips. "But for you, for your coven. You have rules, make this one. That's how you avoid this type of argument in the future."

Alistair steps closer, a small smirk playing on his lips. "Would you make one for us?" he asks in a low voice that feels like chocolate tastes. I can see why Tina kept him around. Both Jasper *and* Lucian look irritated at Alistair's approach.

I clear my throat. "I don't do that kind of work," I say, trying to sound diplomatic when I'd rather run the opposite direction from estate planning *and* vampire politics.

"I can pay you," he wheedles. He dips his hand into the pocket of his suit pants and my eyes widen wondering what the hell he's about to do. With an even bigger grin, he pulls out a handful of rocks and offers them to me. On closer inspection, they're rubies.

"Holy hell," I exclaim, staring down at more money than I've physically seen in my life. Considering the envelope in my purse was *also* more money than I'd seen in my life, I wonder if I should rethink my stance against vamp legal advice. "You just walk around with those?"

"I told you money is different for paranormals," Lucian says, holding back a laugh. He turns back to the others. "I have no concerns with Emily's 'funeral rules.' Severin, please work with Jasper and Alistair to coordinate the distribution of Tina's property."

Severin nods and drags the other two by the collars upstairs, leaving me standing in the threshold of Lucian's home.

"Well, that was a circus," I say, trying to shake off the tension and my crow-like desire to snatch the rubies from Alistair's hands and run off to a deserted island somewhere. But the drama also brought up a question that had been nagging at me. "Why didn't you seem upset about Tina's death?"

Lucian raises his brows.

"I mean, that night," I explain. "You acted all normal, telling me about the fledglings. Stardust was upset, I realize that now." I wince, thinking back at my insensitivity towards Stardust's grief. "But you didn't even mention it."

A little warning might have been nice, honestly.

Lucian sighs like he's carrying the weight of the world. "Death is an inevitability that we never obtain. It doesn't seem that terrible once it finally comes." He leans against the door frame. "For those of us remaining, having lived long enough to see loved ones come and go, it feels as though the vampires no longer with us... have found release."

I'll ponder that back in the solitude of my apartment. "I see. Thanks for explaining."

"And thank you for mediating," he says. "An outside perspective is... refreshing."

I tilt my neck back, half-jokingly asking, "Nice enough to feed from me?"

"Not even a little," he says, his tone dry as century-old parchment. He directs me to the door, a figure cloaked in elegance, his gray eyes shimmering in the moonlight streaming through the window. "But let's not dwell on things that won't ever be. We have more pressing matters."

"Right, the whole 'clearing your name' thing." I run a hand through my hair, securing the strays back into my messy bun.

"The preliminary hearing is Monday." Lucian's voice is as serious as a heart attack. "With me no longer held in the jail, I must appear at the courthouse before sunrise."

I frown. "I guess I hadn't thought about that part. Is the courthouse even open?"

He smiles ruefully. "No. But an officer has committed to meet me at the jail at 6:00 a.m. to aid me through the tunnels connecting them and place me in a private holding cell. The Officer Greene you met tonight, we discussed it prior to my release."

My brows raise high enough to give myself another headache. "Good for her, I guess. Hopefully it works out."

"Indeed. I will remain there until sunset when it is safe to leave."

"With Monday full, shall we hit the ground running tomorrow night? Take Saturdays from the boys and give them to the vamps?"

"Not tomorrow. *After* the preliminary hearing." Lucian stands before me, arms crossed, exuding a confidence that would make a lesser man—or woman—falter. "Although my absence was short, I have duties to attend to."

"Fine. You do that, but I'll get a head start and we—"

"No," he says firmly. "If you are sincere about wishing to help, we must work together. I'll review the case file and we can begin immediately after the preliminary hearing on Monday. Please. Wait for me."

"I'll do my best." The words spill out with more mock solemnity than I intended.

"That's all I can ask." There's a trace of a smile playing on Lucian's lips, a sight that stirs something within me. "I'm grateful, Emily. Few would stand by a paranormal in my position."

"Paranormal or not, we're stuck together now," I say. "It could be worse, being tied to a charming, infuriatingly cryptic vampire." Although God only knows I won't regret it. Maybe there's a psychic paranormal out there and I could ask them their predictions.

"Charming?" He arches an eyebrow, the picture of feigned innocence. "How kind of you to notice."

"Infuriatingly cryptic?" I shoot back, unable to suppress my grin. I don't know if it's the thrill of the chase or the company of the chaser that's got my pulse pounding.

"Merely a side effect of immortality." He shrugs, as if to say 'what can you do?'

"Right. See you in court, Mr. Immortal," I say, offering him a mock salute. "Unless you've changed your mind and need a little blood cocktail from me?"

"Until tomorrow, Emily Lane."

I glide away from Lucian's lair, my boots clicking rhythmically against the cobblestones. I think about ambition, about competition, and for the first time in a long while, I'm not chasing after validation and security—I'm racing toward something unknown, exhilarating. Lucian watches me go, and I sense his smile lingering in the darkness.

"Let the games begin," I whisper to myself and whatever paranormals may be listening in the dark.

CHAPTER 8

The weekend stretches out in front of me like an eternity, and the thought of wasting it is unbearable. With my social life circling the drain ever since Brett and I called it quits, and Lucian's ban on my preferred method of stress relief still active, I'm desperate for something to occupy my time. I'd already tried reading but my dogeared vampire romance was nowhere to be found.

"Come on, Lane," I mutter to myself, firing up the laptop. My hair's pulled back in its usual messy bun, a few stray strands framing my face as I lean in, ready to dive into the digital world. Frank Mitchell's smug digital footprint stares back at me from the screen. Businessman, mayoral candidate, anti-paranormal crusader, and now, a corpse with secrets begging to be spilled.

"Emily Lane, playing Nancy Drew with the supernatural set," I quip, my voice bouncing off the apartment walls in mockery of my plight. "Lawyer by day, paranormal investigator by twilight. What a headline." A career-killer for sure.

I dig into Mitchell's dealings, skimming through years of transactions and personal associations like a hawk eyeing prey. It's meticulous, mind-numbing work, but every so often, a tidbit glimmers amongst the mundane. I scribble notes, the tape recorder sitting unused today—I want only silence and my own rampant thoughts for company.

The clock ticks past midnight when I hit a wall. I need local intel, the kind you can't find on the internet. Matty comes to mind. He'd know all about Mitchell, prepping for the case against Lucian. The question is whether I can sweet talk him after hours.

I hesitate, considering Lucian's stern warning against investigating, and discard it along with my restraint.

Matty picks up after three rings, sounding groggy or annoyed—it's hard to tell which. "Emily? Do you know what time it is?"

"Time for spontaneity, Matty," I shoot back, injecting false cheer into my words. There's a pause, and I picture him rubbing his temples in frustration.

"Spontaneity's for people without day jobs," he retorts. But the telltale rustle of bedsheets sounds through the speaker; he's up now. "You need to stop calling so late."

"Sure. But tell me, did Frank Mitchell have any favorite haunts? Somewhere he'd unwind, away from the campaign trail?" I ask, pressing on before he can protest.

"That's why you called, Emily?" he grumbles. "Jesus, if I'm going to be woken up by a beautiful woman, I thought she'd at least ask what I'm wearing."

I huff a laugh. "The night is young."

His laughter crackles through the phone, rusty and like he's surprised he did it. "Fine, fine. Mitchell was a creature of habit, you know the type," Matty says, sounding more alert now. "He used to frequent a bar downtown called Moonlit Haven."

"Moonlit Haven," I echo. The name conjures grim images of shadowy corners and whispered secrets. And the ghosts in my apartment aren't too thrilled with it either, as I swear a breeze comes out of nowhere and sends my notepad tumbling to the ground.

"Thanks, Matty. You're a lifesaver," I say, already mentally planning my visit to Moonlit Haven.

"Please tell me you're not planning on going there," Matty pleads, his concern evident even through the phone. "What would Brett say?"

"He'd say, 'why the hell are you asking me?'" I reply, rolling my eyes. "We weren't dating, and now we're not even doing that. Don't you worry, Matty. I'll be fine."

"Right. If you're sure," he says, skepticism thick in his voice. "Be safe. And more notice next time, Em."

"More spontaneity next time, Matty," I say. And then I get ready for a night on the town.

As soon as I enter the dive bar of Moonlit Haven, it's like I've stepped into a scene straight out of a film noir, complete with a sassy neon sign and creaky door. The clientele is an eclectic mix of characters that seem like they could be plucked from every bar film known to man. There's a tall man in a fedora nursing a drink at the bar, his eyes hidden under the brim. A group of women in vintage flapper dresses giggle in a corner booth, their laughter tinkling like music. A gaggle of college boys look to be doing a shot contest. And then there's a figure in a long coat with a hood pulled low over their face, sitting alone at a table.

"Can I help you?" The bartender's voice breaks through the haze of smoke and low murmurs. He's got a smile that could make even the toughest mob boss blush, capped by brown eyes that look hungry.

I order a whiskey neat to steel my nerves, taking a seat at the bar. It probably sounds silly, but donating to vamps in the park seems safer than frequenting this place. Sipping on my drink, I discreetly survey the room, searching for any familiar faces or potential informants who might shed light on Frank Mitchell's secrets.

"Looks like you could use another," the bartender says, leaning over the bar, his muscles rippling under his tight black shirt.

"I'd prefer information for a chaser," I say, trying a direct approach. "A man named Frank Mitchell used to come here. Is there anyone who might have seen him?"

The bartender raises an eyebrow in amusement before pointing to a golden-skinned woman in red sitting in a booth. "She might have what you're looking for." He quickly pours two more whiskeys and slides them over to me. "You'll need a bribe to open those lips. Unless you've got something else on offer."

"Drinks it is." After slipping a bill on the bar, I give him a wink as I head towards the femme fatale. *Who knew bartenders were also detectives?*

Bribe in hand, I weave through the crowd, each step measured against the pulse of music that thrums beneath my skin. Something about her screams trouble, but I can't resist a good mystery.

"Mind if I join you?" I ask, offering the drink like a white flag.

"Suit yourself." Her voice is velvet laced with thorns.

Up close, there's an otherworldly grace about her that sets my instincts on edge. It might also be because her hair falls in perfect waves around her face, white blonde and glossy like the feathers of a swan, beautiful in ways my long locks have never behaved.

"Emily," I introduce myself, ignoring the subtle pull of charisma that seems to cling to her. "I'm new around here, looking to make friends."

"Friends," she echoes, a ghost of a smile touching her red lips before fading away. "I'm not in the market for new friendships. I just lost someone... important."

"Sorry to hear that," I say, taking a sip to fill the silence. "Relationship trouble has a way of following me too."

"Trouble?" A flicker of interest sparks in her eyes, the hue of which can't be pinned down—amber, green, something else entirely?

"Ex-boyfriend complexities," I admit, leaning into vulnerability. "He had a talent for making everything complicated." *Should I add a few crocodile tears?*

Tears unneeded, as she continues. "Mine... left me," she confides after a beat, the words stark against the backdrop of revelry. "We'd had three glorious years together."

"I'm so sorry. What happened?"

She pins me with a stare so intense it feels like she's peeling me open to discover whether my sympathy is genuine. I hold her gaze, determined to show her that I'm not just another face in the crowd at Moonlit Haven.

"He was murdered," she finally reveals.

"Frank?" My brain stutters to a halt, the pieces clicking together. *So much for being devoted to Margaret.*

She studies me, guarded now, but nods. "You knew him?"

"By reputation only," I hedge. "His death's been on the news all week."

"I miss him so much," she says, her voice tinged with sorrow. "He'd promised he was leaving his wife for me."

I bet he did. I pat her hand in what I hope is a reassuring manner. "He must have loved you very much."

"He did," she confirms. She tucks her hair behind her ears, revealing the biggest rocks I've ever seen, bigger than Alistair's rubies by a mile. "He gave me these for an anniversary present."

Before I can come up with a suitable reaction to diamonds more expensive than a small country's GDP, a shadow falls over our booth. The shadow clears its throat, and I don't need to turn around to know who's looming behind me.

"Perhaps you should find some... nourishment, Rebecca. It always makes one feel better." Lucian's smooth voice breaks into the conversation, the timbre low and controlled. "There's a group by the piano who look up for some amusement."

The woman perks up at his suggestion, her earlier melancholy momentarily forgotten. "You're right, as usual, Lucian." Her voice holds an edge of something feral, and she slides out of the booth with a grace that's too perfect to be human. She crosses by another man whose fangs peek out when he laughs. As she saunters off towards a group of party-goers, I finally piece it together—this isn't just any club. It's a feeding ground where the supernatural mix with the blissfully unaware.

"What—" I begin, but Lucian cuts me off with a gesture, his long fingers adorned with those family cufflinks that gleam in the dim light.

"Emily, this establishment plays host to many of our kind," he explains, and there's a hint of pride in his voice.

"Some seek companionship, others conduct business—both legitimate, and... less so."

I can't help but note the irony; a vampire saddled with murder charges preaching about legality. "Tell me you don't own the bar," I ask, rolling my eyes at the cliche.

Lucian's laughter rumbles through the air, rich and melodic. "I assure you, Emily, I have no interest in running a bar. Severin is the proprietor."

"You're kidding me." My voice is flat. Drill sergeant extraordinaire owns the bar. What's next? Stardust moonlights as an actuary?

But despite my sarcasm, curiosity gets the better of me, and I lean in, resting my elbows on the table. "If it's a vamp bar, why don't your kids feed here? It's certainly classier than the park."

He smirks, a humorless curve of his lips. "Class has nothing to do with it. Feeding here is uncontrolled chaos waiting to happen." He glances around the club, his gaze sharp and assessing. "In the park, it's easier to manage, smaller. Less possibility of... permanent damage. No one accidentally wanders into the park, but a bar?"

"Was easier," I correct him dryly.

"Was," he agrees, annoyance creeping into his tone. "Until someone stirred up trouble and put us all under the microscope."

"Bad press will do that to you," I say, unable to resist reminding him it wasn't my actions that did it.

His eyes narrow. "Why are you here, Emily Lane? Severin keeps me up to date on all humans that come to Moonlit Haven and your name has never made the list."

"I'd heard Mitchell frequented this place and wanted to check it out," I say, keeping my tone casual.

His face hardens, and the temperature between us drops several degrees. "Investigating without me, after you promised otherwise?"

His anger is a tangible thing, and I'm not immune to its effects, despite my stubbornness. "I said I'd try, and I did. But then changed my mind," I say, matching his icy tone. "I'm not exactly your subordinate, Lucian."

He leans in close, close enough for me to catch the faintest scent of old books and forest earth that clings to him. "We're supposed to be a team," he says, his breath ghosting over my cheek.

"Teams have common goals, not leashes," I shoot back. "Being joined at the hip wasn't part of the deal."

We lock eyes, each refusing to yield. Lucian's gaze flickers with a mix of frustration and perhaps a touch of admiration. Although the latter could be wishful thinking on my part.

"What have you found so far?" he finally asks, changing tactics.

"Nothing yet, except he apparently wasn't *too* anti-paranormal if he was sleeping with one." I gesture towards the woman in red, Rebecca he'd called her, now curling her fingers playfully around a man's neck.

"She had nothing to do with his death," he says firmly.

I lean back in my seat, crossing my arms. "Well, I'm not *her* alibi."

He studies me for a moment, as if weighing his options. "Mitchell, like most humans, was a hypocrite. Rebecca knew that well," he says. "He enjoyed the thrill of forbidden desires until it threatened his image."

I raise an eyebrow. "Not a great look for the face of the anti-paranormal movement. Maybe one of them took offense and took him out."

"Perhaps," he concedes. "Now go home, Emily." Lucian's command slices through the pulsing music, but there's a note of concern beneath the authoritative timbre. "After the hearing, we'll work together. Properly."

"Fine," I relent, standing up and adjusting my jacket. "But only because you asked so nicely." My tone skirts the edge of defiance, and his eyes flash with amusement.

"Of course," he replies, the slightest hint of a smile tugging at the corner of his mouth. "Always a pleasure to accommodate your whims."

"Likewise." I offer him a mock salute before heading toward the exit, the promise of unraveling secrets keeping my steps light. At least it wasn't another evening alone in my apartment.

Chapter 9

The moment my eyes snap open, determination sparks through me like a jolt of electricity. Today's the day I dive headfirst into Lucian's mess. Once Lucian double-swore me not to investigate without him, I spent the rest of the weekend catching up and getting ahead of work.

With a sigh, I sit up and grab my phone. My fingers fly over the screen, firing out a message to the firm: *"Emergency appointment this morning. Unavailable until afternoon."*

As if on cue, the send button is followed by a chime.

"Hope everything's okay," Liz texts back. I can almost see her green eyes wide with worry, that curly auburn mane bouncing as she types, understanding but curious.

"Thanks, Liz. It's... complicated," I reply, my thumbs hovering over the keyboard before adding an ambiguous smiley face. I can't afford to let anyone know where I'll really be. Dropping the phone onto the bed, I push myself to my feet and stride toward the closet.

"Disguise time," I mutter under my breath. The last thing I need is someone recognizing me. I yank out a box marked 'COSTUMES,' a hodgepodge of thrift store finds and office Halloween relics to prove I'm 'fun,' pulling out a mishmash of costume jewelry, oversized sunglasses, and finally—the pièce de résistance—the crappy blonde wig from Friday's jail visit. I stare at its tangled strands; it looks like something a cat dragged in, worse after spending a few hours on the floorboard of my car when I took Lucian home, but it'll have to do.

"Here goes nothing." I chuckle, attempting to wrangle my hair into submission before perching the wig awkwardly on top. It sits like a disgruntled bird's nest, and I have half a mind to throw it out the window. But beggars can't be choosers.

"Hey, wall hobgoblin," I say, eyeing the crack along the plaster where I swear I've heard scuttling more times than I can count. I assumed it was a mouse or maybe a possum, but after Lucian's revelation Friday night, I'm not so sure. "I'd appreciate some privacy while I change. I don't need any peeping Toms, real or imagined."

Of course, the wall remains silent, as always.

"Thanks for the consideration," I add dryly.

Dressed in a jumble of clothes that scream 'not Emily,' I take a deep breath and face the mirror. The woman staring back is a stranger, one with questionable fashion sense and a terrible hairdo. But it'll do. It has to.

The courtroom looms ahead, its tall wooden doors the last barrier between me and what I've unwittingly tied myself to. I push through the heavy doors to the symphony of whispers and shuffling feet. Packed doesn't even begin to describe it—the place is a sardine can of morbid curiosity and ill-concealed prejudice.

"Nice wig," a familiar voice says from behind me.

I glance over to find Matty sliding into the seat beside me.

"I borrowed it from a friend who moonlights as a '40s film noir detective," I say without missing a beat. My joke earns me a soft chuckle, his shoulder brushing mine conspiratorially.

"A regular gumshoe," he replies. "It's nice to hear your voice during more *appropriate* hours, but green isn't your color." He points to a fake emerald hanging from my ear peeking out, smoothing down a rogue strand of my wig to cover it.

"Thanks for the fashion tip," I say, suppressing a smile. The banter is a welcome distraction from the tension in the room, *and* unexpected from the man I've previously likened to the human embodiment of beige paint drying.

My attention shifts as the court comes to order, the buzz of conversation dying down to an anticipatory silence. Ava Sinclair, the District Attorney, enters, flanked by two lawyers who must also be Matty's coworkers. They sit at the prosecutor's table. Sinclair's known as a pit bull in a pinstripe suit. She's draped in designer digs and stiletto heels that clicked and clacked on the courtroom floor like a war drum. Her black hair is swept up in a loose bun, strands of it escaping to frame her soft features, and her brown eyes glitter with a cool, calculated intelligence. Her record is spotless, more wins than the house in a blackjack tournament. It's no wonder the public keeps voting her in.

"Peterson asked for her to keep the case, instead of assigning it out to one of us," Matty whispers. "It's the case of a lifetime, the ability to create precedence for charging paranormals with crimes."

Lucian is brought in next, muzzled and restrained, igniting murmurs of disapproval from the audience. The officer escorting him in isn't Greene, but a reedy looking man, who tries to shove him until he stumbles. Lucian doesn't, his preternatural grace too... graceful for that, but the officer does manage to direct him into a sunbeam from the window. Lucian hisses behind the muzzle as a curl of smoke comes off his arm, and he bends at the waist. A collective gasp ripples through the crowd at the sound, and my stomach drops. But Lucian quickly straightens and allows himself to be dragged to the defense table, his usual composure a mask over what must be a maelstrom of frustration. Even from here, I can see the gray of his eyes, stormy and resolute. Matty leans in, his voice a conspiratorial whisper.

"It's like I told you, no lawyer in town will touch Lucian's case with a ten-foot pole. The prejudice against vampires—nobody wants to get burned," he explains, his eyes scanning the room, taking in the wary glances and the stony faces of those around us. "I can't say I blame them."

"What about a public defender?" I ask, feeling a twinge of disgust at the cowardice masquerading as prudence. Including my own.

"The Judge will be ruling on that this morning," Matty says. "This has become a bigger case than anyone expected."

"The circus here is testament to that." It's like witnessing a storm break over a cloudy sky—sudden and charged with tension. Lightning's going to strike soon, I know it.

"Not just here," he adds. "The crime scene turned into something out of a carnival. Anti-paranormal activists are holding vigils like they're expecting a resurrection, while pro-paranormal fanatics are shouting about rights. It's a mess. Margaret Mitchell complained enough to get a 24/7 police guard on the place while she stays at a hotel."

"Order!" The judge bangs his gavel, and the room falls completely silent. "The public defender assigned to this case has been removed effective immediately due to the defendant's non-person status as per the request of the District Attorney."

Non-person? Since when did existence become a matter of legality?

"Is there no one else?" The judge's voice booms across the courtroom, already knowing the answer.

Murmurs erupt as various lawyers in the audience shuffle papers, avoiding eye contact, their silence a damning testament to the bias pervading the room. Lucian stands alone—literally and figuratively—as the embodiment of everything the law refuses to protect.

"Talk about being caught between a rock and a hard place," Matty mutters, his playful tone now edged with disapproval. But of Lucian or the system for failing him?

"More like between a fang and a stake," I say under my breath, my gaze fixed on Lucian.

Before I can dwell further, the doors swing open with a dramatic flourish, and in strides another figure that commands immediate attention. The pro-paranormal candidate trying to primary Mayor Peterson, Stephanie Evans. If Sinclair is a bulldog, Stephanie is a cat: sleek and uncompromising. Her dark tailored suit fits her perfectly, accentuating her toned physique and contrasting beautifully with her pale blonde hair, and her piercing blue eyes seem to size up the room, taking in every detail.

Evans takes her place at the defense table, a small smile playing on her lips. She glances over at Lucian and nods subtly in solidarity before turning her attention to the judge.

Lucian's brows flutter in what can only be confusion. I discreetly click on the recorder in my purse.

"Your honor may I approach?" Evans asks, her voice clear and commanding.

The judge nods and she saunters confidently towards him, Ava Sinclair following behind with a scowl.

"Although I'm not a licensed attorney, I'd like to speak for Mr. Belmont," she begins, her gaze sweeping across the courtroom. "As he is a non-person, the Illinois Attorney Act doesn't apply."

I glance over at Lucian who remains stoic, his face giving nothing away. He knows as well as anyone that this is yet another step in the inevitable outcome.

Sinclair raises a single brow. "I have no concerns with this, Your Honor. So long as she doesn't act as an attorney and question my witness, Detective James."

"Very well," says the judge. "Ms. Evans, you may speak on Mr... Belmont's behalf." His lips twitch with what must be disgust. "Detective James, come forward and take your oath."

A man in a crisp suit steps forward and is sworn in by the court clerk before taking his place on the stand. He recounts his investigation into Frank Mitchell's murder, and how they've pinned it on Lucian.

"And what about any possible motives for Mr. Belmont's actions?" Sinclair asks when Detective James finishes his testimony.

"We believe it is a hate crime against Mr. Mitchell's anti-paranormal rhetoric," he replies, his gaze flickering towards Lucian, who remains impassive.

"Prosecution rests," Sinclair says.

The judge directs Evans to the stand. She's the epitome of a politician, her words honey and fire, weaving through the room with a passion that makes you believe in something bigger than yourself. She talks of justice, equality, and the inherent right of all beings—living, undead, or otherwise—to a fair trial.

"The accused before you is not merely a paranormal creature, a figure of myth and legend," she says. She moves with grace and purpose, commanding attention from everyone in the room. "He is a being with thoughts, feelings, and a soul as vibrant as any among us. Yes, he may walk in shadows and draw sustenance from a source different from our own, but does that make him less deserving of justice? Less deserving of compassion?" she declares, her tone shifting effortlessly from authoritative to persuasive.

"With humans being the 'source' of sustenance, yes," someone in the audience says. Evans ignores him.

"Mr. Belmont is not merely a vampire; he is a citizen of this city," she continues, her voice rising with fervor. "Let us not forget the fundamental principle upon which our legal system is built: the presumption of innocence until proven guilty. Yet, how can we uphold this principle when the accused is denied the right to speak in his own defense? Is it justice to silence a voice simply because it does not conform to our preconceived notions of what it means to be human? To deny him these rights is to deny the principles upon which our society stands!"

I find myself leaning forward, drawn in by the raw emotion of her plea. I've got to admire her audacity—we know there's no evidence in Lucian's favor now, so she's turning a legal defense into a political rally. I jot down notes, not on what she says, but on how the crowd reacts. It's not the content of her speech that will help Lucian if we can't find the real murderer, it's the public opinion's tide turning, ever so slightly, in his favor.

The gavel's echo slices through the whispers of the courtroom like a knife, and there it is—Lucian, bound over for trial. The sight of him, so isolated amongst a sea of turned backs and averted gazes, ignites something within me, a spark of defiance against the injustice unfolding before my eyes.

"Quite the circus, huh?" Matty leans in, his whisper barely audible over the shuffle of people rising from their seats.

"More like a kangaroo court," I say, forcing a wry smile as I gather my things. "But hey, who doesn't love a good show?"

Matty raises an eyebrow at my tone, a glimmer of worry flickering in his eyes. "You seem pretty invested in this. Why the long face for the vampire?"

I stiffen, shooting him a sharp look. "I told you, Matty. I know he's innocent. It's about justice. Doesn't matter if you're human or... otherwise."

"Right," he says, unconvinced. "Because Emily Lane is all about justice for vampires now." He shakes his head, amused.

"Laugh it up," I mutter. "Maybe someday you'll be charged with a crime and no one will be in your corner."

"Look, I don't understand it, but if this is what you've decided to do—"

"It is," I say, the determination in my voice surprising even myself.

Matty leans close, his spicy cologne undercutting the staid air of legal proceedings, and I'm acutely aware of the warmth from his arm brushing mine. "Then, against my better judgment, let me help a little. Mitchell's house? It's going to be free of its chaperones from 8 to 10 tonight. Shift change shenanigans."

"Really?" I feign nonchalance, but my heart skips a beat. "That's quite the security lapse."

"Isn't it just?" He grins, tapping the side of his nose. "The Sheriff is still ironing out the kinks in the schedule. To the uninformed, it will look guarded and no one will be the wiser if a certain justice-seeking lady takes a peek."

"Thanks for the heads-up," I say quietly, masking my excitement with a nod. This could be my chance to find something everyone else missed.

"Hey, don't mention it," Matty replies, clapping me on the shoulder. "Friends help each other out, right?"

As the crowd files out, I catch Lucian's gaze from across the room. He's all stoic composure, but those sharp gray eyes are electric with silent questions. I take a deep breath and lean back, pretending to stretch. My lips barely move, but the message is clear: "8:00 p.m. Mitchell house."

He doesn't blink, doesn't give a single sign he's heard, except for the smallest nod, almost imperceptible. *Got it.* Thank heavens for vampire senses.

"Before you head off," Matty says. "How about dinner tomorrow night?"

I pause, the offer dangling like a shiny lure. I'm tempted, more than I care to admit. Matty isn't just the guy who color-codes his grocery list and alphabetizes his spice rack, he's pretty and funnier than I remembered. "What happened to needing more notice?"

"I'm trying for spontaneity," he answers, a playful twinkle in his eye.

"Sounds great," I say, my voice as firm as a steel beam despite the butterflies tap-dancing in my chest. "But nowhere with martinis. I can't stand cliches."

"Deal," Matty says, laughter dancing in his eyes. "No eggs either."

Maybe Matty can be my replacement for Brett. *Or maybe once you fix this Lucian problem and make partner you can stop worrying so much and actually try to connect with someone emotionally*, my inner voice says. *Maybe you should stop psychoanalyzing yourself*, another voice responds.

Maybe I should be doing it more if I'm going to continue having conversations with myself.

"Emily?" Matty's voice reels me back.

"Sorry, just... thinking about work." The lie slips out smoother than I'd like. Yeah, work, my ever-reliable scapegoat.

"The eternal grind," he replies with a sympathetic grimace. "Well, I'll text you the details for tomorrow. Can't wait."

"Me neither," I say, allowing a genuine smile. But as he heads out with the tide of bodies, I can't help but wonder where the evening might lead us, or if I even have time for whatever 'this' is.

With the courtroom emptying fast, I slide out of the pew, my movements all calculated nonchalance. As I pass by the defendant's box, I let my gaze linger on Lucian one last time, my presence a silent promise that I'm not giving up on him.

Then I'm out, slipping through the heavy courthouse doors into the bright light of day. I slip my sunglasses on and merge with the flow of pedestrians, my mind already racing ahead.

"Emergency appointment" or not, my inbox won't check itself, and Liz will have her perfectly manicured hands full covering for me. I shoot her a quick text—*"All good. Back soon."*—and accelerate my pace. Partner track waits for no woman, especially one moonlighting as a secret detective in a case that's growing more intense by the minute.

Chapter 10

In the murky depths of an alley, we bide our time until the final police officer retreats, then scurry across the street to Frank Mitchell's home. The townhouse stands at the end of the street, an extravagant display of marble columns, gold trimmings, and grandiose balconies. The exterior is painted a bright and eye-catching shade of yellow, with large windows capped in ornate gold frames and heavy velvet drapes. A lone police cruiser remains, its lights flashing to deter mischief-makers. But I trust Matty's intel; we've got this house to ourselves for a good couple of hours at least.

The moment Lucian and I step past the yellow tape on the sidewalk, a shiver runs down my spine, but not from fear. It's that pre-performance buzz, that mix of anticipation and grit, like stepping onto a stage before the curtain rises. "Become a lawyer, they said. Get security and power, they said. Nobody mentioned covert crime scene visits. They really should've," I say, rolling my eyes for effect.

Lucian chuckles, mischief dancing in his gray gaze under the cruiser's flashing lights. "Perhaps I would have become a solicitor myself had I known the thrills that might await me." He gestures grandly at the gaudy scene around us. "Like trespassing. Who knew being on the side of the law meant breaking it so often?"

"Excuse you," I say, though the ghost of a smile tugs at my lips. "I said 'sneaking' not trespassing. *I* was invited. Sort of."

"Yes, you're a bastion of good behavior," he says dryly, not missing a beat. "Shall I remind you of how we are acquainted? Of your own extra-legal activities?"

"Without my 'extra-legal' activities, you'd still be rotting in a cell without an alibi," I shoot back.

"I shall not forget it," he acknowledges.

With his admission hanging between us, we venture into the townhouse. Once we cross the marble threshold, I slide my hand into my pocket, activating my tape recorder. We creep through the foyer, following the markers to what looks to be Mitchell's study. The setting looks like a macabre stage, dim light casting eerie shadows that seem to creep just out of reach.

"Remember, hands off," I remind Lucian, though my fingers itch to sift through the chaos for clues. "Eyes only. We don't need more evidence against you."

"The risk is greater for you," he says, his voice low. "My genetic traces no longer linger."

I gulp. Better I don't get more caught up in this than I already am. I shove a cap over my head just in case as we walk through the study doors.

Despite the blood (or perhaps because of it), the room resembles Lucian's own library. Books clutter shelves and floor space, while the desk remains clear except for an open whiskey bottle and a lone cup, marred only by a crimson stain. Dust coats my tongue, mingled with a metallic tang, likely from the lingering scent of blood in the air. The sole light emanates from a table lamp, casting elongated shadows that seem to reach out like grasping fingers.

The epicenter of the incident is impossible to miss—a dark outline marking where Frank Mitchell's body once lay, surrounded by splatters of blood painting a violent picture on the hardwood floor. Yellow numbered flags identify the evidence. I crouch down, studying the way the droplets are flung far and wide. It's as if someone shook a crimson-soaked brush at an invisible canvas.

"Most vamps don't do this, right?" I ask, my eyes tracing the patterns. "This isn't... normal feeding behavior?"

Lucian shakes his head, his expression solemn. "No. We are many things, but rarely are we so... messy. Wasteful. And unnecessary violence during feeding? It goes against the etiquette we've cultivated for centuries."

"Etiquette" seems like a strange word to pair with bloodsucking. I straighten up, mulling over the implications. If not a vampire—or at least not one from Lucian's disciplined coven—then who or what would leave such a gruesome scene?

"Could it be a rogue? Someone unaffiliated with any coven?" I suggest.

"Possibly," Lucian concedes, his gaze sharpening as he scans the area. "But even rogues have patterns that echo our own. This..." He gestures vaguely at the carnage. "It's more chaotic than a mere deviation."

"Another paranormal, then?" The words taste strange on my tongue, given two days ago my only experience with the supernatural was getting high off a vampire's teeth.

"An upset werewolf, perhaps, or..." Lucian trails off, his forehead creased in thought. "Mitchell had enemies, many of them paranormals due to his stance on us, but few resort to biting."

"Few, but not none," I point out.

"Indeed," Lucian replies, his gray eyes reflecting the scant light like steel blades. He stalks towards a yellow flag labeled #5 on the corner of the desk, far from where Frank's corpse once lay. "Look at this. There was something here, something small that was removed, likely the cufflink." He points to another corner of the desk without a yellow flag or label. "But there's something missing from here. Something that was covered in blood and removed before the police marked the scene."

I join him, spotting the clean spot amidst the blood splatters, the size of a small box. "The cufflink could have been inside a box, and the murderer took the box with him after he planted it."

"Perhaps," he says, frowning.

I glance around, seeing nothing else of note in the room. After a quick check of my phone for the time, I say, "Let's check around for clues while we still have the opportunity."

Descending the creaking stairs into the basement, I can't shake off the eerie sense that we're stepping into a crypt. Old wood, mildew, and rust combine to create a musty aroma that sticks to my clothes and lingers in my nose. Each step forward sends a shiver through the floorboards. Except Lucian's steps are soundless beside me, a reminder of his otherness in this dreary human haunt.

Until finally, we reach the bottom where the floor is uneven and littered with dust and debris, crunching under our feet. The beam from my phone's flashlight dances over piles of boxes, furniture draped in ghostly sheets, and shelves lined with forgotten trinkets.

"Over there." Lucian nods towards another desk nestled in the shadows. This one is well used, covered in papers and ink.

Amidst a pile of shipping manifests and invoices, a yellowed envelope catches my eye. *'Last Will and Testament of Frank Mitchell,'* it reads in bold, scrawling letters. Void is stamped across the front in red so vivid it seems to pulsate. Idle curiosity has me extract the document, using my jacket sleeves to wrestle it from the envelope until it flutters open onto the desk.

"An outdated will?" Lucian muses, crowding close but careful not to touch.

"Look at this," I say, scanning the legalese for any clue. "A thirty-year marriage clause. If Mitchell dies before then, Margaret gets nothing."

"Harsh terms," Lucian observes, leaning in to peer at the document over my shoulder. His breath is cool against my ear.

"Especially if he's cheating with succubuses," I add, cocking my head. "Or is it succubi? I might get a little stab-happy at that injustice."

Lucian chuckles softly at my comment. "Murder seems excessive, even for succubi entanglements. Divorce court might have sufficed."

I flash him a quick grin before turning back to the will, my mind already racing through the implications of this new-found information. Rebecca is proof that Frank Mitchell's marriage was not as solid as it seemed...

"Twenty-five years," I recall suddenly. "They were married for twenty-five years. She never mentioned it—"

"Perhaps she didn't know of the will. Or perhaps it didn't matter since this is the older version," Lucian draws back, gray eyes alight with speculation, "Or perhaps there's more to this story."

"Maybe the current will can give some insight," I ponder out loud, already thinking ahead. "We need to compare them, see if the terms changed..."

"Or if someone ensured they wouldn't have to wait another five years," Lucian finishes my thought, his voice a low rumble of dark implication.

"Exactly." I carefully refold the will, sliding it back atop the stack.

"See if there's anything else, and then we need to get out of here," I say, my eyes sweeping the room one last time. Something about the quiet feels too loud, the emptiness too full of whispers. It feels as though eyes are watching us. "Before someone catches us."

"I thought you were invited," Lucian says.

"To the crime scene, sure? To snoop through basement mafioso dens? Not likely."

"Let us get caught by someone first," Lucian says, moving to the middle of the basement and crossing his arms. "He'll be able to tell us what the scene did not." He closes his eyes briefly, murmuring words too soft for my ears.

"What? There's someone else—" I start.

A flicker of movement catches my peripheral vision, and there, materializing from the shadows like magic—or more accurately, *because* of magic—is a paranormal being. He stands at barely three feet tall, his body lean and compact. His skin is a deep, rich brown, almost the color of tree bark, and is covered in subtle patterns of scales that glimmer in the low light of the basement. His eyes shimmer like stars as he comes closer to us, his movements fluid, like a dancer caught in a never-ending loop. Grotesque beauty and grace personified.

"Come the fuck on, Vampire Lord!" the being says.

Until it talks, of course.

"Sir, is that how one speaks in the presence of guests?" Lucian chides.

The creature crosses his arms, revealing long nails covered in neon green varnish. At least, I think it's varnish. "It's how I talk when a fuckin' vampire exposes me to humans."

"Hello," I say, half-amused, half-shocked by his appearance. "I'm... Emily. And you are?"

"Not interested in talkin' with humans, how about that?" he says, snarling.

"Emily, this is the house's keeper," Lucian explains. "A hobgoblin, to be precise."

My brows raise. "Hobgoblins like you mentioned yesterday?"

"Quite so," Lucian says. "They dwell in old abodes such as this, sometimes allies, other times tricksters. Shall we see if this one fancies a chat?"

"I don't," the hobgoblin snarls.

"Sounds like he's not one of the former," I say under my breath.

"I apologize for so unceremoniously revealing you," Lucian says. "We seek your insight into a rather... delicate matter."

The hobgoblin chuckles, a dry rasping sound. "You mean the murder?" He mimes what must be Mitchell being attacked from behind and slowly dying. As the hobgoblin lies on the floor, he leers up at us, revealing three rows of haphazard teeth. "I'm not feelin' in an insightful mood."

"Maybe we could trade," I offer. "Something you need for something... we need."

Lucian cringes but the hobgoblin looks intrigued.

"Will be a stiff price," he asserts from his place on the floor.

Remembering Lucian's claimed riches, *and* that he got us into this (and all the other) messes, I say dryly, "Try us."

"Information for information," he says, fixing his gaze upon me, sharp and assessing.

"Let's hear it then," I prompt, eager to keep him engaged and get out of here before the cops return.

"You've heard of the Fae Accords?" he asks, his eyes narrowing with a glint of urgency. "Fuckin' tricked by a pixie into a deal not worth the spit we shook on it."

"Tricked by a pixie?" Lucian interjects with slight amusement.

"Silence, leech," the hobgoblin snaps, baring his teeth, but softens his expression as he turns back to me. "But yes, tricked! And now I'm stuck servicin' her unless I can find a loophole. Or kill her."

"We said information," Lucian warns.

"Yeah, yeah," the hobgoblin says. "So, human lawyer, get me out of the contract and I'll help you out."

"How did you know I was a lawyer?"

Both he and Lucian frown at me. "I'm a hobgoblin," "He's a hobgoblin" they both say in tandem.

I suppress an eye roll. "Okay then. Fine, but only if you can prove you actually have the information about the crime I need." No way am I getting forced into paranormal lawyering for something piddly.

"How dare you!" the hobgoblin says, standing to his full three feet and puffing out his chest.

"She doesn't know," Lucian says, hands aloft as if to soothe him.

"This is my home," the hobgoblin says, his tone sounding dark like storms. "I know every single fuckin' thing happens inside these walls."

I shift my balance to one hip and cross my arms. "Even when you're not here?"

"D'uh," he says.

I flick my focus to Lucian who nods. "Alright. I'm sorry. No harm, no foul. We have a deal," I say, pressing my lips together as I consider the *third* paranormal client I've apparently taken on in as few days. "But this isn't exactly the place for in-depth legal consultations." Especially with the cops coming back.

"Agreed," he rasps, his voice now a blend of gravel and wind chimes.

"Meet me at my house later," I tell him, slipping my tape recorder into the pocket of my blazer and rattling off my address. "We can't stay at a crime scene longer than necessary, especially when the deceased's spirit might be eavesdropping." I shoot Lucian a look that says, 'yes, I'm serious.'

"No such thing as ghosts," the hobgoblin says. "But fine. Your house then. I can visit my cousin."

I wince at the confirmation of my own creepy houseguest. "Great. Meet us there in an hour."

"An hour and a half," he demands, and I wonder if everything he says is supposed to be contrary.

"Fine," I nod, more to myself than him. "Lucian, we should wrap things up here."

"Indeed," Lucian agrees, casting one last sweeping glance around the dank basement.

"Until tonight, then," I say, extending a hand not for a shake but as a signal of temporary parting. The hobgoblin nods once, sharply, and with a flicker of shadow, he disappears from sight, leaving only the echo of our agreement hanging in the air.

"Let's go," I urge Lucian, anticipation building for the evening's rendezvous. For someone who didn't sign up for paranormal lawyering, I can't seem to escape it. Which reminds me...

"Hey, Lucian, what are the Fae Accords?"

CHAPTER 11

Lucian tries to explain the Fae Accords to me as I drive him back to his house. Ever heard of the Rule Against Perpetuities? Ever think that sounded like a lot of legal mumbo jumbo? Now add magic.

My clunker wheezes to a stop in front of Lucian's grand estate, the headlights cutting through the evening's gloom. "We might need a Plan B if I can't help this hobgoblin," I tell him as I kill the engine. "Fae contract law sounds like a migraine waiting to happen."

Lucian emerges from the car with the grace of a panther. "Are you not a lawyer extraordinaire?"

"Sure, for humans," I say, scurrying to the sidewalk. "But throw in some magical fine print, and I'm about as useful as a chocolate teapot."

"I'm sure you'll be fine," he says. "Fae law truly isn't that complicated. Shouldn't you be returning to your home to wait for your new client?"

"Not a client," I say. "Plus, I think we deserve a breather after the week we've had." I tilt my neck in what I hope is a beguiling manner.

"And breather would be me feeding from you?" His eyes blaze again but instead of terrifying me, it lights a fire in my belly.

I throw my hands up in mock surrender. "Hey, you said it, not me."

"I think it's time you develop a new vice," he suggests, his voice a smooth baritone that glides over my skin.

"I tried alcohol, but I'm pretty fond of my liver," I say, but the flutter in my stomach betrays the jest. There's an electric charge between us, a current that sizzles under the surface of our banter, and I'm suddenly not so cold in the night air.

"Whatever it is, choose something less... ferrous." His eyes glint mischievously under the moonlight.

Before I can conjure up a comeback, our little tête-à-tête gets busted up. From the tree line, a shadow breaks free, striding into the scene with a determination that chills me more than the autumn weather ever could.

"Your kind isn't welcome here," the intruder spits venomously, his hand creeping under his coat. The silhouette of a weapon forms against the fabric, and my heart kicks against my ribs like it's trying to break free.

"Emily, get back," Lucian growls, positioning himself between me and the threat. The sudden shift from charming to deadly is disconcerting, yet oddly thrilling.

"Back off, buddy," I say, ignoring Lucian's warning. The tape recorder in my pocket feels suddenly inadequate as a means of defense. "You don't want to do this."

"Stay out of this," the man barks, focusing his hateful gaze on Lucian. "This is about purging your filth from our streets."

"Filth?" Lucian's eyebrows arch, a dangerous calm settling over his features. "Is that what we are to you?"

"Lucian, let's just go inside," I suggest, though my voice doesn't carry the conviction I'd hoped for.

"Too late for that," the man hisses, and with a swift motion, he draws his weapon—a sleek, silver handgun that looks particularly designed for one purpose.

"Silver bullets," Lucian says, more to himself than to me. "Worrisome if I were a werewolf."

"Bullets are still bullets," I say, holding up my fists as ineffective shields. "Unless you're indestructible. In which case, tell me so I can stand behind you."

"Enough talk," the assailant snarls, taking aim.

Lucian shoves me aside with force enough to wind me, and I stumble to the ground, my shoulder connecting with the cold brick of his walkway as my wrists scrape the ground. The world tilts on its axis as I watch Lucian spring towards our would-be assassin.

"Emily, stay down!" he commands, but I'm already scrabbling to my feet, adrenaline igniting in my veins like gasoline to fire.

"Like hell," I say. My parents' chaotic legacy didn't leave me with much, but it did teach me not to run when cornered.

Lucian grapples with the man, silver gun glinting ominously between them. They're locked in a dangerous dance, each vying for control. I scan the area for anything that could help us. And then I see it: a discarded pipe lying just a few feet away. Without hesitation, I lunge for it.

"Stay back!" Lucian grits out, throwing a punch that lands with a sickening crunch against the man's jaw. But this guy, fueled by hatred, seems impervious to pain or reason.

"Sorry, not my style," I say, gripping the pipe.

My heart pounds in my chest as the assailant reaches for his gun, his fingers inches away from pulling the trigger. Without a second thought, I lunge forward and swing the pipe with all my might. The satisfying sound of metal connecting with flesh echoes through the street as the man collapses to the ground. A look of shock crosses Lucian's face for a split second before he regains his composure.

"Nice swing," he says, a ghost of a smirk on his lips despite the chaos.

The man recovers quicker than expected, lunging for the gun. I kick it away, sending it spinning beneath a parked car. Lucian uses the distraction, locking the attacker's neck in a vice-like grip. His strength is a tangible thing, his arms bands of iron as he holds the struggling figure. His eyes are fierce, protective, and something primal stirs within me at the sight.

But I'm no shrinking violet myself. With the attacker momentarily subdued, I leap forward, grabbing the man's wrists and wrenching them behind his back until I hear a sharp crack.

The would-be assassin's body slams against the pavement, his breath a ragged surrender to our combined might. Lucian's grip on him slackens as the assailant scrambles to his feet, a look of wild terror replacing the malice in his eyes. He doesn't look back as he bolts, disappearing into the murky embrace of the night.

"Looks like we scared him off," I quip, trying to steady my voice, but it trembles like a leaf in the wind. The taste of triumph mixes with the copper tang of fear on my tongue. We did it; we're still standing.

Lucian and I lock eyes, an unspoken communication flowing between us. His lips part in a half-smile, the hint of fangs visible for a split second before he composes himself. "We make quite the team, don't we?" he says, his tone light, but the concern in those stormy gray orbs is palpable.

"Let's not make it a habit though, okay?" I manage to say, though my insides are still doing somersaults. If there's one thing I'm good at, it's defusing tension with humor. I force a shaky laugh, the adrenaline crash leaving me feeling raw and exposed.

"Are you hurt?" Lucian's question slices through the fog of adrenaline.

"Nothing bruised but my ego," I say, checking my limbs. They're all functioning, albeit shaking like I've just downed six espresso shots. But as the rush fades, the reality of our close call sinks in, wrapping around me like a cloak. It could've gone sideways so quickly.

"You could have been killed," he scolds me softly, but I hold up a hand.

"I know. Just... give me a second. I need to... just breathe." I draw in the cool night air, letting it fill my lungs, feeling the ground beneath my feet, solid and real.

"Okay," he agrees, and we stand there in silence, letting the world slow down around us. There's something about almost dying that really makes you appreciate... not dying.

Except for the fact that Lucian's already dead.

"Thanks, by the way." I meet his gaze again. "For not abandoning me to the trigger-happy jerk."

"I would never abandon you, Emily," he replies, and something warm flickers in his expression, something that has nothing to do with vampire heat. It's genuine, human, and it hits me then how much I enjoy hanging out with this immortal paranormal, near-death experience or otherwise.

The rhythmic thud of our hearts gradually fades into the background noise of the night.

"We should disinfect your hands," he finally says.

I look down at my hands, which are trembling slightly. The skin is scraped raw, little droplets of blood dotting the surface. Tiny bits of gravel are embedded in the cuts. "Vampire super-senses, huh? Must be handy."

He takes my hand gently, inspecting the damage inflicted by the scuffle. "They are, but I knew you'd fallen on them. The extent of the damage was merely conjecture. Though you failed to admit it when I asked." His voice turns mockingly stern, "and someone needs to keep you from infection. That killed people in my day."

It's both comforting and disconcerting to have someone care, but I brush it off with a small chuckle, my nerves still jangling like a poorly tuned guitar. "You got me, grandpa. I'll avoid my hands going gangrenous. But I've got a first aid kit at home."

Lucian nods, his eyes lingering on my scraped hands with a mix of concern and... something else. Admiration? Regret? Maybe even desire, hidden under centuries of control. If I were more poetic, I'd say it was a longing to keep touching me, but more likely it was just the sight of blood.

I clear my throat and pull my hands back to my sides. "You should come with me."

Lucian's gaze flickers from my hands to my face before he nods in agreement. "I can escort you but I must return—"

"No," I interrupt. "You can't go back to your place tonight. It's not safe." No more jokes now, this is serious.

Lucian's stance goes rigid, his posture that of a commander assessing the battlefield, but there's no denying the flicker of concern in his steel-gray eyes. "I cannot leave my fledglings."

"You're the target, not them, and you don't want to lead any other fanatics back here," I say. "Can't you use some supernatural magic and protect them and then hide out somewhere else?"

"Not.." He trails off, like he's thinking through what I've suggested. "Perhaps. Where do you suggest I go? I cannot remain in vampire territory then."

I suck in a breath and repeat my impulsive offer. "My place."

"You think *your* apartment will offer better protection?"

"Better than a potential crime scene? Yeah, I do." I cross my arms, trying to match his cool composure. "No hotels will have you, right? And Sara's place is... well, it's full of dead people."

"Occupational hazard for a mortician," he says, but the humor doesn't quite reach his eyes.

"Which wouldn't do much for your reputation if you're found there. Unless someone pulls the records and finds my name bailing you out," which I'm desperately hoping no one will ever do, "they'd never guess you'd stay with me. So, what do you say, roomie?" The tease slips out, but my pulse quickens at the thought. Sharing space with Lucian means more than just safety; it's an admission of trust.

He hesitates, a shadow passing over his face so briefly I might've imagined it. "I suppose it makes some sense," he concedes, though I catch the reluctance in his voice. "Until I can place a few more wards..."

"I'll invite you in, and even that second-in-command of yours for slumber parties-slash-meetings," I wheedle, hoping to sweeten the pot.

The raised brow is back. "That's a myth. But," he continues, "you've convinced me, Counselor. Your place it is."

"Great!" My heart does a little victory dance, even as I keep my expression neutral. "But if you even think about using my toothbrush, we're going to have words."

"Rest assured, Emily, I've survived centuries without borrowing personal hygiene products." A smirk plays on his lips, the tension between us shifting again, becoming something charged and electric.

"Good to know," I say, feeling the corners of my mouth lift into a smile. "Let's go before another loser drops in."

The lock clicks, and we step into the dimly lit foyer of my spartan apartment. Lucian's hand hovers near the small of my back, a tantalizing brush that sends a ripple of awareness through me.

"Nice place," he says, his voice smooth like aged whiskey, warming me more than I care to admit. He leans close, his breath ghosting over my face.

"Thanks." My attempt at modesty is halfhearted at best, the secondhand furnishings speak for themselves. "It's my little corner of—"

"Human!" A gruff voice slices through our moment like a sharp knife through a ripe tomato.

We both whirl around to the source of the interruption. There, perched on my scratched coffee table with his knobby knees drawn up to his chest, is the hobgoblin from Mitchell's house. He wears a lopsided grin, displaying his three rows of pointed teeth that could probably open cans.

"Fantastic timing," I deadpan, while Lucian shoots me a silent question with his raised eyebrow.

"You said an hour, here I am," the hobgoblin says.

"You said an hour and a half," I retort, massaging my temples. I turn to Lucian, hoping for a miracle. "Please tell me you know some paranormal that can conjure wine."

"I thought alcohol wasn't your new vice of choice," Lucian says with a laugh. But even his charm can't ease the irritation burbling in my stomach.

I sink into the worn cushions of my lumpy couch. "Okay, hobgoblin—"

"Wilkin," he grunts.

"Wilkin. You've got my attention. You mentioned getting out of the contract. Do you have a copy for me to review for loopholes?"

"Nope," Wilkin announces, leaping down from the table with the unpredictable movements of a coiled spring. "You need to get it."

I lean forward, resting my elbows on my knees as I glare down at him. "Usually I don't need to sing for my supper. When someone wants me to help them out of a contract, they *give me* the contract."

"This is the deal," Wilkin insists, his eyes suddenly serious. "You get the contract, I get you the information. And it is *good* information."

"I thought this was an *exchange* of information," I snap back, all the tension and stress of the day returning. "Not a game of fetch."

"The contract's literally information. Not my fault you weren't more specific," he says, crossing his bony arms around his naked chest.

Freakin' fae tricks, apparently.

"Fine," I concede begrudgingly. "Where do I find it?"

"In the Underground," Wilkin announces.

Lucian's face darkens beside me, capturing my attention. "Is that bad?" I murmur from the side of my mouth.

His noncommittal shrug doesn't inspire confidence.

"Nah, she'll live," Wilkin says to no one in particular.

"Who are you talking—" I start, but Wilkin cuts me off.

"My cousin," he confirms with a toothy smirk. "The one in the walls of your buildin'."

"Of course, how silly of me." I press my fingers against my forehead. Ten minutes ago, I was imagining Lucian licking my neck (and elsewhere), now I'm planning a B&E with the buddy of my very own wall-monster.

Lucian watches me, his gaze steady. "The Underground is incredibly dangerous for humans, even with an escort," he says softly. "We can find another avenue for the information we need. There is still the will to consider."

I purse my lips. The will could be a red herring. But Wilkin could also be trying to pull a fast one like he did with the 'information for information' game.

"Wilkin, what did your cousin—"

"Herle." It sounds more heaving than a word.

I let out a heaving sigh. "What did *Herle* say to make you think I might not survive?"

He leers, revealing those ominous teeth again. "No un-bonded human's been to the Underground before. No telling whether you'd live. Herle thinks you're too soft."

"And Herle's been spying on me since I moved in?" I ask wearily.

Wilkin nods, his expression earnest. "He also thinks you'd be prettier if you cut your hair and threw out that ratty bra you got on."

"Your opinion is noted, Herle," I say to the walls before turning back to Wilkin. "I'll see what I can do about the contract."

"Oh, I know, human," he replies before vanishing in a puff of brimstone-scented smoke.

Lucian turns to me. "I don't like this, Emily," he says, his voice laced with concern.

"Well, neither do I, but I think Herle's been here longer than me."

Lucian huffs. "I mean about the Underground. Even with me beside you, it's treacherous."

"No, I know," I say. "How bad would it be? You saw me earlier. I can handle myself."

His jaw tightens. "All your fears about ruining your reputation for helping me will no longer matter. Because you'll be dead."

A chill slithers down my spine, but I shove the weight of his concern aside. "What about that 'bonding' thing he mentioned? Unbonded humans haven't visited, which implies *bonded* humans have," I say. "Could I—"

"Absolutely not." Lucian's tone is granite.

"What do you mean, 'absolutely not'?" Indignation bubbles up quickly, all my emotions close to the surface.

"I mean exactly what I said," he replies firmly, his eyes flashing. "Bonding with a paranormal creature is one of the most dangerous things you could do."

Ever curious, I begrudgingly ask, "Why?"

Lucian hesitates for a moment before answering. "Because once bonded, your soul will be tied to theirs forever," he says gravely. "You will become dependent on them, and they on you. If anything were to happen to them, it would also happen to you."

My heart sinks. Bonding with an underworld creature would mean putting my life in their hands completely, which sounds slightly... awful. "But wouldn't that also mean they would protect me?" I counter weakly.

Lucian gives me a look like I just suggested jumping off a cliff. "Certainly, in exchange for eternal attachment. But do not overlook what I've said. If they stub their toe, you'll feel it. If they die, you die. Is that worth the risk?"

"The immortality part might be nice," I mutter to myself, though I know he heard. To him, I say, "But if it's the only way to survive in the underground..." I trail off. The thought of backing down now doesn't sit right with me. I've always been stubborn to a fault, and there's no way I'm letting some creature underworld intimidate me just because I haven't *eternally bonded* with a paranormal.

Lucian shakes his head. "There are other ways. And bonding is not an option."

I chew on the inside of my cheek. Part of me wonders if he's bonded, and that's why it's no-go. To Sara maybe? To another man or woman somewhere in a nicer apartment with a better grasp on paranormal affairs, one not strongarming their way into things?

Taking a deep breath, I turn to Lucian, my tone as resolute as his was. "Well, it seems like we've got ourselves a lovely little suicide mission on our hands."

Lucian's eyes widen, his surprise evident. "This isn't a game. Traversing the Underworld is not something to be taken lightly."

I flash him a wry smile, trying to mask the tremor of fear that snakes through me. But if I'm about to risk my skin, I'll be damned if I do it without my trademark sass. "Who said anything about taking it lightly? I'm simply stating the obvious."

Lucian's gaze searches mine. "Let us see about the will first. Then we can discuss you attempting to infiltrate the Underground unbonded. Please."

"Okay," I assure him, though the promise tastes bitter on my tongue. "Shall I show you the bedroom?" I fall back onto humor again. "I did mention this was a one-bedroom joint, right? We'll need to snuggle."

His hand reaches out, fingers brushing against mine in a fleeting touch. "Goodnight, Emily. Sleep well, *alone*."

Chapter 12

The next morning finds me hunched over a sea of paperwork that's swallowed my desk whole, the widow's will in my hands like a lifeline—or maybe it's a smoking gun. Stuart did me a favor by uploading it into the system, sparing me the humiliation of begging him for a copy on my hands and knees.

Liz enters, and I swiftly conceal the will beneath the Jenkins brief. "Here," she says, handing me a stack of papers. "Just filed in NorthMark. I've noted the due date."

I thank her and add them to the towering stack of tasks awaiting my attention. Who knew that my side gig as a paranormal investigator would wreak such havoc on my day job? At least my social life has taken a nosedive to make up for it—with Lucian refusing to let me donate and Brett no longer offering his services on demand. *Emily Lane, lawyer by day, murder mystery sleuth by night, pariah through it all.* Although I briefly remember Matty's invite, and the possibility of a date tonight. That'll give me a reprieve from my hermit status for an evening.

When Liz returns to her cubicle, I retrieve the will. A small part of me—very small—registers the ethical quandary I'm in now. Oh, if my law school professors could see me now, they'd have a field day with my very own exam question:

when can confidential client information be used to potentially save a life? Does the equation change when that life isn't human?

Frankly, I'm not losing much sleep over the ethics of it. Trying to save an innocent vampire is ethical enough. But risking disbarment? No, thank you.

Just don't get caught, my inner voice says. Surprisingly, none of the other voices disagree. With that consensus, I squint at the legalese, searching for something helpful. And then I find it—the golden ticket. My pulse quickens as I trace the line where the 30-year marriage clause used to be. It's gone. Vanished. Margaret inherits everything no matter how long they've been married. And underneath it, Frank's signature, dated just a week before his untimely demise.

"Gotcha," I whisper to the empty room.

I tap my pen against the will, plotting my next move. I've got a widow with a will that reeks of motive and now I need evidence to back it up. And I bet that evidence is sitting snugly with Frank's former campaign manager, Tom Turner, a man who wears success like a second skin, especially after his client's sticky end.

Liz's habits have rubbed off and I've trawled the online news streams for the last week. That or my even-more solitary status means I have more free time. Either way, Tom has been making the rounds, talking up poor Frank and the need for a strong anti-candidate contender to replace his dearly departed client.

"Here goes nothing," I say, standing up, straightening my jacket, and checking my reflection. My dark hair is pulled back in its perpetual bun, a few rebellious strands framing my face. Today's armor includes a sharp blazer that doesn't quite hide the scratches on my wrists from the scuffle last night. At least the marks from Alice's feeding have faded nicely, allowing me to wear v-neck blouses once again. And my blue eyes are fixed with purpose; they've seen things, these eyes, and they're about to see a whole lot more.

As I prepare to depart, Liz appears, eyeing me expectantly. "Where are you headed?"

"Just some routine investigation on the Mitchell matter," I reply casually, not wanting to tip her off to the true nature of my mission. It's half-true, anyway.

Liz salutes and returns to her cubicle down the hall.

"Watch your back, Mrs. Mitchell," I whisper to her imagined presence, slipping a copy of the altered will into my briefcase. "Because I'm coming for the truth, and I've got a feeling it's going to be one hell of a reveal."

The elevator dings open on the 30th floor, and I step into a reception area of sleek lines and polished surfaces, a place where success isn't just expected, but flaunted like a badge of honor.

"Can I help you?" The receptionist doesn't even glance up from her monitor when she greets me.

"Emily Lane, to see Tom Turner," I say, clutching my briefcase like it's my trusty sidekick.

That gets her attention, and she stands, simpering, "Of course, Ms. Lane. Mr. Turner is expecting you. Right this way."

She leads me down a corridor lined with glass walls, offices displaying their occupants like exhibits. I catch glimpses of the movers and shakers within, each engrossed in their own little worlds.

Tom's office is no exception. The door swings open to reveal a space that screams ambition. Awards line the shelves, photos with high-profile figures are strategically placed, and there's Tom, standing behind his mahogany desk with the confidence of a man who knows he's made it, his bright white teeth and tanned skin a beacon against the silky black of his perfectly tailored suit. The door closes with a soft click, sealing me inside the campaign manager's domain.

"Emily, a pleasure!" He beams, extending a hand that feels like it's shaken more important ones than mine.

"Tom," I greet him with a half-smile, "thanks for agreeing to meet with me."

"Anything for Frank's widow... and pretty lawyers," he says with a wink that makes me want to scrub my hand with bleach later.

I settle into the chair across from him, clicking my recorder on and crossing legs clad in my best 'don't mess with me' pencil skirt.

"Let's cut to the chase," I start, leaning forward. "Frank's passing has been... unsettling for everyone involved. It throws things into disarray, including some significant campaign plans, I imagine."

"Unsettling, yes, but life goes on," Tom replies smoothly, yet there's a glint in his blue eyes that suggests he's already three moves ahead on the political chessboard.

"Indeed, it does," I nod, playing along. "But let's talk about before everything went sideways. As you know, Mrs. Mitchell wants to rain justice down on anyone under her thundercloud. And image is everything in these lawsuits. We'll need to show her as a devoted spouse, get the jury fully behind her. How was Frank's relationship with her? Any tensions we should be aware of?"

"Emily, they were like any power couple—fiercely loyal in public, but behind closed doors..." Tom trails off.

"Behind closed doors is where the truth tends to hide," I say, tapping a finger against the side of my nose. "And truths have a way of emerging, especially when there's a potential wrongful death claim looming over someone's legacy."

"The legal dance." He smirks, leaning back in his chair to cross one long leg over the other. "It's always about what you can prove, isn't it?"

"Always," I agree, holding his gaze. "So, anything you can share that might help clear the murky waters? For the sake of Mrs. Mitchell's case—and Frank's memory, of course."

Tom hesitates, weighing his words like they're currency, but then something firms in his expression and he splays his hands. "Between us, Emily, there were always rumors about them, her part in his business. Money changing hands, strange meetings at odd hours... But hey, that's politics, right?"

"Right," I echo, my voice tinged with irony. Politics, or the perfect cover for something much more sinister? It's not like someone trafficking in large shipments doesn't have the opportunity. Enough movies were made on the subject, after all.

"And... it's a little strange, isn't?" He leans in, as if sharing a secret. "She found her husband dead, body still warm. She was at a campaign event I signed her up for, some Ladies Auxiliary shit. Wasn't supposed to end until midnight, but she leaves after twenty minutes and happens to find Frank bleeding out?"

"Are you suggesting...?"

"I'm not suggesting anything." He chuckles darkly. "Just that I've seen her type before. Always one step ahead, even in heels. Would have been an excellent candidate herself."

"What about her background? Any skeletons I should worry about? For the lawsuit, of course," I prod, sensing the undercurrents of gossip swirling beneath his polished exterior.

"She wouldn't be out of place in a den of vipers. They say she's always at the right place at the right time—or the wrong one, depending on your perspective."

"Right place, huh?" My heart beats a staccato rhythm against my ribs. There it is—the hint of a motive wrapped in innuendo and sealed with a knowing look.

"Exactly," he affirms, a conspiratorial glint in his eye. "You didn't hear it from me, but that woman knows more than she lets on. And Frank signing over everything to her just a week before his... untimely exit? Raises questions."

"Anything else?" I prompt, sensing there's more he's holding back.

"Let's just say, if walls could talk, Frank's house would be a veritable cacophony." Tom smirks, seemingly pleased with his own turn of phrase.

"Charming imagery," I say dryly, my mind wandering to Wilkin. I might still need to venture into the Underground for his information. But so far, all signs point to Margaret being the mastermind behind Frank's demise.

"It's quite the opportunity, regardless of the circumstances," Tom continues, his eyes gleaming like a predator who's just spotted his prey.

"Opportunity?" I parrot back, crossing my arms as I lean against the edge of his desk. It's all chrome and glass, much like the man himself—transparent in intent but unyielding in resolve.

"Frank's death," he starts, pacing before the floor-to-ceiling windows that showcase the city's skyline, "has... simplified things. People want stability, Emily. And those paranormals—" He spits after, as if he's tasted trash. "But the anti-paranormal sentiment? It's through the roof now. Frank's death is just the martyrdom we needed to push the agenda. A real rallying point, you know?"

"Peterson sounded like he was falling on Frank's side of the aisle with that press conference," I say, frowning.

Tom stops, spinning to put his back to the windows. "Mayor Peterson's stance? He's been playing both sides now, which might win him some of Frank's supporters, so long as he can keep playing the idiots with paranormal-loving hearts." He fists his hands on his hips, looking like every villain in a superhero movie pleading for the audience to understand the merits of his evil plan. "But I'll be the one to bring back order."

"You're running?"

"I have to. People are scared, Emily. They want someone to blame, and now they've got a face for their fear, and a man to rally behind. For Frank's legacy, of course," he says, with a sly smile.

"Of course," I repeat dryly, watching his chest puff out with every breath.

"Frank's death was tragic, yes," he explains, "but politically convenient for those of us on the anti side."

"Almost too convenient," I muse. But I've found my murderer, no reason to talk myself out of it. "Any worries about Stephanie Evans?"

"Stephanie?" He chuckles, a sound devoid of humor. "She's on the fringe now. Couldn't primary a paper bag. But politics make strange bedfellows. She could become a client someday." Tom's grin is quick, fleeting. "Hell, Peterson even sent me a 'welcome to the race' present." He flicks his hand towards the small box on the console table beside me.

With his go-ahead, I snap open the lid, revealing two engraved pens.

"Nice shit, right?" Tom says, looking down at them. "Steel nibs, sharp as sin and custom-made. Have to specially ship in the ink from France."

"They certainly are something," I say diplomatically, closing the box before I rise to leave. "Thanks for your time, Tom. You've given me plenty to... digest."

"Be careful, Emily," he calls after me, his voice dripping with mock concern. "People in my line of work have accidents when they get too nosy."

"Thanks for the advice," I shoot back, stepping into the hall towards the elevator. "I'll be sure to watch my step."

It's clear that Tom Turner loves the sound of his own success almost as much as he loves the game of politics. But beneath that slick exterior and those carefully chosen words, he gave me exactly what I needed.

CHAPTER 13

The interview with Tom leaves me more drained than I care to admit. As I walk through the door of my apartment, the click of the lock behind me sounds like a closing argument; final, resolute. My heels come off with two satisfying thuds against the hardwood floor. Home. My remaining work can be done from here, in the solitude and comfort of my own poorly outfitted sanctuary.

Work and committing ethical malpractice against a client, that is.

After finishing up and checking off a few more items for the job that actually *pays* me, the sun is just beginning its descent. I'm halfway to freedom—my couch—when the shrill ping of my phone slices through the quiet.

Text incoming from unknown number. *Great, because who doesn't love a good mystery after a day of... actual mysteries?*

"Autopsy report's in," the text reads, and I know it's business before pleasure. But the sender could be anyone in Lucian's orbit.

"Who is this?" I text back.

"It's Sara. Got the autopsy back. Lucian wants your eyes on it."

I exhale, picturing Lucian's piercing gaze in my mind, that unnerving way he has of making you feel seen and scrutinized all at once. *"Can it wait?"* I type, my thumbs moving deftly over the screen. *"I have a date."*

"Of course, you do," comes Sara's swift reply, and I can practically hear the eye roll. *"I'll be sure to explain to Lucian that you getting laid is more important than proving his innocence."*

Her words sting with a snark that's sharper than the edge of any legal brief I've ever encountered.

"Fine," I text back, my fingers stabbing the virtual letters with more force than necessary. Guilt is an annoying itch. *"Text the address and I'll be there in fifteen. I'll stay as long as I can."*

She sends directions, ending the thread with an overly cheery *"See you soon."* The message hangs there, a digital reminder that my very limited personal life is now officially on hold. And it's Lucian's fault. Again.

I toss the phone onto the couch, feeling its weight echo in my chest. The irritation inside me is squashed by a stronger sense of duty, or maybe it's just my relentless ambition. Either way, the fight is over before it begins.

"Obligations take precedence. Work over fun," I say to the empty room, repeating a truth I've live by. Grabbing my tape recorder, I make a quick note about the interview with Tom before the night gets away from me. With a sigh, I scoop up my phone again.

I tap Matty's name, and he picks up on the second ring.

"Hey, Emily," his voice comes through, warm like a shot of whiskey on a frosty night.

"Hi, Matty," I start, twirling a strand of hair around my finger. "Look, I'm going to need to push dinner back by at least an hour. Something's come up at work that I can't ignore."

"Everything okay?" Concern laces his voice.

"Nothing life-threatening," I reassure him, leaving out that it indirectly involves someone else's potential life sentence. "Just a last minute... consultation. I'll make it up to you, I promise."

"Sure thing, Em," he replies without a hint of hesitation, something surprising given his reputation for being in love with regimented schedules. "I'll push back the reservation until 8:00. See you soon."

"Thanks, you're the best," I say, meaning it more than he knows. The call ends with a soft click.

The drive over to Sara's is a blur of traffic lights and the same three chords repeating from a pop song that's been overplayed to death. I switch the radio to the news just as they're interviewing Tom for the seventh time. His campaign spiel blares out until I give up and finish the drive in total silence.

When I pull up to Sara's place, it looks like every other cookie-cutter townhouse in the row, except for the faint glow of candles flickering behind closed curtains—a mortician's touch, perhaps.

I knock twice and the door swings open to reveal Sara, her platinum hair cascading in waves that somehow look both meticulous and wild. Beside her stands Lucian, tall and imposing in the dim hallway light, his ponytail a dark streak against the crisp white of his shirt.

"Emily," Lucian greets me, his voice smooth, a carefully modulated tone that carries centuries of persuasion. "Thank you for coming on such short notice."

"Wouldn't miss it," I say, trying to steady the flutter in my chest that his presence has provoked. Damn that missing endorphin rush. If I'd found a new bedmate or donated blood again, he'd surely not make my body quiver just by his presence. Probably.

Sara moves beside him, leaning against Lucian's arm as if they were long time partners, but in what, I don't know. "At least you have your priorities straight now," she says, causing Lucian to smirk down at her. His hand rests comfortably on her shoulder.

I step inside, brushing past them, feeling the charged air of their camaraderie like static. "How'd you get here so fast? The sun's barely down."

"The tunnels," both Lucian and Sara answer in unison.

"So you didn't need my getaway car?" I ask, arching an eyebrow.

"Not unless it's a Tin Lizzie," Sara says, her inflection rising like she's made a great joke.

Apparently she has, as Lucian releases a chuckle as dark as chocolate.

"What's so funny?" I ask, trying to keep from frowning. I know I'm an outsider to their inside jokes and shared history, but they invited me here; they could at least include me.

"Oh, just one of Lucian's anecdotes from the 1920s," Sara says, her hazel eyes twinkling with a shared secret. "You know how it is, some stories are timeless."

"Right," I say, dragging out the word as irritation gurgles in my gut. "Unfortunately, time isn't something we have the luxury of wasting tonight," I remind them, slipping back into lawyer mode. It's all about control: keeping my focus sharp, my wit sharper, inside jokes be damned.

"Let's get down to business, then." Lucian's expression shifts, the levity gone as if shed like a second skin, and suddenly it's all grave seriousness—the kind that commands attention without raising a voice. "After all, we have a mystery to unravel."

I shuffle the papers, my fingers tracing the stark black lines of text as Lucian and Sara lean in, forming a triangle of intense scrutiny over the autopsy report spread across Sara's cluttered dining table. The scent of eucalyptus in Sara's house is overtaken by the sterile smell of ink and paper filling the air as we pore over every detail.

"The tox report showed traces of brandy in his system but nothing else," Sara says, shuffling through the pages.

"No brandy at the scene," I remind Lucian. "Only whiskey. Unless the cops used the crime scene as their own private liquor store."

Lucian frowns. "And no exsanguination, as Sara previously surmised."

Which fits Sara's theory that a vampire wouldn't kill him. Why waste the blood. The words "puncture wounds" catch my eye, and I snort.

"Yes, but punctures from thin blunt instruments," I muse aloud, tilting my head to one side. "That's vague enough to be anything from a rod to, I don't know, vampire fangs?"

"Pencils, pens, ice picks," Sara adds.

"No trace of lead or ink in the wounds," Lucian says, his gaze fixed on the report as if searching for hidden clues between the lines.

"What about hairpins?" I ask, cocking my head curiously. I cast my memory back to my first meeting with Margaret, her hair perfectly coiffed, not a strand out of place, secured by ornate hairpins. She'd been wearing them during that first press conference too. "Sharp, likely metal, easily concealed. Probably messy if you're trying to stab someone in the neck that's resisting you."

"An excellent thought," Lucian acknowledges with a nod.

"We should investigate that angle further," Sara chimes in, gaze as sharp as those hypothetical weapons.

Who is the 'we' in that sentence?

"Margaret Mitchell wears hairpins," I blurt out, unwilling to let Sara take my part in this so-called team.

"But she discovered the body well after time of death," Lucian counters, his brow furrowing as he looks through his notes. "According to the case file, she was at a dinner event and returned home to find him dead."

I wave a dismissive hand. "She left the dinner early, she could've slipped out with no one noticing. What if she wasn't truthful about when she left, came home, murdered Frank, and then waited around before calling it in?"

Lucian frowns. "How did you come across this information about the dinner?"

"It was work related," I say nonchalantly, unwilling to admit I'd been investigating without him. "I just happened upon the info."

"Fair enough," Lucian concedes with a nod. "But there would likely be surveillance footage or witnesses that could confirm when she left the dinner."

"Don't forget time of death is wiggly anyway," Sara interjects. She'd been watching us play ping pong and apparently wanted back in the game. "It isn't an exact science. Just a minor mistake, and suddenly the widow is home at the exact right time."

I look down at the report in front of us and feel a sense of satisfaction. "I think we've got it. With the changes to the will and Margaret's questionable behavior, she's looking pretty shady."

"Was the will *also* work related?" Lucian asks, a half-smile tugging at his lips.

"In fact, yes," I reply with a smirk.

He leans in. "So long as you aren't investigating without me."

"It looks like you might not need to anymore," Sara interjects, pushing herself back into the conversation. "If what Emily is saying is right."

"It is," I say.

"I'm not sure," Lucian counters, ever the realist. "This isn't the smoking gun we'd hoped for."

"It's just as good," I insist. "Consider it the cooling bullet. Margaret can't leave Frank if she wants his money, because of the 30-year marriage clause. He's cheating, with a paranormal being no less. Maybe Margaret gets wind Frank is promising said paranormal his commitment, true or not. She's pissed at the betrayal, or the end of her gravy train. Because who is going to vote in an anti-paranormal candidate who struts about with a succubus on his arm? She convinces him to change the will, she'd been the loyal one after all so why keep it? And then stab! Murder by hair accessory."

The blaring sound of my alarm interrupts our discussion, reminding me that I have plans tonight and need to get ready. I quickly silence my phone and stand up from my seat. "I should probably head out, but I really believe we've cracked the case. We should bring our findings to the police."

"Let's consider it further," Lucian suggests. "There could be ramifications in revealing our findings too soon."

"It'll be fine," I assure him, shrugging on my jacket. "I'll see you tonight at mine?" I ask, glancing back at them sitting so cozily at Sara's table. For some reason, the sight irritates me.

"Naturally," he says, smiling. "We can discuss the next steps in how to reveal what we've learned about Margaret."

"Sure, maybe," I call out as I make my way to the door. "See you tonight!"

Chapter 14

Okay, *maybe* I should wait until Lucian is home, or revisit all the facts. But I'm itching to call Matty and tell him what I've learned. After all, the pieces all line up.

"Hey there, Herle, what do you think?" I ask my silent sidekick, who still offers no response. I'm starting to think Wilkin made him up just to mess with me. *Although a pretend housemate is probably healthier than talking to myself. Maybe.*

But with no answer in the negative from Herle or myself, I dial Matty's number, each beep a staccato prelude to the bombshell I'm about to drop. Better do this before the date, instead of mixing work and play. Holding the phone to my ear, I lean against the cool surface of my kitchen counter, feeling like a kid on Christmas eve—tingling with secrets and imminent revelations.

"Pick up, pick up," I mutter as the phone rings. But maybe luck—or fate—is on my side.

"Emily? If you're canceling on me now, you're setting a new record for me and women." Matty's voice is dry as week-old bread, but it's music to my ears.

"Nope, dinner's still on. But prepare to be dazzled," I say, unable to contain my excitement. "You're going to want to sit down for this."

There's a rustle on the other end, followed by a low chuckle. "Alright, hit me."

"Frank Mitchell's better half is crying crocodile tears," I begin, pacing now, my free hand gesticulating as if he could see me. "She's practically swimming in motive and opportunity. And guess what? The puncture wounds are a red herring. It's not a vamp's style to leave evidence like that. Too messy, too... human."

"Emily," Matty interrupts, his skepticism practically reaching out and tapping me on the shoulder. "You can't seriously think—"

"Can and do," I cut in, undeterred. "Look, Matty, Margaret Mitchell has more red flags than a Bulls' game. All I'm asking is for you to take these findings to your office, poke around, maybe lean on the police to take a second look. You already *know* he's innocent, this is extra proof."

"Emily." His sigh crackles through the line. "Even if there's a speck of truth in what you're saying, how do you expect anyone to take this seriously? You're talking about paranormals, vampires—"

"Exhibit A: Prejudice," I retort, spinning on my heel. "Matty, you've got to trust me on this. I wouldn't stake my reputation with you if I wasn't sure."

"Stake, huh? Cute," he says flatly. "But alright, I'll take a look. I can't promise anything though."

I can tell from his tone he's already bracing for the paperwork avalanche I'm about to unleash on him. But the DA's had it easy so far, with a defendant that can't testify and half-theories about a cufflink, they can handle reviewing some *real* evidence.

"But Emily, this better not be a wild goose chase," he continues. "You're completely kept out of it, I haven't told anyone about your alibi yet. But I might need to if I'm pointing the finger at a grieving spouse. And if this blows up..."

"It won't," I assure him, my confidence a suit of armor I wear better than any couture. "Thanks, Matty. You're a gem, even if you don't sparkle in sunlight."

"Hilarious," he replies. "See you in thirty," he adds before hanging up.

I toss my phone to the counter. The game's afoot, and I've just made the first move on the chessboard—a queen's gambit, no less. I just hope my reputation isn't the sacrificed pawn.

I stand before the full-length mirror, scrutinizing my reflection with an intensity usually reserved for cross-examinations. My little black dress hugs curves that usually hid behind legal briefs. It wasn't my first choice, that's my blue standby used for those few and far between dates, but there was a mustard stain on one of the shoulders. Considering I don't own mustard and haven't had a takeout burger for a few weeks, the stain was a surprise.

But the fabric of my *second* choice whispers against my skin, a silent promise of allure and professionalism mixed with just enough rebellion to make it interesting. As I twist my hair into an elegant chignon, a rogue strand falls, framing my face in casual defiance.

Tonight, it's not about ambition, it's about... something else. Something like butterflies doing the tango in my stomach.

"Stop overthinking," I mutter to my reflection, dabbing on just enough lipstick to look intentional without screaming 'trying too hard.'

"What do you think?" I ask the walls. Herle stays silent, but I imagine he's va-va-vooming in whatever invisible realm he's inhabiting.

"Okay, Emily, you're just going to dinner. With Matty," I remind myself, though the pep talk sounds more like a closing argument to a jury of nerves. I grab my clutch—no room for a tape recorder tonight—and head out.

The restaurant gleams under the soft glow of streetlights, a beacon of civilized dining amidst the jungle of the city. I push open the door, the murmur of conversation wrapping around me like a warm shawl. And then I see them—Matty, Megan, and Brian—seated at a table meant for four, their laughter punctuating the air.

Surprise skitters up my spine, followed by a shiver of disappointment I quickly squash under the heel of my poker face. So much for intimacy over appetizers.

"Emily, you made it!" Megan calls, waving me over with an enthusiasm that contrasts with my awkward stride.

"Hey guys," I say, my voice steadier than I feel as I slide into the chair next to Matty. His eyes meet mine, and there's a silent exchange I can't decipher.

"Didn't know we were making this a law school night," I quip, though the joke lands like a lead balloon.

"Well, you've missed out on the last..." Megan taps her purple painted lips thoughtfully. "What is it, Brian, eight outings?"

Brian nods, already signaling the waiter.

"And Matty missed the last one," Megan finishes. "So, this is perfect. We can make this a regular Tuesday night hang!"

I force a smile, but it's brittle, threatening to crack under the weight of disappointment. I glance at Matty, hoping for a lifeline, but he remains neutral, an unreadable mask that frustrates me more than any legal jargon. As the waiter approaches, I hastily order a glass of red wine, feeling the need for its fortifying presence. I've got nothing against a law school dinner, but a warning that I'd misinterpreted Matty's invite might have done wonders for my heart.

Dinner unfolds in courses—appetizers, main dishes, and frustrations piled high on my plate. It gets worse when Stuart comes by.

"Emily, fancy seeing you here. And with your... friends, no less," he drawls, his smile as insincere as a politician's campaign promise.

"Stuart," I acknowledge, my tone frostier than the pinot I'm shotgunning. "What brings you out of your coffin?"

I inwardly wince at the vampire joke and tell a silent apology to Lucian, Stardust, and the rest of them. Matty looks at me, a silent question in his expression but I shake my head.

"Business dinner with a client," he replies smoothly, his eyes flicking between me and the others. "You know what a client is right, Emily? Something you're supposed to bring into the firm?"

Stuart's smirk widens and I fight the urge to throw my drink in his face. Instead, I smile sweetly, hiding the storm brewing beneath the surface.

"Of course, Stuart. Thanks for the reminder," I say through gritted teeth, my polite facade barely concealing the seething anger within. "I'll be sure to bring it up at my partnership interview."

Megan isn't so polite. "Harsh, dick. Who peed in your pasta?"

Stuart's smile tightens. "Charming." And then he excuses himself with a scowl.

Dinner drags on, my appetite lost amid the tension simmering beneath the surface. I stab at my food with more vigor than necessary, trying to channel my frustration into something less destructive than hurling insults at coworkers in public.

When Matty finally pulls me aside, there's a tension in his shoulders that mirrors my own.

"Emily, I didn't plan for a group thing," he confesses, his voice a low rumble. "Megan heard about us meeting up and assumed..."

"Got it," I cut in, the disappointment a tangy note on my tongue.

"Next time, I'll make sure it's just us," he promises, and the sincerity in his voice chips at my carefully constructed walls.

"Next time," I echo, letting the words hang between us like a dare. Matty might be a chance for something real. As scary as that sounds, I lean in closer, unable to resist the pull, until our lips are mere inches apart. But just as our lips ghost over each other, the sound of approaching footsteps breaks the spell, and we pull away, leaving me breathless and wanting.

When dinner finally wraps, we all mull outside the restaurant.

"Let's do this again sometime," Matty suggests, and the look in his eyes tells me he means just us. Just Emily and Matty, minus the unexpected audience.

"Sure," I say, my smile genuine but my heart still thumping a complicated rhythm. As I bid everyone goodnight, it feels the evening was both a misstep and a step forward, leaving me adrift in a sea of what-ifs.

"Mayor Peterson, a retrospective," the news radio announcer starts when the engine turns over. "Raised by his grandmother Eleanor Peterson, nee Carter, Michael was a conscientious boy..."

I quickly click it off, preferring the sound of my own thoughts. As I drive home, to Lucian, the city lights blur into streaks of color, painting the night with possibilities. Lucian's image haunts the edges of my thoughts, a ghostly presence that's become all too real. I'm a woman who prizes logic over fantasy, evidence over emotion. Yet here I am, feeling caught between two men...

"Get a grip, Emily. You're not some damsel in a gothic novel," I scold myself, though the flutter in my stomach betrays me.

The key turns in the lock with a faint click and I push open my door, stepping into the quiet coolness of my apartment. It's dark, only moonlight streaming through the sheer curtains, casting long shadows across the floor. I toss my keys on the entryway table, the clatter louder than I expect in the silence.

"Rough night?" Lucian's voice comes from the living room, smooth as silk and just as comforting.

I flick on the light to find him lounging on the sofa. He looks up, gray eyes catching the light, and there's an unreadable expression on his face.

"You could say that," I admit, kicking off my heels and padding towards him.

"I have a few moments before I must depart, if you'd like a sympathetic ear." He pats the space beside him, but I don't take the bait, not yet.

"Actually, I've got news." The excitement bubbles inside me despite the letdown of the evening. "Matty's going to look into Margaret Mitchell for Frank's murder. She has motive aplenty, and I'm sure she's our girl."

But instead of sharing my enthusiasm, he looks disappointed. "I thought we were going to wait."

"I know we mentioned wanting to think about it," I begin, my voice hesitant as I carefully choose my words. "But the opportunity presented itself, and I couldn't just ignore it."

His expression remains inscrutable, and a knot of anxiety twists in my stomach.

"Come on, be an optimist," I continue, my voice more determined now. "What's the worst that can happen?"

"What indeed," he replies, but there's a shadow lurking behind his words, something I can't quite catch.

The shadow doesn't deter me. I move closer, even more emboldened by the strange cocktail of disappointment and desire swirling inside me. And alcohol, of course. I'm riled up enough not even to care about a potential hobgoblin audience. "So... how about we celebrate your impending freedom?"

"Emily—" His voice is a warning, but I ignore it.

"Come on, Lucian. Just one little victory dance?" My fingers trail along his arm, feeling the coolness of his skin beneath the soft fabric of his shirt.

He catches my hand, his touch gentle but firm. "As tempting as that is, I think it's best if we keep things professional."

I pause, logic peeking through the haze of my feelings, remembering our near-moment yesterday. "You're not bonded, are you?"

He shakes his head silently and I slide even closer.

"Okay, then. I'm not asking for a ring and a house, just sex," I tease, leaning in until our faces are inches apart. I can feel his breath on my skin, cool and steady.

"Don't tempt me." His thumb brushes against my wrist, sending a shiver up my spine. "I'd rather not complicate matters further."

I tilt my head, searching his gaze for any sign of capitulation. "Complications can be fun."

For a heart-stopping moment, he hovers there, his cool breath brushing against the sensitive skin of my neck. *His teeth in my neck might be as nice as a kiss*, I think dazedly. I brace myself for the piercing sensation.

But the bite never comes.

"Emily." There's a note of finality in his tone this time, and he leans forward, his lips hovering over mine for a fraction of a second before he pulls back. "Go get some rest. You've had a long day."

"Rest is for the faint-hearted," I say, my last-ditch attempt at flirtation falling flat as he doesn't react.

Deflated but oddly electrified, I stand and head toward my bedroom, pausing at the doorway to glance back at him. "Goodnight, Lucian."

"Goodnight, Emily."

The sheets feel cool against my skin, but they can't quench the heat swirling within me. Tossing and turning, I can't shake off the frustration of two near-kisses lingering like ghosts in my mind.

"Focus, Emily," I mutter to myself, attempting to rein in my thoughts. Professionalism, boundaries—terms that suddenly feel as outdated as the vampire lurking in my living room. A small, treacherous part of me wonders what it would be like if he had blurred those lines. Would the ground beneath us quake?

I shift again, pulling the blanket up to my chin. The gears in my brain churn relentlessly, analyzing, predicting, preparing for the next move in this legal chess game. Which brings me to Matty, him another kind of challenge I'm itching to meet. Could we—would we...?

"Stop it," I scold myself. "One heartthrob at a time."

But it's no use. The 'what-ifs' circle like vultures, refusing to let me sleep. I close my eyes, and in the darkness behind them, images of Lucian and Matty intertwine—a game of desire and duty that leaves me both breathless and exasperated.

The clock's slow march taunts me—11:47 p.m., 11:48... I roll out of bed, my feet hitting the cold floor as if to shock some sense back into my life. I've done the horizontal tango with my pillow long enough, and it's clear who's leading. Hint: not me. So, I decide to burn off the restless energy with a midnight raid on the fridge.

Lucian's nowhere in sight, and I tell myself I'm not disappointed his gorgeous backside isn't gracing my couch.

"Let's see," I muse aloud, swinging the fridge door open. "What's a girl got to eat around here to exorcise her emotional demons? Ah, leftover Chinese takeout. Perfect for a side of self-pity."

With a container of Moo Shu pork in hand and a fork as my weapon of choice, I settle onto the couch, still in my PJs—a pair of old sweatpants that have seen better days and a tank top that reads 'Legal Briefs by Day, Vampire Slayer by Night.'

The irony isn't lost on me.

"Maybe I should add 'Dating Disaster' to my resume," I say to the empty room, flicking through the TV channels like they're defendants on the stand, each one pleading their case for my attention.

"Infomercials, reality TV, oh, a documentary about the mating habits of snails—riveting." My sarcasm could cut glass but hey, it beats dealing with the silence. And maybe Herle will emerge just to shut me up.

I'm about to commit to the love life of gastropods when my phone vibrates, jolting me upright. Speak of the devil—it's Matty.

"Emily, did you email that information?" His voice is all business, which I guess is fair considering it's nearly the witching hour.

"Sent them after dinner, hotshot. Check your inbox before you accuse the innocent," I say, balancing the phone between my shoulder and ear as I dig into my late-night snack.

"Got it, sorry. I was too excited after dinner and got sidetracked," he admits.

Warmth suffuses my skin and I'm back bouncing through the thoughts that kept me awake in the first place. I consider a phone tête-à-tête but my indifference to Herle's voyeurism vanished along with the remains of my tiny buzz.

"Relax, counselor. Margaret Mitchell's innocence is shakier than my commitment to getting a good night's sleep. Once you sift through that info, even you'll start believing in vampires—or at least innocent ones."

He chuckles, and I can almost picture the skeptical arch of his brow. "You really think Lucian's off the hook?"

"More than I believe in my chances at partner this year. And trust me, that's saying something."

"Get some sleep," Matty says, his tone softening a fraction.

"Sleep is for the well-adjusted. I'll settle for more Moo Shu and bad television. Night, Matty."

"Night, Emily."

I end the call and toss my phone aside, letting out a sigh that feels heavy enough to carry all my doubts with it. But it doesn't. Instead, it settles back down around me like an unwelcome blanket.

Just as I'm about to zone out, the soft click of the door catches my attention. I glance over, and there's Lucian, leaning casually against the doorframe.

"Mind if I join you?" he asks as he gestures towards the couch.

I swallow, suddenly feeling a rush of nervous energy coursing through my veins. "Not afraid I'm going to come on to you again?"

"With that shirt? I'd be more afraid for a stake through my heart," he says as he crosses the room and settles onto the couch beside me.

We sit in silence, the glow of the TV casting flickering shadows across the room.

"Is this your newest vice?" he asks, voice barely heard over the tv. "Lack of sleep and television?"

"Healthier than drugs," I shoot back.

He laughs, something low and growly and I clench my legs together as heat trails down to my core at the sound.

Come on, Lane, get it together, I tell myself, focusing on the screen where snails are apparently locking lips, or whatever equivalent they have to lips. If they can find love, surely there's hope for a hapless lawyer. Lucian shifts beside me, our knees grazing.

"Hope" being a relative term, of course.

Chapter 15

I strut into the office with a spring in my step, the satisfying click of my heels against the polished floor echoing like a victory march. The corners of my mouth are practically dancing with smugness. I've solved Frank's murder and now I can focus on making partner.

"Morning, Emily," chirps Jenny, the receptionist, but I'm too wrapped up in my own world to do more than nod and flash what I hope is an appropriately professional smile.

Shutting the door to my office behind me feels like sealing myself off from the chaos. I toss my bag onto the chair and prepare to get down to the brass tacks of legal wizardry. Inbox checked, computer booted, I head to the news for a dose of my own victory parade, otherwise known as the news of Mrs. Mitchell's arrest.

I'm in luck as Peterson is doing a new press conference on the Mitchell murder. I quickly click the link and adjust the speakers, ready to bask in the glow of my success.

But no basking occurs. Instead of triumph, I get a sucker punch. Beside Mayor Peterson is Margaret Mitchell, hair wound tight enough to control her thoughts, two sparkling hair pins poking out like devil horns.

"...paranormals responsible for the death of my husband..." Margaret's voice quivers with the perfect cocktail of mourning and malice while my high spirits deflate faster than a punctured tire. "It grieves me to see how quickly certain facets of society have attempted to shift blame onto me, onto one of our *own*, the humans who are simply trying to survive against such paranormal violence. Although paranormal advocates have attempted to throw mud onto me—" She sniffs dramatically, patting her eyes with a gold-threaded hanky. "The police have fully exonerated me from any wrongdoing."

Peterson places a comforting hand on Margaret's shoulder, his warm green eyes now throwing daggers at the camera. "We stand united against these attempts to undermine our community and sow discord. As such, I am announcing additional rules for paranormal beings. They will be subject to curfews and restricted from all areas outside their respective quarters. Furthermore, any attempts to impede ongoing investigations or cast aspersions on law-abiding citizens will be met with swift and severe consequences."

"Damn," I mutter, sinking into my chair as the weight of the world plays piggyback on my shoulders.

"O.M.G., did you see this?" calls a voice from beyond my office walls—Jeff or Sandra, no doubt itching to discuss the newest development. But I barely hear them over the rush of blood in my ears.

I snatch up my phone, typing out an apology to Matty with fingers that suddenly feel too thick, too clumsy. The message reads like a white flag, each word heavy with defeat.

His reply pings back almost instantly, just two letters that slice through any pretense of camaraderie or any hope for a do-over of the not-date from last night: *"OK."*

I send a similar message to Sara, knowing she's more likely to see Lucian before I do tonight, a fact that chafes.

"I heard. We all know. Will follow up later," she responds.

"Great," I say to no one. The screen blurs as I blink rapidly, refusing to let my eyes betray me. If there's one thing worse than being wrong, it's being wrong and having everyone know it.

My day just gets better as I'm immediately summoned to meet with the litigation team, including the partners responsible for pushing my promotion forward. The conference room is a pressure cooker, and I'm the main dish being served up for everyone's criticism. Not for my paranormal moonlighting (that's still under wraps) or my *slightly* unethical actions against Margaret Mitchell (those are going to my grave, if I can help it), but for the day job the former two activities keep interrupting.

I stand tall at the head of the polished mahogany table, but it's less like a position of power and more like I'm about to get a royal dressing-down from the top brass.

"Emily, your delay in filing the Mitchell suit is unacceptable," Mr. Davenport, the head partner in our branch, says from his seat, which seems more like a throne of judgment than office furniture. "We needed those papers filed yesterday."

"Sorry, sir," I start, but before I can continue, Stuart chimes in.

"Perhaps Emily has been too busy socializing with her. .. interesting circle of friends to attend to her professional obligations," he says, the word 'interesting' oozing sarcasm like pus from a wound.

I shoot him a look that could sear steak. "My personal life doesn't interfere with my work, Stuart. And why are you here? You're not even on the litigation team."

A few partners suppress laughs while other associates shuffle uncomfortably, hoping my verbal crosshairs won't swivel their way.

"Look," I say, steering the conversation back on track and pulling out any Hail Mary's I can think of. "The timing of the lawsuit is critical. If we file now, we risk jumping the gun. Lucian's trial is the linchpin here. A guilty verdict would set a precedent, solidifying our case."

"Lucian is obviously guilty," someone mutters from the back, another voice echoing agreement.

"Clearly just because he's a vampire," I snap, irritation making my words sharper than intended. "But we deal in facts. We need that concrete guilty verdict. Otherwise, it's just hearsay and speculation, and a jury could decide we brought the case against the wrong party. You must have heard the news reports, the preliminary hearing had a politician campaigning on paranormal rights, for God's sake. Get enough sympathy for the vampire community and we're toast."

The room falls silent as my argument sinks in. Even Stuart's smug grin wavers, and I can practically feel the tide turning. They might not like it, or me much right now, but they can't argue with logic.

"Fine," Mr. Davenport finally concedes with a sigh that speaks volumes of his skepticism. "We'll delay the lawsuit. But make no mistake, Emily, your career is riding on this. Do not disappoint us."

"Understood," I reply, my tone ironclad. I've danced on tighter ropes than this, and I won't let them see me stumble.

The meeting adjourns with a scatter of chairs and low murmurs. I gather my papers, poised to prove myself once again.

That night, I'm hunched over my laptop, the glow of the screen casting spooky shadows on piles of work I should be focusing on instead. My fingers fly across the keyboard, each click a step further from Frank Mitchell's mysterious list of enemies and deeper into the rabbit hole of new suspects: the anti-paranormal fanatics who'd love nothing more than to see Lucian burn. Or whatever vampires do when they die.

"Paranormal hate groups..." I mutter as I type in the search query. It's a dark corner of the internet I'm diving into, a cesspool of hate and fear-mongering. I wince at the first few hits—a smorgasbord of forums and articles painting paranormals as the root of all evil. But somewhere within these digital screeds must lie a clue, a motive strong enough to pin a murder on an innocent vampire. Add in Mitchell's hypocritical love affair with a succubus, and you've got a murder. I'll be damned if I don't sniff it out.

"Interesting choice of research." Lucian's voice cuts through the silence of my apartment. I didn't even hear him come in, but his reflection in my screen snaps me to attention, locking eyes with those gray pools of mystery.

"Just expanding the net," I say, swiveling to face him, bypassing the 'Margaret mistake' entirely. "Maybe Frank wasn't Mr. Popular with his allies if they knew about Rebecca. If it's not the widow, he could be the match to light more anti-paranormal drama."

"An astute observation," he concedes, leaning against the kitchen doorframe, arms crossed. "However, have you nothing else to say?"

I sigh, standing and crossing the room. So much for the 'if I don't mention it, it doesn't exist' plan. "Look, I'm sorry about pressing ahead on Margaret, really," I start, injecting a dose of empathy into my tone. "But I'm sure the answer is out there. And I mean to find it."

He steps forward, closing the gap until we're almost toe-to-toe, the air charged with something that feels like more than just tension over strategy. "You need to stop," he says.

I meet his gaze head-on. "I know I messed up. But I'm on the right trail now. Someone framed *you* and used Frank's corpse to do it. If it isn't about Frank, then it's got to be about paranormals. If that means ruffling a few feathers or baring some teeth, then so be it."

A flicker of something dark flits across his face, gone before I can decipher it. "It is no longer safe for you to investigate."

"I'm a big girl," I say, trying to sound more casual than irritated. "I can handle myself."

He steps even closer, invading my personal space in a way that I'd have welcomed last night. Hell, I'd have welcomed it thirty seconds ago, too. But his tone is serious and urgent, the energy hostile. "It is not about your safety. Nor is this about your capabilities, Emily. It's about protecting my people. You cannot rush off with half-formed ideas like you did with Mrs. Mitchell."

I cross my arms, leaning back against the wall for both support and distance from his frostiness. "Don't patronize me."

"Emily," he sighs, his gray eyes locking onto mine like he's trying to beam a message straight into my mind. "It's not patronizing you. It's putting my people first. It's a matter of life and death for my kind. I cannot afford for you to make reckless moves."

I push off the wall, affronted and angry at being treated like a child. "Reckless? I'm only trying to find the truth."

His expression darkens. "You are a brilliant lawyer, and I am thankful that you posted my bond and allowed me freedom. But your tunnel vision in this matter is dangerous," he says firmly, his voice laced with frustration. "You fixated on Margaret Mitchell as the culprit solely because of the will and a hairpin theory, ignoring any other possibilities that could have led us to the real culprit. Now the entire city knows we're investigating, and my people are being punished for it."

"Maybe you're right," I concede through gritted teeth, swallowing my pride like bitter medicine. "I might have rushed in, guns blazing. But I can't sit back and watch, Lucian. Not when every moment lost could mean another step away from the truth. Your trial isn't waiting for us to figure things out."

He approaches me again, his presence intimidating but no longer unfriendly. "I understand your drive, Emily. But rash actions, like those you've just taken, could lead to consequences neither of us can foresee." His hand reaches out before dropping back to his side. "They already have."

I meet his gaze. "So, what, then? I sit on my hands and wait for permission from you to pursue leads?"

Lucian shakes his head, regret flickering over his features. "No. I cannot allow you to investigate further."

"You can't allow me?" I shoot back, my voice sharp with defiance. "Who are you to stop me?"

He reaches out again, like he's aiming for a peace offering, his hand landing heavily on my shoulder. "I'm the coven leader, responsible for my people's safety. And right now, your actions are putting them at risk."

I shrug off his hand, his words crushing down on me like an anvil. "So, what? You're going to play Mr. Overprotective and expect me to twiddle my thumbs while you call the shots?" I let my voice rise, fueled by a mix of anger, embarrassment, and rebellion. How dare he try to put the brakes on me like this? "You may be the coven leader, but I am not one of your vampires to command at will."

Lucian's eyes darken. "I am not trying to control you," he says, his tone unwavering. "But we do not need outsiders who act on their own accord and only cause chaos in our world."

I take a step back. "I'm in this now, Lucian. My name on the bail form. My name as your alibi." Because after possibly making him look like a fool at work, I doubt Matty's covering for me as his source against the widow now. My reputation is staked on this thing, no pun intended, and time is running out.

"I know exactly what you're risking. But the lives of my people outweigh it," Lucian says, shaking his head. "I'm returning to my coven tonight," he continues. "I need to ensure their safety under the new restrictions. Once they're secure, I'll pursue my exoneration and investigation without your involvement."

He grabs the few things he left in my apartment and heads for the door. With his hand on the handle, he calls over his shoulder, "I've tightened the restrictions in the vampire district. You'll not be welcome anywhere within."

The door slams shut behind him, the sound echoing through the empty apartment like a final punctuation mark on his departure. I stand there in the silence that follows, my heart hammering in my chest, a mix of anger and hurt swirling within me like a storm. Lucian's words linger in the air, heavy with the weight of his authority and the finality of his decision.

How dare he dictate my actions, confine me to the sidelines like some helpless observer?

If Lucian thinks I'll meekly abide by his wishes and twiddle my thumbs while he takes charge, then he doesn't know me at all. And considering we had our first actual conversation a week ago, he doesn't. And he's in for a surprise.

"Hey, Herle!" I call out. "Let Wilkin know I'm ready to work. Just tell me where to find the entrance to the Underground." There's no response, but I think I sense the acknowledgment.

Let's see how far my tunnel vision takes me. No pun intended.

Chapter 16

I shimmy through the grimy bars of the sewer entrance, a scowl twisting my lips as the stink of city rot smacks me right in the mouth. Herle hadn't passed on any message, but I'd whistled loud enough outside Mitchell's house to get Wilkin's attention. His raspy laughter still rings in my ears, the 'directions' he'd so kindly provided a tangled mess in my brain.

"Down the old tunnels," he wheezed, sounding like gravel in a tin can. "Humans actually can't see it. But hey, not my circus, not my monkeys."

The tunnel before me is an artery of shadows, barely lit by the occasional flicker of a bulb hanging on for dear life. I keep my back straight, trying not to think about the gallons of literal filth that have probably passed through here, or the paranormals that call this gloom home.

"Fantastic," I mutter, forging ahead. I'm no stranger to tenacity; I've fought tooth and nail for every scrap of success at my job. But this? This is a whole new level of ambition. All I've got guiding me is the promise of justice for Lucian and my reputation, Wilkin's ghostly directions, and a stubborn streak that maybe should've taken a vacation.

"Find the contract in the sewers," I scoff under my breath, the absurdity of it echoing in the dank air. "How hard could it be?"

Harder than making partner. Harder than keeping a friend, apparently.

The deeper I delve, the heavier the silence becomes, smothering any hope of a simple solution. I'd expected. .. what? A bustling shadow market, perhaps? Paranormal creatures haggling over enchanted items? Instead, nothing but emptiness. Just me and the quiet drip-drip-drip that mocks my every step.

I pause, a plan simmering to life despite the desolation around me. Empty or not, there has to be something here—some clue, some sign of hidden life. I just need to tap into that same persistence that's fueled my career, that same drive that won't let me walk away from a challenge. The same stubbornness that had me leap into the sewer at midnight without backup.

"Alright, Emily Lane," I say to myself, summoning a smile that feels more like a grimace. "Time to live up to that reputation for being relentless."

With renewed determination, I press deeper into the bowels of Chicago, ready to peel back the layers of mystery that shield the underground world from prying eyes like mine. Soon enough, the concrete and steel of the sewers give way to caves, the walls transforming into jagged, rocky formations.

But still, the wet and winding caves are empty. Ordinary.

The sound of my own footsteps, a sloshing beat against the damp stone, is interrupted by an unexpected tune. A soft humming, melancholic and strangely familiar, filters through the stale air. I freeze mid-step, heart thumping like a bass accompaniment, as the melody weaves around me like the ghost of a forgotten hit single.

"David Bowie's 'Starman'?" I murmur, both amused and bewildered. "Here?"

"Seems fitting for an Underground escapade, wouldn't you say?" the performer says, laced with a mock-serious tone.

I round the corner to find Stardust, a splash of vibrant color amidst the grime and shadows: all sparkle and swagger, his wild blonde hair catching what little light seeps into this forsaken labyrinth and reflecting it off some ridiculously glittery shades over his eyes.

"Stardust," I say, unable to mask the relief flooding through me. "What are you—"

"Emily Lane," he interrupts, removing the shades to reveal one eyebrow arching above a flash of blue eye shadow. "Still sticking your nose where it doesn't belong, I see."

"Guilty as charged." I retort, unwilling to let his sardonic tone derail me. "But for a good cause, this time."

His expression flickers, something akin to respect—or is it pity?—crossing his features.

"I heard you joined up with Lucian. Trying to clear his name?" He asks, crossing his arms. "Was thinking, that's not our Emily Lane, who doesn't care about nought but her next bloodletting."

I wince. "That's not completely true." I cared about my job too. And was trying to be less selfish on that account.

Otherwise, why the hell would I be rooting around the sewer in my good shoes?

"I also heard *you're* to blame for the new restrictions," he adds.

"*Also* not entirely accurate," I mutter. "Not that it's affecting you, apparently."

"Peterson's pissed off the only beings that could actually force us to stay in our areas," Stardust says. "The witches wouldn't even give him a meeting, assuming he figured out how to ask. And he doesn't know about the tunnels," he adds, gesturing around us.

So the Underground is more than some supernatural hotspot, it's an entire network of channels, like those Lucian used to get around in the sunlight. *And something that humans can't see.* It's a wonder we found *anything* during Prohibition.

As I'm having my eyes opened, figuratively since the tunnels are still empty, Stardust chuckles, the sound echoing off the walls, and shakes his head in disbelief.

"I'll give you credit; you've got guts, Emily."

I echo his movements, gesturing towards the empty tunnels. "Thanks, but I'd trade guts for a clue right about now."

"Perhaps I can assist with that." His hand moves to the glinting frames now hanging from his silk shirt. "These aren't just a fashion statement." He removes them with a flourish, handles held delicately between thumb and finger, offering them to me. "They're... handy for humans. Ray borrows them when we venture down here. They might give you a clearer view of things."

"Handy," I repeat, taking the glasses with a nod. I slip them on, everything tinted a soft pink. I blink, waiting for some magical reveal, half expecting unicorns to waltz past or something equally fantastical.

"Give it a moment," Stardust advises, watching me with an unreadable expression.

"Right, because all good things take time," I say, rolling my eyes behind the rosy lenses. *Including exoneration and finding elusive contracts in Chicago's underbelly.*

He holds out his elbow. "Shall we?"

With no better way to find Wilkin's contract, I let him lead me deeper into the dark.

The world warps under the rosy tint, distorting like a reflection in a carnival mirror. The narrow sewer morphs into an expansive cavern of vibrant noise and color.

"Stardust," I breathe out, my voice a mix of awe and fear, "I think it's working."

"Told you," he says, satisfaction lacing his words.

Whatever I imagined the Underground to be, it wasn't as incredible as this. It's like a farmer's market from a fairy tale—or a nightmare.

My gaze flits from one stall to another where goblins hawk rusted keys and mercurial potions. A banshee wails softly, advertising her services of foretelling doom, while a ghoul hobbles past, indifferent to the human suddenly in their midst. Fairy-like beings with gnarled wings flutter above us, their eyes tracking our every move. A group of trolls stand nearby, their grotesque features illuminated by the flickering light of torches. It's a world where magic and horror coexist in uneasy harmony.

"Welcome to the Underground," Stardust says. "The most perilous place for both humans and paranormals alike—except for vampires and sunlight."

"Ha ha," I say faintly, trying my best not to gawk at the paranormals around me. "All those bedtime stories got it right. Trolls, fairies, the whole shebang."

Stardust smirks. "And then some. Not every paranormal lets humans catch a glimpse. You're one of the lucky ones. Assuming you live through this."

I swallow hard.

"Don't worry," Stardust assures me. "I'll make sure no harm comes to you. Gotta protect my investment." He playfully flicks the glasses on my nose. "And if something down here kills you, Lucian can't, which would be a real letdown for my entertainment now that the park's shut down."

I throw him a look of mock outrage, trying to mask the unease and wonder still swirling inside me. "Your concern is touching."

He flashes a grin that seems to outshine even the most dazzling paranormal around us, one that's sharp in the corners. "Just taking the lead from you, Miss Missy, and all your care and concern for me and mine."

I wince but Stardust doesn't let me wallow *or* offer apologies, instead dragging me deeper into the Underground.

We walk through stalls draped with spider silk and bones. Pendants crafted from giant iridescent scales hang next to potions claimed to be made from the blood of mythical beasts. My fingers itch with temptation but I resist the urge to touch anything.

"Do you come here often?" I ask Stardust as he leads me past a stall filled with glowing orbs. His sparkling attire blends into the bizarre surroundings beautifully.

"Only when the supermarket isn't the 24/7 variety," he says. "And the theme nights. As good as the Haven is, it's got nothing on the costume parties here."

I follow him towards a stall at the end of an aisle. The paranormal behind it resembles a human woman but her skin is pale as snow and her eyes glow an otherworldly blue.

"Greetings, Miss Emily Lane," she says in a voice that draws me in against my will. "How can I assist you?"

"You can't," Stardust says, baring his teeth. He drags me from the stall and, I have no idea why, but I fight him on it.

"Emily, come on," he snarls, his fingers digging hard into my forearm.

I snap back to reality, tearing my gaze from the alluring woman. Maybe Lucian was onto something about not venturing here alone. I'd have walked through fire if she asked me to, sliced off my own hand and eaten it if she'd suggested it. Thank God for Stardust.

"Thanks," I tell him sheepishly, twisting my arm to get the blood flowing back into it from his tight grip. My heart hammers a discordant rhythm that echoes against the stone walls.

He raises a glittery brow. "Told you, protecting my investment. She likely smells the open bond on you."

"Good to know," I say, swallowing down a shudder. "Let's get to business. I'd rather avoid another encounter like that." I square my shoulders, letting the unease fall off my shoulders and onto the wet ground. "I'm here for a contract—a pixie's contract with a hobgoblin. It will give us... *me* evidence to proving Lucian's innocence."

"Stealing from a pixie," Stardust muses. "When you commit, you commit."

"No challenge too hard," I say, chin up.

"Except getting bespelled by a kelpie," Stardust says.

I ignore him, strutting forward full of unearned confidence. Stardust follows until we slip through the throngs of paranormals, in search of something resembling a pixie.

"Over there," Stardust whispers, his breath warm against my ear. "Pixie's den, only one that deals with hobgoblins—third stall on the left."

"Third stall, got it," I mutter under my breath, memorizing the path as if it were a clause in a contract. We glide past a sea of scales and feathers, our steps measured and silent. I can't afford to alert the pixie until I'm ready—or worse, attract the wrong attention. My hand hovers over the tape recorder in my pocket, a habit more than necessity in this lawless lair.

Before I rush forward, I stop, hesitant and more out of my depth than I've been in a while. Or in a few hours, at least. "Is there anything I need to know about pixies?"

"Well, they have sticky fingers," Stardust replies in a hushed tone. "Watch your belongings and don't make any deals with them lightly. Pixies are tricksters, and their contracts are bound by magic, not law. *Oh*," he adds with a laugh. "And they can be hypnotized by music. Even shitty music. It's hilarious."

I nod, absorbing his advice as we approach the third stall. A soft glow envelops the area, tiny orbs of light dancing in the dimness of the underground. A small figure flits between jars of glittering dust and vials filled with iridescent liquid, her wings beating so quickly they're almost a blur.

"There's your girl," Stardust murmurs, his eyes fixed on the delicate being before us.

"Excuse me," I start, projecting confidence despite the butterflies fluttering in my stomach.

She turns towards us, her wings buzzing softly like a hummingbird's. Her skin is the color of an emerald, sparkling with every movement, and capping her head is a shock of short pink hair. *Is that where we get the term 'pixie cut?'*

"Well, well, what do we have here?" Her voice is melodious but tinged with mischief. "A human in my den? This is a rarity indeed."

"We don't mean to intrude," I say, trying to sound as diplomatic as possible. A big part of me can't believe I'm even having this conversation. "We're here on business."

"Business?" The pixie tilts her head, her eyes glittering with curiosity. "And what might that business be?"

"I'm hoping to make a deal. Is that something you do?"

The pixie's laughter tinkles like wind chimes in a gentle breeze. "Oh, human. You misinformed thing." She snaps her tiny fingers and hundreds of gossamer sheafs of paper appear on her desk. "I love deals. *Especially* with non-pixies. I tend to deal with hobgoblins but..." She trails her tiny gaze over me. "I'd bargain with a human."

I nod respectfully. "Excellent. I've heard there are several reputable dealmakers down here, so I'm looking for the best."

Stardust shifts beside me.

The pixie's eyes sparkle with pride as she flutters closer, her wings leaving a trail of shimmering dust in the air. "You'll find I am the best."

"I can't accept that just on faith," I say, injecting respectful regret into my voice. "I need proof."

She flits closer, her delicate features almost ethereal in their beauty. "And what proof could I offer?"

I splay out my hands. "I need to see your contracts. Check out your terms. Make sure you're really the best dealmaker around."

Stardust leans against the counter and lowers his voice, as if he and the pixie are in on a secret. "Lawyers, right? Can't take them anywhere."

The pixie's expression shifts, a mix of contemplation and amusement playing out across her face. She hovers in front of me, studying me intently. "Very well, human. You may peruse my contracts."

With a wicked glint in her eyes, the pixie snaps her fingers again, and the papers on her desk scatter like confetti, rearranging themselves into a neat stack. She gestures for me to come closer, her wings softly humming in the air.

I lean in to examine them, searching for Wilkin's. But I can't help but be impressed. The terms are written in a script that looks ancient and mystical, a far cry from the boring print I deal with in my everyday life. But still, the language is familiar, a give and take revealing that magical law and human law aren't all that different. Minus the magical consequences, of course.

Stardust leans in beside me, his breath warm against my ear as he whispers, "What's the plan here? Not get horny over legalese, I assume?"

I shoot him a quick glance. "I'm hoping for a distraction of the musical variety?"

"I'm *very* good for a distraction," he says, already stepping away with a swish of his cape.

He launches into an impromptu performance, belting out lyrics from a time when disco reigned supreme. The market-goers are captivated, their eyes drawn to the spectacle as if by magic.

After waiting for Stardust's voice to belt into the bridge, I check on the pixie. "These are... fascinating," I murmur, running a finger over the elegant writing crawling over the many pages. "Do you write them all yourself?"

But the pixie is preoccupied, her jewel-like eyes focused on Stardust like a moth on a bug zapper. With her attention elsewhere, I zip through the pages, searching for Wilkin's name. And there it is. With the stealth of a shadow, I tuck the paper inside my jacket.

"Time to go," I signal to Stardust, my voice barely a whisper.

"What about an encore?" Stardust says, batting his mismatched eyes down at me.

"No," I hiss.

"Spoilsport," he pouts.

"Well, thanks for the look," I tell the pixie once she's blinked away the effects of Stardust's song. "I've got a lot to think about. I'll be in touch!"

I yank Stardust by the arm and scurry away from her stall. We weave back through the market, Stardust's flamboyance now a shield as we navigate the serpentine paths. A naga hisses nearby, its forked tongue tasting the tension in the air. An ogre lumbers close, too close, but we sidestep its bulk.

"Almost to the exit," Stardust assures me, but I feel it—a prickling at the nape of my neck, a gaze that lingers too long. We may not be alone in our knowledge of the theft.

"Keep moving," I urge, pushing down the fear that tries to claw its way up my throat.

We emerge from the bowels of the city, the night air crisp and biting against my flushed skin. I heave a breath, the contract secure against my side. But as we put distance between us and the subterranean world, I can't shake off the feeling of being watched.

But there's no time to worry about watchers when my own watcher is there, hunched like an accusation beneath a flickering streetlight. Wilkin's impatience is almost palpable.

"About time," Wilkin snorts as he eyes us emerging from the depths. He extends his gnarled hand expectantly. "Got it?"

"Keep your scales on," I say, my voice breathless but buoyant. I fish out the pilfered contract from my jacket pocket and slap it into his green tipped palm.

With the precision of a surgeon and the glee of a pyromaniac, Wilkin unravels the parchment and tosses it into a newly-lit barrel fire. The flames greedily lick up the paper as if starved for the taste of illicit magic. It crackles and hisses, transforming into ash before our eyes.

"That required a lawyer's touch?" I ask him, aghast. "I thought I was supposed to be reading it and finding the loophole once I grabbed the damn thing."

"Always with the questions and the sass," Wilkin chuckles, his reptilian eyes gleaming in the firelight. "Herle was right about that." He slides his gaze up and down me. "And about the hair."

I narrow my eyes at him even as Stardust squawks out a hearty laugh.

"You should'a read the Fae Accords," Wilkin says, brushing his hands on his scaly stomach.

I clench my jaw. "I'll add it to my list. Now how about my side of this bargain?"

"Keep your pants on, human. I uphold my bargains," Wilkin says.

"Except with pixies," Stardust mutters from behind us.

Wilkin ignores the jab, even though Stardust's not wrong. "Frank Mitchell's death—it was a crime of passion. He and some man were talkin' and drinking' and Frank said something the man didn't like."

"What did the man look like?" I ask.

He squints, likely casting his memory back. Or he's just a squinter. "Looked like an older Lucian. Didn't have the stink of blood on him though, all pale and pallid."

"That's all? Did you not hear what they talked about?" I'm desperately trying not to shriek 'I risked my life through the underground for that?'

"Look, I had a friend over and was a little distracted," Wilkin says, scowling. "The guy took a box with him and dropped two bits of metal." He hands me a cufflink, glinting ominously in the firelight.

"Good thing you nabbed one of them, or else my entire evening would have been a waste of time," I say only partly sarcastically, turning the cufflink over in my hand. It's heavier than it looks, and similar to Lucian's pair, down to the scent of lavender polish on the metal. But it opens more doors than it closes. What kind of guest would Mitchell have over for drinks? An anti-paranormal, sure, but Mitchell's cozy with the other side too, whether he knew it or not. His frequenting Moonlit Haven is a testament to that.

Stardust extends his hand, and I drop the cufflink into his palm. Before I can ponder further on the intricate design etched into the metal, Severin materializes from the shadows like a well-tailored phantom. His eyes narrow at the sight of Stardust and me, together outside of the Underground's treacherous embrace.

"Richard," Severin says, his tone clipped and authoritative. "Lucian requires all vampires to check in nightly now. New protocol."

"Blame her." Stardust jerks a thumb in my direction, but his expression suggests he's more amused than annoyed.

"Ms. Lane," Severin acknowledges with a nod that's more curt than courteous. "Still meddling, I see."

"Meddling's my middle name," I snap back, defiant despite the creeping weight of responsibility. His gaze lingers on me, assessing, calculating.

"Show him." I nudge Stardust, who presents the cufflink to Severin with a flourish fit for a stage magician.

"This is the twin to the cufflink found at the scene," I explain. "*I* retrieved it."

"Made an enemy out of a pixie, even," Stardust adds.

"Interesting," Severin murmurs, taking the cufflink between his fingers. "It looks nearly identical to Lucian's."

I hold out my hand, but he pockets it. "Hey!"

"Lucian says no more investigating for you, so I'll be keeping this. Richard, five minutes," Severin declares before turning on his heel, vanishing as quickly as he appeared.

"How does he do that?" I ask under my breath.

"Always a pleasure," Stardust says with a deep bow. I can't tell if he's sincere. Then he melts into the night, leaving me with my rose-tinted glasses and a flurry of unanswered questions.

Chapter 17

The next morning is an exercise in futility as I scroll page after page of recent cufflink sales on the digital marketplace, trying to find a match for the pair found at the Mitchell house. If I'm lucky, it's a common design *unrelated* to Lucian's family.

Wilkin's information was a breadcrumb trail to nowhere: a man that looked like an older Lucian? That's any tall dark fox in town. *Thanks a bunch, Wilkin.* If this office building were older, I'd be having words with whatever hobgoblin pal of his must live in these walls. But instead, I'm left with the mind-numbing task of combing through endless listings, praying for a breakthrough and cursing Wilkin silently.

"Emily, you have a 1:00 p.m." Liz's voice, a bright interruption, sails through my doorway, her sauntering steps just a beat behind. I glance at the clock—12:58. Well, there goes my sense of time.

"Who's it with?" I ask, not recalling any scheduled meetings. My personal clientele typically consists of referrals who can stomach—or appreciate—my brand of candor. Which, admittedly, isn't many. And Mark usually gives me a head's up before siccing me on one of the firm clients.

"No idea. Name's Mr. Montgomery. Walk-in. Says he needs the best, and somehow, he got pointed your way."

"Flattering," I mutter, the sarcasm dripping so heavy it could stain my notes. Clients don't ever stumble into my office; they're usually dragged, kicking and screaming, and only *after* a partner talks me up. I straighten my blazer, the fabric stretched taut over ambition that's crammed inside me like last year's files in my bottom drawer.

"Think it's legit?" I thumb through the pages of my docket, not finding much room for a new mystery guest, social life solitude or otherwise.

"Seems loaded," she quips, green eyes gleaming with mischief. "Could be helpful for your partnership interview."

"Show him in, then," I say, masking the churn of anticipation with a practiced grin. "Let's see if Mr. Montgomery is here to make my day or ruin my week."

The door to the conference room swings open with a silent assertion, as if the hinges themselves know better than to squeak in his presence. Mr. Montgomery steps inside, and the air seems to shift, like the calm before a storm.

He stands tall, his posture impeccable, and his sharp features are framed by a neatly trimmed beard that's dark against his golden-brown skin. He's not just a man who fills a room—he commands it, every corner bending to accommodate his dominant presence.

"Ms. Lane," he rumbles, voice gravelly and deep. His handshake is firm, almost predatory, and I wonder if I'll get my hand back or if it's now part of some unspoken deal.

"Mr. Montgomery," I echo, matching his grip out of habit more than bravado.

He's dressed like he stepped off the set of an old gangster film—pinstripe suit tailored to within an inch of its life, glossy black shoes you could use as mirrors, and a silk tie knotted with precision. But it's the little things that snag my attention: the sharpness in his hazel eyes, the hint of something feral; the way his nostrils flare slightly, as though scenting the room; how his presence seems too large, somehow more than human. Although he could just be tall.

"Let's skip the pleasantries," he says, easing into the chair across from me with the grace of a predator claiming territory. "I'm here on business."

"Business is my specialty," I reply, letting a smile play at the corner of my lips. I lean back, trying to ignore the primal part of me that's suddenly very aware of the exit routes.

"Good," he nods, brushing imaginary lint off his wrist. "I need an attorney. Not simply for the courtroom antics—you'll be on retainer for... various matters. I want the best, and your reputation precedes you."

My brow arches involuntarily. 'Various matters' doesn't sound like legal jargon so much as mob code. Yet, the way he says it, coupled with the unmistakable aura of wealth surrounding him, weaves a tempting web I'm not sure I want to escape.

"Retainer?" I prod, feigning a nonchalance I don't feel. "What's the catch? There's always a catch."

"Let's call it an investment," he suggests, his smile revealing teeth that seem a touch too sharp. "In your capabilities. And your discretion."

"Discretion" is another one of those words that carries weighty implications. My mind races as I consider the implications. This isn't just a job offer; it's a golden ticket served with a side of danger. It promises security, the kind I've been clawing after my entire career—but at what cost?

"Riches, Ms. Lane," he continues, leaning forward. "Enough to make even your loftiest ambitions look like child's play."

I can hear my heartbeat in my ears, thrumming with a mix of excitement and caution. The Mitchell lawsuit looms over me like a guillotine, its delay testing the firm's patience. Doubt whispers in the corridors, questioning my competence, led by Stuart and others jealous of my partnership invitation. And partnership feels like a distant dream, one that could slip through my fingers if I'm not careful, especially with my new habit of moonlighting as a paranormal detective. If partnership eludes me, having this client in my pocket would keep me fed for years.

"Riches are tempting," I admit, my voice steady despite the turmoil inside. "But I need details. I'm a litigator by trade. What exactly am I getting myself into?"

He produces a satchel from thin air, dumping folders onto the table. I reach out to accept a thick stack of documents, but my gaze snags on something far more intriguing than the legalese I'm about to wade through. His cufflinks glint under the fluorescent lights—a pair with a crest etched into the design, silver wolves mid-howl and arrows circling the edges. They're similar to the ones I've been searching for, different crests, of course, but the fancy kind you don't just find at any department store.

"Those are interesting cufflinks," I say, nodding toward his wrists as I take the papers. My tone is casual, but there's a detective within me, unable to resist chasing a lead.

"Ah, these old things?" Mr. Montgomery gives a nonchalant glance down at his sleeves. "Family heirlooms, passed down through generations."

"Really?" I lean back in my chair, giving him a once over. Recognition flickers in his eyes, as if he knows precisely why I'm intrigued. "They're unique. But I've seen similar ones before."

"Have you now?" His lips pull up at one corner in a way that suggests he's enjoying this little game of cat and mouse. "The world's a small place, Ms. Lane. Especially for those who... stand out."

"Is that so?" I drum my fingers on the desk, contemplating. If these trinkets are more than fashion statements, they could be the breadcrumb trail leading to answers I didn't even know I was searching for. "Well, they certainly caught my eye. I suppose you wouldn't know where I could find a pair of my own?"

"Not with the history these have," he replies with a chuckle that sounds like gravel being churned beneath heavy tires. "But there is a reputable establishment in town that dabbles in repair of the... exclusive." His choice of words hangs between us, laden with unspoken understanding that we're no longer discussing mere accessories.

"Exclusive," I echo, rolling the word around in my mouth like a piece of hard candy. It's a clue, a puzzle piece sliding into place, and I'm itching to see the bigger picture. "How does one gain entry?"

"Ms. Lane," he says, voice smooth as silk, "to join my circle, one must earn my trust. And I only conduct business with those I trust. Jewelers, valets, brokers... lawyers."

And there it is. Information in exchange for an agreement to his offer. My mind races, weighing the pros and cons like a seasoned prosecutor building a case. Ambition tugs at me, while instinct whispers warnings of treacherous waters ahead.

Buying time, I skim through the pages before me, jumbles of business jargon and deals, an entire world of legal demands.

"Alright," I hear myself say, the word slicing through my hesitation.

His lips curve into a triumphant smile, sharp and knowing. I extend my hand, sealing the deal with a firm shake that doesn't betray the tremor of uncertainty coursing through me.

"Welcome to the fold, Ms. Lane," he says, rising from his seat with the confidence of a predator who knows the hunt has ended in his favor. "I believe this is the beginning of a prosperous partnership."

I escort my new client through the labyrinth of beige corridors to the elevators. He moves with unsettling ease, as if more accustomed to shadowy back alleys than the sterile halls of legal offices.

"Quite a place you've got here," he remarks.

"Thanks," I say, the word clipped as I scan our surroundings, half expecting the walls to have ears. "We pride ourselves on... adequacy."

He chuckles, a low rumble echoing deep in his chest. "I expect we'll meet in different locales from now on."

"Is that so?" I raise an eyebrow.

"Indeed. I'll send you a message with my first assignment. I believe you'll enjoy it," he says, his eyes glinting. "And my jeweler's address, of course."

"Looking forward to it," I lie through my teeth, because let's face it, anticipation is for birthday presents and lottery results, not for meetings shrouded in cryptic conversations and The Godfather-like warnings.

As he departs, I'm left feeling like I've made a deal with a devil who wears cufflinks as talismans.

Liz appears beside me, watching him enter the elevator. "He looks... interesting," Liz remarks, her green eyes narrowing as she studies the man's retreating figure. "Did he just walk out of a gangster movie or is it just me?"

I let out a surprised breath, my mind still reeling from the whirlwind of the encounter. "You could say that. I didn't get the impression he's your run-of-the-mill client."

"I looked him up," she reveals, her voice lowering. "He gives a *lot* of money to pro-paranormal groups."

"The firm will probably forgive him for his politics for the size his pocketbook," I say dryly.

Liz raises an eyebrow, her freckled face a mix of curiosity and concern. "This whole thing feels sketchy. Should you bring in one of the partners, just in case?"

I offer her a reassuring smile, though it doesn't quite reach my eyes. "Don't worry about me, Liz. I've got it."

Because there's no one else I'd trust to try.

The quaint Victorian-style brick and plank-sided homes that mark the entrance vampire quarter pass by in a blur. I tighten my grip on the steering wheel, the familiar grooves of the leather comforting against my skin as I coast to a stop down the street from Lucian's gothic mansion. The only sound is my car groaning, sounding like it was dragging itself out of the grave, a stark contrast to the usual buzz of restrained chaos that permeates this area. Killing the engine, I'm met with an eerie silence, stretching out like an unwelcome guest.

"Guess it's just you and me," I mutter to the dashboard, which doesn't have much to say on the matter. Slinging my bag over my shoulder, I step out into the cool air, locking the car with a beep that feels like a gunshot in the stillness. The park where the vampires and their donors usually perform their bloody dance of give and take is empty, the swings creaking softly like they're sharing ghost stories. Lucian's new rules, and Peterson's retributive response, has turned this place into a literal cemetery. The quarter's usual nocturnal whispers are absent tonight, making my approach to Lucian's house feel more invasion than visit.

"Montgomery better come through with that jeweler info," I whisper, a mantra to keep myself moving forward towards Lucian's place. Or perhaps I'm trying to convince myself that this isn't a colossal waste of time. Then again, I have nothing better to do tonight.

Being alone is something I've grown accustomed to, almost too comfortable with, like a favorite sweater worn thin at the edges. I'd not cared when it was a handful of dinners with the law school gang, donating with Tina, sex with Brett. But it feels different now, what with the vamps being punished for my actions (and Mitchell's murder, let's put fault where fault is due). And I'd been getting used to spending my evenings with company.

I can't drop the investigation. Besides the hope of partnership, it's all I've got. My potential with Matty is up in smoke, no further texts from him after the damning "*OK*." The few I'd sent trying to reschedule our not-date were left on 'read.' And donating blood is out of the question with

Lucian's new regime. My budding friendship with Stardust is as dead as he is or will be when Ray shows up and Stardust remembers he doesn't like me all that much. All I've got is my work and the mystery of who framed Lucian. And until I tie up the latter, the former's still in peril.

"Who needs personal connections when you've got ambition, right?" I scoff, kicking at a stray pebble. It skitters away, the sound sharp in the quiet. The joke lands flat, even to my own ears.

"Come on, Em," I chide myself, pushing past the creeping vines of self-pity. "You didn't get this far by giving up."

I fish out my tape recorder, clicking it on, the soft whir a prelude to the verbal notes I'll spew into it. But I pause, the red light blinking patiently.

"Note to self: figure out why you're so damn stubborn," I say into the device, the words more for me than any future case reference. Maybe it's the fear of failure, or maybe it's the reluctance to admit that there's nothing else waiting for me outside of this case. If I solve this, if I untangle the threads of mystery and pull the truth into the light... then what?

"Then you'll find another case, one that pays this time," I answer my unspoken question with a wry smile. There's always another case, another puzzle to piece together. Because in the end, that relentless drive, that need to prove myself—it's the closest thing I have to a love affair.

With a final bracing breath, I push open the door to Lucian's place without knocking, because I'd rather ask for forgiveness than permission.

Inside, it's chaos wrapped in velvet and brocade, a house party gone sour with vampires all but baring their fangs at each other. My eyes dance over the crowd, searching for Severin amid the snarls and hisses.

"Looking for something?" Severin's voice slithers into my ear from behind.

I spin around, and there he is, dangling the cufflink like a carrot before a particularly determined horse. "Hand it over," I demand, locking onto his mocking gaze.

"Not for all the blood in the world," he sneers, pocketing the bauble.

"Severin, you would test the patience of a saint," I say. We're on the razor's edge here, and I'm not about to start a brawl—I mean, unless absolutely necessary.

"I see no saints," he says, staring down at me.

"This isn't a game. I got the cufflink and I need it," I say, trying to keep my voice level. "You know, to uncover the frame job on your fearless leader?"

Severin's frown twitches, something like guilt flashing across his features before he regains his composure. "I have orders, Ms. Lane. And one includes keeping you away from here."

"Give me the cufflink and I'll be on my way," I demand.

Severin's eyes narrow, defiance brewing beneath the surface. But before he can respond, a familiar voice interrupts.

"What seems to be the trouble?" It's Lucian, cutting a sharp figure as always amidst the chaos. His gray eyes, usually a stormy sea, now reflect emotions I can't decipher. His gaze shifts between Severin and me, assessing the tension that crackles in the air like static electricity.

"Lucian," I acknowledge with a nod.

"I was escorting her from the property," Severin says. "Before one of the young ones loses control."

I blanch. I hadn't considered that consequence of Lucian's—and Peterson's—restrictions on the fledglings. *If donations are dwindling, am I in danger?*

"You've been told the new rules, Emily. You need to stop playing with monsters," Lucian says mildly.

"Only when they stop playing with me," I grumble under my breath. "I just need my property, and I'll leave." I motion towards Severin, hoping Lucian will play referee without stopping me.

Lucian raises an eyebrow at Severin, who reluctantly produces the cufflink.

"You're still chasing shadows?" Lucian asks. His gaze is penetrating.

"Shadows have a nasty habit of being cast by something real," I say, holding his gaze. "I don't plan on stopping until I've turned every stone, shined a light in every corner."

"Should have known," shouts a voice that sounds like Stardust from behind me, his voice tinged with a mix of admiration and disbelief. "Don't you get how single-minded Emily is? Like a dog with a bone."

"More like a cat with a laser pointer," I throw back over my shoulder, never breaking eye contact with Lucian.

"Did I tell you what she did to that pixie in the underground?" Stardust continues. "Man alive, she'll be in trouble when that pixie comes to collect."

My cheeks flush as Lucian's eyes narrow. Lucian doesn't need to know about my trip to the Underground. There's a tension in the air that could shatter glass, and I don't need Stardust adding fuel to the fire.

"Stardust, maybe you should take your glitter somewhere else," I mutter without looking away from Lucian.

"Don't point that barbed tongue at me," Stardust says, his tone sharpening. "Some of us bite back and not in the fun way."

I wince. If the friendship wasn't dead, the verbal weed killer I'm spraying will take care of it.

"A pixie?" Lucian asks.

"I needed what she had to give," I admit, unable to keep the sheepishness from my tone.

"In the Underground?" His eyes darken. "*Wilkin*," he nearly spits out.

I tilt my chin up challengingly. "It was my deal." And it's the right thing to do, no matter that it feels like the wrong one.

"As you continue to remind me, you're not part of my coven." Lucian studies me for a moment longer. "Severin," he commands. "The cufflink."

Severin hesitates, his defiance warring with obedience. "What of the consequences?"

Lucian drags his gaze over the vampires. "How much worse could it get?"

I swallow a mouthful of guilt as Severin reluctantly holds out the cufflink. Before I can snatch it, the sound of a fallen decanter shatters the moment, sending shards across the floor. A ripple of snarls weaves through the crowd, two vampires at the center of the brewing storm and at each other's throats.

"Enough," I snap, stepping forward with confidence, even though my insides felt like they were doing the Macarena. "This isn't solving anything."

A chorus of hisses greets my interjection, and a dozen resentful gazes pin me in place. I'm an outsider here, the architect of the legal chains that now bind them tighter to the shadows. But old habits die hard, and I can't stand by when there's a conflict begging for resolution.

"Silence, human!" a vamp spits, venom dripping from his words. "You've done enough damage with your laws."

I stand my ground, meeting his glare. "And yet here I am, trying to help," I say, staring them down. "So why don't we cut through this posturing and get to the heart of the matter?"

"Which is?" Lucian prompts, his voice carrying over the discord.

"Blood," I say without hesitation. "The restrictions have limited your movements so you can only get donations from a nurse or people who risk heading into the quarter."

"Perhaps the counselor understands our ways more than we thought," Severin muses, begrudging admiration in his tone.

"Or maybe I just understand bullheaded men like you," I say, allowing a wry smile to dance on my lips. "Even with the restrictions, the laws on blood donations can't be ignored. That's not how statutes work, no matter what the mayor may claim. Call a blood bank and demand an accommodation for them to come to you." I whip open my phone and tap out a few searches. "The closest is by the downtown hospital. Get one of your less volatile vamps to call."

"I'll handle it," Lucian announces. "To the rabblerousers, talk it out or take it outside. But do remember the sun will be up in a few hours."

The room falls into a reluctant silence, and with a few murmured words and begrudging nods, the tension ebbs away as the two vampires retreat into the shadows to hash out their differences.

"Interesting as ever, Ms. Lane," Severin remarks, stepping closer. He extends his hand again, revealing the cufflink.

"Never underestimate the power of common sense," I say, taking the cufflink. The cold metal serves as a reminder of the stakes.

"Nor the determination of a woman with nothing left to lose," he says.

"Especially not that," I agree quietly, tucking the cufflink safely into my pocket.

Lucian's piercing gaze meets mine, and I can see a myriad of emotions swirling in those gray depths—concern, frustration, but also a glimmer of something else, something unreadable. "Don't forget your restrictions again," he says, opening the door and gesturing out into the night. "I would hate to ward the area against you."

And with that, I leave the vampire quarter behind, heading back to my apartment alone.

CHAPTER 18

Saturday finds me knee-deep in the chaos of kitchen cabinets, where the expired food resembles tenants who've overstayed their welcome. As I sift through a box of ancient takeout menus, the shrill ring of the phone sends me banging my head against the shelf above. Rubbing the sore spot, I fish the phone from my pocket.

"Emily Lane," I answer, trying to conceal the fact that I'm in the midst of a battle with kitchen storage.

"Ms. Lane, it's Montgomery." His voice is like oil poured over gravel, and impossible to ignore. "Your presence is non-negotiable tonight."

"Montgomery?" I feign ignorance, mostly because I can't imagine why he'd call on a weekend when he hired me 24 hours ago. The hefty retainer check cleared, hence why I didn't hang up the second he spoke. "To what do I owe the pleasure?"

"Pro-paranormal fundraising dinner. It's imperative you attend," he insists, urgency lacing every word like a corset pulled too tight.

"Imperative? Is there a subpoena I should know about?" Sarcasm drips from my words, but Montgomery is unamused.

"Consider this a personal request from your client who—need I remind you—is paying handsomely for your discretion and cooperation."

"Ah, right, that personal request that sounds suspiciously like an order." I sigh, flipping through a mental calendar I keep pristine out of a lacking social life. "Fine, send details."

"Excellent. And as promised, your jeweler information—the shop is called 'Elegance in Metals.'" He pauses, and I can almost hear the smirk in his voice. "Be prepared, Ms. Lane. This event could be... enlightening."

"Enlightening," I mutter, jotting down the name of the shop before disconnecting. Social gatherings aren't usually described that way, but tonight might be an exception. I glance at my reflection in the toaster—my messy bun more mess than bun—and grimace.

"What do you think, Herle," I call to the walls. "Should I wear the knockout dress?"

In the depths of my closet, hidden behind business suits and sensible shoes, lies the knockout dress. One of the few pieces of my wardrobe I spent top dollar on. It's red, sleek, and screams 'I'm here to make a statement or possibly commit espionage'. Had my rendezvous with Matty (or Lucian) panned out differently, they might have seen it on dinner #3. Slipping it on, I catch my reflection; the professional lawyer façade gives way to something more enigmatic, someone who might frequent paranormal sympathizer dinners for fun—or profit.

I trace the teeny straps laying against my pale shoulders and wonder if attending this event could backfire spectacularly. My career teeters on the edge of partner status, and I can't afford political missteps. Not more than I've already made, what with bailing out Lucian and losing the new ally in Matty. Yet, if Montgomery, with all his wealth and influence, thinks this is important, it shouldn't tarnish my reputation by association. At least, that's the gamble I'm taking.

My makeup is minimal, a nod to professionalism among the unknown. As I secure my hair into a more sophisticated version of my usual updo, I allow myself a moment to ponder the curiosity of it all. Who attends these dinners? What passes for polite conversation amidst paranormal sympathizers when the paranormals themselves are never invited?

Slipping into heels that promise both elegance and discomfort, I grab my clutch with the tape recorder tucked inside and steal one last glance in the hall mirror. Emily Lane, attorney-at-law, is ready to mingle with the mysterious and influential—or so I hope.

"Wish me luck, Herle," I say. And with a deep breath, I step out into the evening chill, the air heavy with anticipation of the unknown.

The banquet hall shimmers under the warm glow of chandeliers, casting a golden hue over the assembly of the pro-paranormal sect, each table an island of murmurs and clinking glasses. Despite the negative press for paranormals, the event boasts an impressive turnout. I stand at the back, my arms folded, as Stephanie Evans takes the stage, her presence commanding immediate silence. That and the gorgeous pantsuit she's wearing. Before the speeches start, I click my tape recorder on, ready to capture whatever insights Montgomery deems necessary.

"Good evening, ladies and gentlemen," Stephanie begins, her voice smooth and clear. "We gather here tonight not only in solidarity with our supernatural friends." She pauses for effect and applause. "But to address the prejudices that still fester in the shadows of our society."

The crowd hangs on every word, a collective nod spreading through the room like a wave. Stephanie has a way with words that could almost make me a believer, if I wasn't already one step ahead in my support.

"However," Stephanie says, a sharp edge entering her tone, "not all paranormal creatures have their community's best interests at heart. There are individuals, like the vampire coven leader Lucian Belmont, who is accused of killing my former competition, Frank Mitchell, whose allegiance rem ains... questionable."

My irritation flares instantly, curling my fingers into fists. The murmurs rise again, laced with uncertainty and whispered agreements.

Stephanie continues, "We must be vigilant, my fellow supporters. We must not allow ourselves to be misled by those who claim to be on our side, only to harbor dark secrets and commit heinous acts against humans. Paranormals who cannot abide by our principles of coexistence have no place among us. They must be held accountable for their actions."

"Lucian has contributed more to his community than probably anyone else in this room," I snap to the woman beside me, who raises an eyebrow in surprise but doesn't respond.

While Lucian may have his flaws, painting him as a villain intent on disrupting the delicate balance between paranormals and humans doesn't sit well with me. I frown, recalling Tom's comments. Stephanie seems to be courting the paranormal community while attempting to sway centrists by denouncing Lucian.

After what feels like an eternity of veiled accusations and political maneuvering, Stephanie steps down amidst applause. My frustration only grows as the next speaker, a werewolf activist, takes the stage and amplifies Stephanie's sentiments about Lucian even further.

"And that's why we stand behind Mayor Peterson's proposal to limit vampire rights, a move that will benefit all paranormals—"

The political spiel fades into the background as I push through the crowd, trying to find Montgomery among the sea of faces. Spotting him near the front, I weave my way through the clusters of people until I reach him.

"Emily," he says with a smirk. "Having fun?"

"A real hoot," I say, my tone indicating otherwise. "I'm trying to figure out what I'm supposed to be doing here, aside from enduring stump speeches that use murder as campaign fodder."

Montgomery chuckles. "Not one for idle nights out?"

"Not when I'm technically on duty."

Leaning in, Montgomery adopts a more serious tone. "Be social, Ms. Lane. You're part of the Montgomery brand tonight. Make your presence known."

Before I have a chance to press him further, Montgomery is pulled away by another guest and disappears into the crowd. Left alone with my thoughts once again, I can feel doubt creeping in as to whether taking Montgomery on as a client really *was* a good idea.

I navigate the crowded room, dodging elbows and spilled drinks as I make my way to the bar. Stephanie Evans stands there, exuding elegance in her sleek black pantsuit as she sips on a martini. I approach her with a polite smile.

"Ms. Evans," I greet her, injecting a cool professionalism into my voice, "Emily Lane. Nice to meet you."

She turns to me, a sly smile playing on her lips. "Emily Lane, is it? The rising star attorney Frances was telling me about." She sizes me up with practiced ease.

I blink. *Frances?*

"Frances Montgomery," she clarifies. "Great dress," she adds, looking me over with an appraising eye. "But you'd be a real goddess if you did something with your hair. It's too long for you."

I offer a polite smile, continuing to conceal my irritation beneath a façade of composure. "You're not the first to suggest that."

She reaches into her clutch, producing a sleek black box identical to the one Tom had shown me earlier. With nimble fingers, she retrieves what appears to be an ink cartridge and inserts it into the pen inside the box. She then scribbles down a name on a slip of paper and hands it to me. "My hairdresser," she says casually.

"Thanks," I say, studying the elegant handwriting on the paper. "Nice pen."

She proudly turns the pen over in her hand, revealing a personalized engraving on the side. "A gift from the mayor," she boasts. "It's a hassle to make sure there's an ink cartridge in it, since you have to remove the ink before it can fit back in the box for storage." She removes the cap and twists the pen open, exposing a tiny chamber holding the ink that she tips out and into her bag. The pen is carefully replaced in the box. "But it gives me a sense of professionalism and officiality, so the slight inconvenience is worth it."

"And speaking of professional," I start, "your speech was certainly... enlightening."

Stephanie's smile widens, her eyes gleaming with a hint of challenge. "I'm glad you enjoyed it. Your presence here tonight is quite the surprise, Ms. Lane. I wasn't aware Montgomery had such... versatile connections."

I arch an eyebrow, meeting her gaze with steady resolve. "I like to keep an open mind and social calendar."

Stephanie chuckles softly, her gaze flickering towards the crowd before returning to me. "Well, let's just say this isn't anyone's usual scene. Paranormals and their allies walk a fine line these days."

I lean casually against the bar, mirroring her relaxed posture. "And which side of the line do you fall on, Ms. Evans?"

She tilts her head, a calculating glint in her eyes. "Oh, I prefer to keep my allegiances fluid. It makes for better... negotiations."

Her cryptic response sends a prickle of unease down my spine. "How does one negotiate on whether paranormals are considered equal to humans?" I ask sharply.

Stephanie leans in, her voice barely above a whisper. "That's the million-dollar question, isn't it?" Her eyes gleam with a mixture of mischief and something darker. "Some believe they are no more than beasts to be controlled, others see them as equals to be respected. It all comes down to power in the end. Even amongst the paranormals themselves."

I raise an eyebrow. "Is that so?"

"Surely you don't expect them to be a monolithic group," she teases. "Vampires versus werewolves—a classic rivalry, you know." She takes a sip of her drink, a secretive smile playing on her lips. "And that's before you consider ghouls, succubi, and more. There are paranormals out there you couldn't even imagine, each vying for power."

I've been to the Underground, I think petulantly. *I've seen paranormals you've never even dreamed of.*

"Any other paranormal conflicts I should be aware of? Specifically of the vampire variety?" I press, tapping my finger against my clutch where the tape recorder lies dormant.

"You'd have to ask a vampire that," Stephanie says. "And because of Lucian, none of them will be outside the vampire quarter for quite some time. At least you know where to find them."

With that, she winks and disappears into the crowd, leaving me to ponder her words. After last night, I'm not tucking my tail and asking the vamps themselves. But, whether intentional or not, she *has* provided me with a new set of suspects regarding Lucian's frame-up: werewolves.

Chapter 19

The morning sunlight filters through the delicate gossamer curtains of "Elegance in Metals" as I arrive at a time when I'd rather be snuggled up in my bed. There are two signs in the window, one older than me that announces the morning hours of the shop, which is why I'm here so early instead of sleeping off my evening adventure. The other is newer, a paper sign proclaiming 'HELP WANTED. NO EXPERIENCE NECESSARY.'

As I push open the door, a small chime announces my arrival. The air inside is imbued with the scent of polish and the aura of old-world craftsmanship, as if the shop itself is a relic from a time when pocket watches were more necessity than novelty. The shop owner, a wiry figure sporting spectacles precariously balanced on his nose, looks up from his workbench.

"Can I help you?" he asks, masking his curiosity beneath a veneer of professionalism.

"Emily Lane," I say, extending a hand he doesn't take. "I've got a cufflink here and I'm wondering if you've seen it before or seen one like it." If there are dozens of 'family heirlooms' out there—Lucian's, Montgomery's, whoever owned this one—then maybe it belongs to an enterprising werewolf family that has a thing against fangs that aren't their own.

The older man wipes his hands on a cloth and rises, joining me at the counter.

"Let me look," he mumbles, reaching out to inspect the cufflink I slide across the polished wood. His eyes widen imperceptibly as he turns the silver piece in his hands, examining it under the soft light. After a few moments of silence, he finally speaks.

"This is a unique design. Exceptional craftsmanship, but not one familiar from our usual clientele. Something the old families liked to have made, to set them apart from the other landed gentry of the time."

My eyes do a quick waltz around the shop, taking in the velvet-lined trays showcasing rings that look like miniature thrones for pampered royal fingers. My suspect list keeps expanding. "How many of these kinds of cufflinks do you think are out there?"

"Dozens, surely," he says, his gaze narrowing in contemplation. "However, I believe I've encountered this design recently."

"Do you recall where?" I ask, leaning forward slightly. "I'm trying to track down the owner to give him the one he lost."

After a tense heartbeat, he sighs, shuffling through a ledger with wrinkled hands that have held countless treasures. "They were indeed brought in recently. Cleaned and returned to the owner."

"Fantastic." I beam, resisting the urge to fist pump the air. "And the owner's name is?"

"That, Ms. Lane, remains between me and him. A matter of professional discretion."

The confirmation that the owner is male is a slight improvement. I lean casually against the glass counter, hoping he can't detect the thunderous pounding of my heart. "Is there *anything* else you can tell me? Maybe not about the owner, but about the cufflinks themselves? You said they were unique."

The shop owner hesitates for a moment before nodding. "Well, these cufflinks are quite exquisite craftsmanship. Definitely not your run-of-the-mill accessory. It was clear they were well-taken care of, polished often." He shakes his finger. "Someone who recognizes the value of history, not letting these sit and tarnish in a drawer. And the silver is likely sourced from centuries ago. And see how the—"

"Did you say silver?" I interrupt, a sinking feeling settling in my stomach.

"Yes," he confirms, his lips pressing into a thin line.

"Thank you for your time," I say, a little sharper than intended as I retrieve the cufflink.

Silver. A material werewolves avoid unless they harbor a masochistic streak.

Stepping outside, I let the fresh air clear my head. So, werewolves are out as suspects, after I'd only just put them on the list.

Fantastic.

The sun dips low, bleeding crimson across the skyline as I return to the Moonlit Haven. With the doors to the vampire quarter slammed shut and my list of allies dwindling faster than my luck, desperation's dragging me to this last-ditch rendezvous with the unknown. The mystery of the cufflink weighs heavy in my pocket, a reminder that Lucian's case is more tangled than a spider's web after a hurricane. I need answers, someone who gets the predator-prey dance. What I wouldn't give for a lead that doesn't bite...

I push the door open, hinges squealing like a chorus of disgruntled bats. It swings wide to reveal a room swallowed by shadow, except for the shards of light clawing their way through grimy windows. Once teeming with life—or something close—it's as abandoned as an old ghost story. There's a sign above the bar that says, 'FUMIGATION IN PROGRESS,' but the place only smells of stale beer and lost dreams. If I were a betting woman (and with the odds against me lately, I'm not), I'd say the recent restrictions closed the place and the sign is a halfhearted explanation to the human camp to keep the bar's paranormal secrets from exposure.

I slump onto a cracked leather booth, the dim light barely reaching the corners. I've hit a brick wall in Lucian's case, unraveling a sweater only to find more knots.

I wonder about the real hideouts paranormals corralled in before they were discovered. "Speakeasy" sounds too quaint for what those places must've been. They'd gather in dens like these, camaraderie and competition pulsing through their veins as thick as the liquor they couldn't enjoy. I trace my fingers over the bar's surface, worn smooth by countless elbows and clandestine meetings. I picture them—the vampires, werewolves, and things without names—leaning in close, whispers spilling secrets that could ignite wars or forge fragile truces.

"Didn't take you for a masochist, Emily," a sultry voice cuts through the silence. I swivel around to find Rebecca, the succubus I'd met on my first and only visit here, leaning against the doorframe, eyes sharp under the exit sign's neon glow.

"Rebecca." My voice is flat, no hint of surprise. In this world, coincidence is just another word for fate meddling. "What brings you to this monument to pathos?"

Her pouty lips twitch into a ghost of a smile, weariness clinging to her like a second skin. "Smelled a human. The Haven used to be a safe place for my... dietary needs. But with the new restrictions, it's as barren as a church during a vampire mass."

"Ouch," I murmur, offering a sympathetic grimace. "That bad, huh?"

She slides onto the seat next to me, all allure and enigma. "And you? Why are you here, poking at shadows?"

"Looking for breadcrumbs," I admit, rolling the cufflink between my fingers. "I found this at the crime scene. There's a story behind it, how it got to Frank's. I was hoping for a lead."

"Lucian warned you off, didn't he?" Rebecca arches an perfectly sculpted eyebrow, curiosity lighting up her golden features. "Yet here you are, digging deeper into the mire."

I shift uncomfortably, the weight of her observation pressing down on me. "You know about that?"

"Word travels fast when humans meddle in our affairs," she says, a tinge of reproach coloring her words.

I lean back against the worn leather of the booth, tapping a finger against the table's sticky surface. "I can't just stop now," I mutter, almost to myself. The bar's dim light casts long shadows that seem to nod in agreement.

"Because you're on Lucian's bail form?" Rebecca's voice is smooth as silk, but there's an edge to it that slices through my thoughts.

"Partly. And there's a part of me that wants to stick it to Lucian. He's not the boss of me."

"Is that the only reason?" Her eyes are piercing, and I'm suddenly aware of how much she sees—how much she understands.

I hesitate, my rebellious streak warring with a growing unease. "I'm not sure anymore." It's a whisper of doubt that even surprises me.

Rebecca leans in, her gaze unyielding. "You think you're doing the right thing, but you're not the one who'll pay the price if you're wrong. Our lives—the paranormals' lives—they get messier because of your little crusade."

"Little crusade?" I bristle, but the truth stings. "I'm trying—"

"Trying isn't good enough when you're playing with fire." Her words are a cool balm to my heated pride. "You need to do better, or you might burn us all."

Her words hang heavy, a ghostly presence at the table. It's true; I've been so focused on unraveling the mystery that I haven't considered the tapestry I might be destroying. The heat of my anger and irritation kept me from hearing Lucian's reasoning on why I should stop. I focused on my own spite and desire to succeed, ignoring how the consequences don't affect me.

"If you're sure about this path forward... before you dive headfirst into another disaster, look into the silver angle of that bauble." Rebecca's tone shifts, intrigue lacing her words. "Old stories, records never erased—if they exist, they could lead you somewhere."

"Silver?" I echo, my curiosity piqued despite the risk. The word seems to hang in the air, like I could reach out and grab it.

"Only rumors and speculation," she says mysteriously.

"Anything more concrete? You knew Mitchell well. Is another paranormal really the answer?" I wasn't abandoning my 'anti-paranormal crusader' idea just yet, but I could continue on this detour until I hit another dead end.

"I never said that," she replies, her eyes flickering like flames in the dimly lit room. "My Frank was a powerful man, and his death raises many questions. Who in his sphere would stand to gain from his death? No one has stepped forward to take over his enterprise, except his wife and we know she's innocent." She raises a single eyebrow at me, her perfectly manicured nails clawing on the armrest of the booth. I fight the urge not to squirm under the weight of her glare.

"But he dealt with many creatures, not just me," she continues. "There are some who may have taken issue with his affiliation, but his death reeks of something sudden and unplanned. A paranormal business deal gone wrong is my guess, with a being who couldn't turn to the law for aid and had to take matters into their own hands."

Someone who didn't play by the rules because they weren't protected by them. Like someone in the paranormal world. "And how does framing Lucian fit in?" I ask.

"Power," she says with an enigmatic smile. "Lucian holds a lot of influence and assets that other paranormal creatures might desire." She pauses, her gaze flitting to the shadows lurking in the corners of Moonlit Haven. "But you didn't hear it from me."

"Silver angle, Frank's associates, and a sudden business deal... this is starting to sound like a game of chess with lives as the pieces," I muse.

Rebecca's eyes soften, a rare flicker of empathy shining through her usual aloof facade. "It's always been a game, Emily. But sometimes, the players forget the stakes until it's too late." She gives me a look that could melt steel. Or silver.

"Yeah, I get it," I say glumly, feeling the weight of each past decision pressing down on me like a lead blanket. "Thanks for the tip, Rebecca."

She stands, smoothing the fabric of her dress with a casual grace that doesn't match the seriousness of her advice. "By the way, if you ever decide to come out of the shadows and reveal your connection to us, give me a ring. I'd like to hire you."

As she disappears into the shadows, I'm left with a choice: heed the siren's call to unravel the mystery of Frank Mitchell's death without considering the consequences or take a step back. Rebecca hadn't warned me off, just warned me to reconsider my methods. I clutch the cufflink in my palm. The allure of uncovering the truth battles with the fear of causing irreparable harm. With the taste of irony on my tongue, I wonder if my ambition has finally met its match in the hidden world of supernatural creatures.

Chapter 20

"Silver: the metal steeped in purity, adored by many, but feared by a select few creatures of the night. And perhaps the key to Frank's untimely demise, if one of those creatures dealt in silver. Perhaps they even *created* the copy," I whisper into my tape recorder.

My eyes remain glued to the computer screen, devouring ancient texts as they glide past, digital pages flipping with ghostly whispers. "Succubi," I add, "affinity for silver... unlikely *assassins*, but can't rule them out if they dealt with Mitchell." After all, even Rebecca could have a motive. I add a mental note to investigate her alibi if my silver trail doesn't pan out.

After a night rethinking my approach, I decided to keep going forward with the investigation. But with *subtlety* this time.

"Next," I say, fingers dancing over the keyboard, bringing up another file. "Ghouls—a plausible scenario, considering the research from the 1300s." A trace of exhilaration seeps into my tone; any of these supernatural entities could have orchestrated Frank's demise and inadvertently dropped the telltale cufflink.

"Emily?"

I startle at the sound, nearly knocking over my coffee mug. *So much for subtlety*. Mark stands in my doorway, his thin-rimmed glasses catching the light, glinting like a cat's eyes in the night.

I straighten up, clicking away from the paranormal database. "What's up, Mark?"

"Partner interview," he announces, "this Friday. They're all abuzz about you landing Montgomery." There's a hint of surprise in his tone, but it's overshadowed by the unmistakable undercurrent of dollar signs ringing in his ears.

had phoned me earlier, extending his congratulations. Montgomery isn't just a big fish; it's the whale Johnson & Marcus has been angling for since I donned these heels and power suits, paranormal sympathizer or no. I can't help the smile spreading across my face, satisfaction unfurling like a victorious banner in the wind.

"That's great news," I say, trying, and failing, to keep the thrill from my voice. I live for this—the recognition, the success. It's like a hit of adrenaline, and boy, do I crave it. The best feeling besides a vamp's teeth in your neck.

"Keep it up, Lane," Mark says, retreating to his world of numbers and billable hours. "This could be your ticket to partner."

"Could be?" I scoff to myself as he disappears. No, it will be. I've worked too damn hard for it not to be. And once I solve Frank's murder and obliterate any impediments in my path, they'll have no choice but to etch my name onto that shiny brass plate.

With renewed vigor, I turn back to my research, the mysteries of the night waiting to unravel beneath my fingertips.

The instant I can escape the confines of the office, I'm retracing my steps through the labyrinthine passages of Chicago's sewers. Rebecca was right, I needed to do better. And since I got the paranormals into this mess, the least I can do is clear Lucian's name and, hopefully, get them out of it.

Descending into the underground, I weave through the maze of shadows and dimly lit corridors. Armed with Stardust's distinctive glasses, I embark on a quest to uncover someone—or something—with a penchant for silver and secrets. The culprit responsible for handling that cufflink and leaving Frank lifeless in his wake.

"Emily Lane. Looking for trouble again, I see."

I stop short at the voice, as unmistakable as his wardrobe. There, leaning casually against the wall, is Stardust, exuding an aura of glitter and nonchalance.

"Stardust," I greet him with a nod, stifling a relieved smile at his appearance. My new plan for subtlety didn't call for getting murdered in the Underground, and I still needed a guide. "Still unfazed by the recent restrictions, I see."

"You only live once," he drawls, pushing off the wall to stand before me. "Or twice in my case. Now what brings you here again?"

"Just following a lead. You wouldn't know anyone with an affinity for silver, would you? Besides yourself, of course."

"Silver's not really my style," he says, smirking. "But I can think of a few paranormals who can't keep their claws off the stuff."

"Care to share? Or is this the part where you play coy for your own amusement?"

"Ah, but life without amusement is like a song without rhythm." His grin widens. "However, seeing as I'm cataclysmically bored, I might be persuaded to assist a damsel in distress."

"Distress is a strong word," I retort, arching an eyebrow. "Curious, maybe."

"Nosy, surely," he shoots back. "I'm not the only one ignoring my restrictions."

I scowl. "Lucian doesn't control me." He's the one who gave me back the cufflink, after all.

"I'd like to hear you say that to his face," he says with a teasing leer. "I bet that vein in his neck bounces like a killer beat."

"I already have." I cross my arms. "Are you going to help me or are you back to hating me?" I try not to inject the hurt that wants to appear in my tone.

"Help, most definitely. Since this damsel carries a *tape recorder* instead of a sword, I figure she could use a sidekick." He flicks a glance at my bag, where the recorder indeed lies. "So, what's the plan, partner?"

"First, don't call me partner. We're not in some buddy cop movie," I grumble, though a part of me bubbles up with happiness at having someone watching my back. "Second, we track down the list of suspects and see who had the opportunity to frame the vampires."

"Sounds like a proper caper." Stardust claps his hands together, the sound echoing off the stone walls. "Lead the way, Emily. Let's unravel this mystery together."

"Try not to get us killed," I mutter under my breath, though loud enough for him to hear.

"Darling, I'm already dead," he says with a wink.

With a swift stride, Stardust overtakes me, moving with an uncanny grace through the shadows, his sparkling attire contrasting vividly against the murky backdrop of the underworld.

"Keep up, Emily," he teases over his shoulder, his voice a playful lilt in the gloom. "We wouldn't want to lose you to a ghoul with a grudge."

"Hilarious," I say, my tape recorder snug in my hand, ready to document our findings—or my untimely demise. We slip past a den of succubi, their eyes glowing like coals as they size up Stardust. He winks at them outrageously, prompting a chorus of disgusted hisses.

"See? Pure loathing," he whispers triumphantly, scribbling down their names on our list. "They've despised us since the eighties when I outshone them on stage."

"Because that's clearly the only reason," I deadpan, though I'm secretly impressed by his ability to draw out reactions without causing a full-on supernatural incident.

We continue winding through the labyrinthine tunnels. When we round a corner, a flutter of delicate wings breaks the silence, and my heart lurches in my chest. Before I can react, a figure darts into view—the pixie from days earlier, her iridescent wings shimmering like opals in the dim light.

Stardust's eyes widen. He gestures for me to duck behind a cluster of glittering stalagmites.

"Exactly how worried should I be about her?" I whisper urgently, my pulse quickening at the sight of the ethereal being flitting about, her tiny form darting in erratic patterns.

His lips curve into a sly grin, his voice barely above a breath. "The ways of mischief these pixies possess are as varied as the colors of the rainbow. And that's for those they like. *You* stole from her." His words hang in the air like an ominous warning, his eyes glinting as the pixie flutters closer to our hiding spot.

"Just what I need," I mutter.

Stardust eyes me. "For someone not that interested in getting involved in the supernatural, you sure changed your tune."

"It's a wonder what spite and curiosity will inspire," I say in a hushed tone, my eyes flicking nervously between the pixie and Stardust.

Stardust chuckles softly, watching the pixie as she hums a melodic tune, her tiny hands plucking at the air in front of her as if playing an invisible harp. "I can only imagine what you'd do if you actually *liked* us."

A prickle of something like guilt pokes at my skin. "I *like* y—"

But I'm interrupted by a sudden burst of light as the pixie darts off into the darkness, leaving us in her wake. I let out a sigh of relief as Stardust helps me to stand.

"Now, who is next?" he asks, rubbing his hands with glee. I let the acknowledgement of my feelings and repentance stay behind.

Our investigative escapade continues—Stardust strutting into a ghoul poker game, tossing a silver coin into the pot and watching the players recoil. One even spits at him, a glob of ectoplasm narrowly missing his shiny boot.

"Nope," I say, scratching them off the list.

Our next stop is a hidden alcove where a group of shapeshifters are rumored to congregate. Stardust's flamboyant entrance draws curious glances from the paranormals gathered there, their forms rippling and undulating.

"Good evening, my ever-fluid friends," Stardust greets them with a theatrical bow, his voice carrying across the alcove with practiced flair. "Hope we aren't interrupting anything too sinister."

One of the shapeshifters, a tall figure with sleek fur and piercing amber eyes, steps forward, eyeing us both warily. "Fuck off, vampire." Their voice is a melodic blend of growls and whispers.

He pouts theatrically. "Would your opinion change if I left you some coin?"

The shapeshifter cocks their head to the side, considering Stardust's proposition as if weighing the worth of his words against his offer. After a moment of tense silence, a low, rumbling chuckle escapes their bared fangs. "We deal exclusively in silver."

"Checkmate," Stardust crows, as I jot down another entry.

My brain thrives on this—the gathering of evidence, the narrowing of suspects. It's just that my usual witnesses aren't usually so... undead.

"Alright, Stardust. What's our next move?" I inquire, momentarily switching off the tape recorder once we're out of the shapeshifters' line of sight.

He pauses, tilting his head as if listening to a silent melody only he can hear. "Time to visit the coven," he declares, a mischievous glint in his eye. "Party off our success."

I hesitate, my stomach knotting. "What about Lucian's edict?"

"He's all bark and no bite," Stardust says dismissively. "Or all hiss and no fang, if you will."

"And what about the others who hold me accountable for the heightened restrictions?" Restrictions that some of them, like Stardust, aren't concerned about, but still...

Stardust winks, his iridescent eyes gleaming mischievously. "My dear Emily, don't worry your pretty little head. I'll handle the negotiations. Follow my lead and try to look less... edible."

"Fine," I concede, more bravado in my voice than I feel. "But if this is some elaborate setup for vampire karaoke night, I'm out."

"Perish the thought," he chuckles, leading the way once more. "Though maybe you'd bring the house down with those pipes of yours."

"Flattery will get you nowhere," I say, but the corners of my mouth betray me, twitching upwards. This partnership may be reluctant, but there's no denying that slipping back into Stardust's world brings back a sense of belonging I didn't realize I missed.

Stardust takes me back to Lucian's house, and the vibe is miles better than it was a few nights past. Instead of growls and grumbles, there's laughter and music spilling out into the street.

Stardust swings open those hefty oak doors with flair, like he's the star of some show, and announces our entrance in a burst of shimmering light.

Lucian, surrounded by a group of vampires, turns towards us, his gaze immediately locking onto me. The entire room appears to hold its breath.

"Stardust, you've brought a guest," he says, his face impassive. He's paler than usual, his eyes not as piercing. And he looks nearly a decade older.

"Lucian, darling, never a dull moment with me around," Stardust says, bowing dramatically.

"Make yourself at home, Emily," Lucian says, his voice lacking its typical authoritative timbre. There's a vulnerability to him that I didn't think vampires ever showed. Almost... like he's under the weather. *Do vampires get sick?*

The moment Lucian's guard drops, I can sense the shift in the atmosphere. The usual tension melts away, replaced by something surprisingly cozy. It's less like a lair of ancient beings and more like a college hangout on a chill Saturday night. I try to blend in with the others lounging around in the plush room I hadn't explored before. Velvet couches host vampires of all ages, bantering like college roomies. They glance my way, curiosity flickering in their ageless eyes, but there's no hostility—just a welcoming intrigue.

"Join the fun," Stardust beckons, all theatrics and sparkle.

"What's changed?" I murmur as he guides me to one of Lucian's many couches.

Stardust shoots me a sly smile. "Let's just say Lucian's in need of a little... pick-me-up, and we had to sample the goods first. And it wasn't through a straw," he adds in a hushed tone.

I touch my neck, raising an eyebrow, and he nods, tapping his nose.

So, Lucian's allowing them to accept blood donations again.

"Emily Lane!" Alistair, the vamp I helped with Tina's estate, calls, pulling me from my thoughts.

"Ever played 'Mortal's Gambit'?" His teasing leer suggests he already knows the answer.

"Can't say I have." I adjust my ponytail, channeling my courtroom confidence.

"Excellent," Jasper chimes in, pushing a stack of cards toward me. "Beginner's luck is as imaginary as ghosts. We could use a fresh loser."

"Hey!" I feign offense, but laughter spills from my lips. "I'll have you know I'm a quick study."

And just like that, the game's on. It's a mix of poker and supernatural strategy, but they guide me through it with a patience I wouldn't expect from immortal beings.

"Got any fours?" Stardust asks, wiggling his eyebrows which seem to be dusted with actual stardust.

"Go fish," I reply, the words a familiar echo from childhood games, yet so bizarre in this context. My gaze flits between Alistair's amused expression and Jasper's mock frustration.

"Never thought I'd see the day," Jasper says, leaning back as he takes in the scene. "A mortal outwitting a vampire."

"Guess there's a first time for everything," I shoot back, unable to suppress a grin.

"She's not just any mortal, Jas," Alistair says, their earlier disagreement long forgotten. "Still hoping to get her to write me a will."

"Not over your dead body," I reply with a wink.

As the night wanes on and the clock strikes midnight, Lucian reappears. "I must step out for a moment," he says, his voice a mix of authority and apology.

"Everything okay?" I ask, trying to keep my tone light, but there's an undercurrent of concern I can't quite mask.

"Nothing to worry about," Lucian assures me with a half-smile that doesn't reach his eyes. "I'll be back well before sunrise." And with a swift, graceful motion, disappears into the shadows.

"He's finally replenishing his stores," Jasper explains.

I nod, unsure how I feel. Not about being left alone with the vamps, but who Lucian is getting 'replenished' from.

The game continues, each round bringing more laughter and banter than I would have ever imagined sharing with vampires when I don't have their teeth in my neck. Alistair's charming smile and Jasper's competitive edge blend into an odd yet comforting camaraderie. Stardust, ever the showman, tries to distract me with tales of his wild escapades from the '70s while slyly helping me strategize my next moves. And I'm getting a class in Vamp 101.

"No on the invitation and the camera thing. What else have the books lied about?" I prod. "You guys aren't compulsive counters or hydrophobic, are you?"

Alistair chuckles, "Jasper's quite wary of water. But that's his own quirk, not a vampire trait."

Jasper shoots Alistair a glare, but the corners of his lips betray his amusement. "That is a legitimate concern. You won't catch me anywhere near a large body of water, especially not in bat form."

"So shapeshifting is real?" I ask incredulously, my eyebrows raising in surprise.

"Vamp's secret, love," Stardust says slyly, tapping the side of his nose.

As if on cue, Alistair stands up and with a wink to Stardust, his figure starts to blur as he morphs into a majestic black panther.

My jaw practically hits the floor as I witness the impossible unfold. The panther saunters with a grace that's simply mesmerizing. It's as though I'm witnessing ancient magic resurrected in the dimly lit room.

Stardust leans in close and whispers, "Vampires are full of surprises, Emily. We've been around for centuries, after all."

Perhaps, I inwardly muse, somewhat shakily, *the were-wolf-vampire rivalry all stems from a hint of prowling envy. No wolf could be that suave.*

When the first light of dawn creeps through the windows, painting the room in hues of gold and pink, my body protests every moment I've stayed awake. The vampires, unaffected by fatigue, watch the sunrise with a quiet reverence that borders on melancholy.

"To the tunnels," Stardust says, pouting.

Alistair wraps an arm around his shoulders. "Molly said Ray will return tomorrow."

Stardust's expression brightens. "I'd nearly forgotten. Let's go."

I pull the glasses from my bag. "Do you want..."

Stardust looks me up and down and smiles, an expression that's all teeth. "Keep them for now, love. I'll recover them when Ray needs them."

The trio leave together, disappearing somewhere in the bowels of the house.

And then Lucian's there, standing in the doorway, the rising sun casting an ethereal glow around him.

No, that's the smoke from his body.

I quickly leap for the curtains, forcing them closed before turning to face him. My pulse quickens, not from fear, but something far more dangerous.

"Miss me?" he asks, a playful edge to his words as he closes the distance between us. He still looks older, pale as milk, but there's a feral glint in his eye, a hunger I've never seen on his face.

"Maybe a little," I say. I'm exhausted, but the sight of him feels like I've plugged into a power source. "Did you have a good... feed?" I ask, wincing at how idiotic I sound.

His face flashes, his eyes nearly flickering red. "I was... unable to sate my hunger." His hands are gentle as they cradle my face, tilting my head to expose the delicate skin of my neck. His breath is cool against my flesh, sending shivers down my spine. "May I?" he asks.

"Please," I breathe out, giving myself over to the moment, to him.

His fangs graze my skin, and it's a pinch, a sting, a rush of sensations that meld into pleasure. As he feeds, his arms wrap around me, pulling me closer, and I cling to him, feeling protected and cherished in a way I'd never felt when Tina fed from me, in a way that defies logic.

His touch is both icy and scorching, setting my skin ablaze with an intoxicating mix of pain and pleasure. Every nerve ending in my body is alight with a fiery passion that consumes me from within. The room fades away, the only sound the rhythmic beat of our hearts echoing in sync. His lips leave a trail of kisses along my neck, each one sending a wave of desire crashing over me.

As he pulls away, his eyes meet mine, a hunger burning within them that mirrors my own. Without a word, he leans in closer, his breath mingling with mine and our lips meet in a kiss. It's soft, sweet, a contrast to the wildness of what we've just shared, even though it's tinted in the iron rich taste of blood. I'm lightheaded, giddy, and when he pulls away, my own wonder is reflected in his eyes.

"Thank you," he murmurs, his voice a tender rumble in the quiet of the dawn.

I let out a soft chuckle, the sound bouncing around the cavernous room, now empty except for the two of us. "Anytime," I say, my voice breathier than I'd like.

His thumb brushes against the tiny puncture wounds on my neck, a gentle touch that causes a tremor in my core despite the warmth spreading through my veins.

Locked in his mesmerizing gray gaze, a million questions swirl through my mind. My fingers trace the contours of his perfect jawline as I ask the first that springs forward, "Can *you* transform into anything?"

"Perhaps," he says, leaning in, his lips inches from mine.

But alas, time ticks away. The clock strikes six and he reluctantly pulls back.

I pout, resting my head against his chest. "I have to go to work."

"You're welcome to return tonight," he says warmly, brushing a stray lock of hair behind my ear. "Perhaps we can discuss what you've learned from your independent investigation."

"And maybe you'll reveal your shapeshifting skills?" I run my hands over his chest and up to his shoulders.

He huffs a restrained laugh. "Don't push it."

"That's the Emily Lane special," I tease. "See you tonight."

Chapter 21

Overnighters are for college kids and vampires, not badass lawyers. Each file I shuffle through feels heavier than the last, reminders of the sleepless night clinging to my eyelids like stubborn cobwebs. I'm halfway through a particularly dense deposition when the sound of Liz's high-pitched squeal pierces my concentration.

"Emily, look who's here!" she exclaims, her voice bubbling with excitement.

I glance up, and there he is—Matty standing awkwardly, his hands occupied by takeout containers that waft a scent promising relief from the stale office air.

"Hope I'm not interrupting," Matty says, tilting his head in a way that softens my resolve a touch, "but I thought you could use a lunch break."

My heart does a little flip—a reaction I silently scold myself for. I eye him, the corners of my mouth betraying the hint of a smile while my brain fires off a thousand reasons why this is a bad idea. It's been a rollercoaster with him, soaring one moment and plummeting the next. It lasted as long as a roller coaster too, short and fast. Things I normally like from my bed partners but damned if I'm getting tired of it.

"Thanks, Matty, but you know, surprise lunches and billable hours rarely mix." My attempt at humor doesn't quite mask the hesitation in my voice.

He sets the food down and leans against my desk, keeping a respectful distance. "I know I've been... not my best lately. That lead on Mitchell's case falling through—it hit me harder than it should've. Sinclair was all over me. But shutting you out was a mistake, Emily."

I take a breath, letting the apology hang between us. It's genuine, I can tell by the way his eyes hold mine, no hint of evasion.

"I understand," I say, my tone softer now, the tight knot in my chest easing slightly. His honesty catches me off guard, revealing a vulnerability I hadn't expected. "We all have our off days. You made me feel a little like a black hole, but I'll live. Especially when it's partly my fault."

Matty's lips twitch into a rueful smile. "I wasn't expecting forgiveness just yet," he admits. "But hey, it's always worth a shot when a heart's on the line."

"So, what's in the boxes?" I nod towards the takeout containers, trying to steer us away from the emotional minefield we're tiptoeing around.

"Ah, right!" Matty grins, seemingly relieved at the shift in topic. "Food, glorious food. Thought a spontaneous lunch might win me a few points." He pops open the lid of one container, revealing an assortment of sushi rolls, neatly arranged like a vibrant mosaic of flavors and colors.

My stomach grumbles in response, and I huff a laugh. "Well, you came prepared. Can't say no to sushi."

Liz, who has been watching our interaction with keen interest, nudges me playfully. "He's a keeper, Em. Bringing you sushi is like the lawyer's version of flowers and chocolates."

Matty laughs at her remark, shooting me a hopeful look. "So... lunch date?"

I glance between Liz's teasing grin and Matty's earnest expression. He watches me with those bright eyes that first charmed me into saying yes and letting myself get penciled into his structured world. A date that now feels like eons ago, something that wasn't even a date. But he'd tried spontaneity for me, the least I could do was return the favor.

"Alright," I finally concede with a mock sigh, "but only because I'm starving, and sushi is my weakness."

He doles out the food as Liz makes herself scarce.

"Spicy enough for you?" he asks, a playful note in his voice. As part of the law school gang, he knows too well my penchant for heat—not only in food.

"Never as spicy as I want," I say, meeting his gaze.

Matty's hand reaches across the table, hovering just shy of mine. "Emily..."

I swallow hard, the rice suddenly a lump in my throat. "Matty, I—"

"Would you let me take you out?" His words tumble out, rushed and raw. "On a proper date this time, not something our friends crash. I know I messed up, both times, and I want to make it right. Please?"

His vulnerability is a tangible thing, hanging heavy between us. A part of me wants to leap back into the possibility we were about to explore. Another part screams to tread carefully, the memory of Lucian's kiss burning bright.

"Matty, I need..." I trail off, searching for the right words amidst the chaos of my thoughts. "I need time to think. I've

got my partnership interview scheduled finally, and I'm stil
l... handling that side project for our sharp-toothed friend."

"You're still doing that?" he asks, his voice tinged with frustration.

I shoot him a piercing look. "Yes, I am. It's not something I can pick up and put down like knitting. It's important, Matty."

"I know you think he's innocent, but there's chatter about—"

"He is," I say firmly.

He raises his hands in surrender, realizing he might have overstepped. "Okay, okay. I get it. I'm sorry. I assumed when you hit a dead end, you'd moved on."

"A man's life is at sta—on the line," I respond quietly, swallowing the inadvertent pun. "Hitting a dead end means backing up and trying a different route, not getting out of the car entirely."

"Understood," he says, pulling his hand back, but his eyes betray the flicker of disappointment. "Take all the time you need, Em."

We finish our lunch with small talk that skates over the surface of things, careful not to break the thin ice beneath. Before Matty finally leaves, he leans down and ghosts a gentle kiss over my lips, one that speaks of deeper desires and demands.

And there I am, alone with the echo of closing doors and the touch of two different sets of lips, wondering when I'll need to choose.

The taste of wasabi lingers, a reminder of Matty's olive branch—or was it a peace offering? Either way, it's enough to keep my thoughts tangled up in him even as I slide into my chair and try to refocus on the Wilson brief.

"O.M.G., have you seen this?" Liz's voice slices through my haze, her face alight with a mix of concern and excitement. She thrusts her phone at me, pointing to a news alert that screams for attention amidst the clutter of app notifications.

"Assassination attempt on Mayor Peterson foiled," I read aloud, feeling a chill snake down my spine despite the stuffiness of the room.

"Who would want to hurt Peterson?" Liz muses, her brow furrowed.

"Good question," I murmur, already tapping into my phone to pull up articles and cross-reference facts. Peterson has been nothing but a beacon of progressivism until recently—a point that's earned him both admiration and animosity, depending on who you asked.

"Maybe it's political... or personal?" Liz suggests, leaning over my shoulder to scan the headlines.

"Or maybe it's something darker, a plot against the mayoral candidates," I reply.

"Government conspiracies," Liz whispers.

I skim through the articles, my mind racing faster than my fingers can scroll. Political rivals... disgruntled citizens... adversaries within the paranormal society. The last one gives me pause. This and Mitchell's death can't be connected, no matter my quip. Sure, there's been increased strife in the paranormal communities since Mitchell's death, but an assassination attempt seemed extreme even for them.

Liz squeals, pointing at the latest breaking news. MAYOR PETERSON SPEAKS: LUCIAN BELMONT TRIED TO KILL ME.

Son of a bitch.

A local reporter stands outside what I can only assume is Peterson's home, the structure surrounded by a swarm of police officers. Her microphone is directed towards the imposing iron gates as she launches into her live report.

"I'm coming to you live from the mayor's official residence, where pandemonium broke loose in the early hours of the morning as the mayor fell prey to a daring assault."

The image cuts to stock footage of flashing police lights and yellow caution tape as the reporter's voice narrates over it. "While most of the city slumbered, the paranormal citizens that inhabit our streets were wide awake. And it seems one such paranormal had murder on his mind, none other than local vampire leader, Lucian Belmont."

As her words echo in my office, a knot tightens in my gut.

The reporter reappears on screen, eyes darting off camera.

"Wait, it looks like something is happening." The camera jostles and shifts as the cameraman and reporter rush towards the driveway, joined by a throng of other reporters and news crews.

"Mr. Mayor, Mr. Mayor!" they clamor as Peterson steps out of a sleek black car, flanked by his entourage and sporting bandages wrapped tightly around his arms. His usually sharp green eyes look bloodshot and weary, but he still exudes an air of authority.

"Everyone," he addresses the crowd, "the police will release more details as they become available to the public. What I can share at this time is this: at approximately 3 a.m., I was roused from my slumber by a raven flying into my window, which transformed into Lucian Belmont. He then attempted to snap my neck. I fought him off, sustaining these injuries to my arms, but thankfully I am otherwise unharmed."

"Mr. Mayor, how can you be sure it was Lucian Belmont?" one persistent reporter shouts out.

Peterson's demeanor shifts to one of cold resolve. "I know."

With that final statement, he turns and strides back into his home, followed closely by his team. The reporter turns back to the camera, her voice tinged with shock and urgency.

"And there you have it, folks. As the city reels from this shocking and brazen attack on its mayor, many questions remain. Was it a targeted assassination attempt? Or is this part of a larger uprising among paranormals? And why was Lucian Belmont not still in detention for his previous crime - the murder of businessman Frank Mitchell? Is his bailout part of the plot? Suspicion and speculation run rampant as the investigation continues."

My phone pings and, in a daze, I tap open the message. It's from Matty.

"I won't say I told you so, instead I'll ask if your timetable has moved up? Let me know. I'm free Friday night and will hold it for you."

Chapter 22

With a fierce determination, I kick open the heavy wooden door to Lucian's home. I've got my game face on, my jaw set so tight it could crush diamonds.

Severin's in the dim hallway, his usual scowl swapped for concern at the fire in my eyes. "Ms. Lane, what's wrong?" he asks, stepping back cautiously as I stalk towards him.

"As if you don't know," I snarl, pushing past him into the opulent library. But Lucian's nowhere to be found. Panic grips my chest at the thought that he may have already turned himself in to the authorities, and the media will be closing in on my name on the bail form. The room suddenly feels suffocating, and I spin to Severin, demanding answers. "Where is he?"

Severin hesitates, pity and worry flickering in his eyes. "I'm afraid I can't say, Ms. Lane."

Ignoring him, I storm through Lucian's maze-like home, with Severin trailing behind me, barking orders that I ignore.

I burst into Lucian's bedroom and immediately spot the cufflinks sitting on his dresser. I withdraw the one I received from Wilkin. They're a matched set. Expected yet still unsettling. With a swift motion, I snatch all three and shove them into my bag.

"Occam's razor, Sev," I snap. "If this second pair was truly lost, why do they show the same signs of wear and tear? These weren't sitting in someone's attic collecting dust; they have been worn repeatedly, cared for by someone that valued them. By an *older* looking Lucian, or perhaps a *hungry* Lucian?"

Severin holds his hands out. "Ms. Lane, you need to leave Lucian's bedroom."

"Oh, don't worry, I will."

A soft rustle sounds from behind me, and I turn to see Lucian lurking in the shadows, his expression unreadable.

"What do you transform into?" I demand, my anger bubbling at the sight of him.

He blinks but doesn't answer, so I turn my ire back to Severin.

"Do you know?" I ask him. "Does Lucian transform into anything?"

Severin glances at Lucian, who remains still and silent as a statue. "That is not common knowledge, Ms. Lane," Severin ends up saying, sounding reluctant. "I cannot answer that, nor could any of the coven."

"Convenient" I mutter.

"Thank you, Severin," Lucian says, finally coming to life. "You're dismissed."

Severin hesitates before vanishing, leaving me alone with Lucian.

"Emily, please, let me explain," he starts, but I silence him with a sharp gesture.

"Explain? What's there to explain, Lucian? You were caught red-handed, and now you're hiding in the shadows like a coward," I retort, my voice laced with anger and hurt.

"Believe what you will," he says, his gaze boring into mine. "But I am not behind any assassination plot. Nor have I ever taken a life without just cause."

I narrow my eyes at him, searching for any sign of deceit. "Then tell me this: what do you transform into?"

His response is quiet and almost pained. "A raven," he admits. "But I can promise you, I haven't transformed since my sister's death. It was a joy I provided to her, not something I'd use recklessly."

"Right." I shake my head in disbelief. "Where were you last night then? Your vampires told me you were getting blood but when you showed up this morning, you looked like a dried-out crypt-keeper when you asked me to bare my neck for you."

His expression remains unreadable as he responds, "I was with no one."

"Sure," I scoff, feeling the heat rise to my cheeks. "And I suppose all those inconsistencies are just... what? Clerical errors?" Tallying all that I'd learned still puts him in my crosshairs. I watch for a flicker of guilt, a crack in his composure.

"Emily," Lucian's voice grows firmer, but he doesn't lose his cool. "You're looking for a monster where there is none."

"You know better than anyone that monsters often wear the most convincing masks," I snap. "Think about how this looks: *your* cufflink, *your* description at the crime scene, *your* raven, *your* hands on Peterson's neck, now that he's pushing Mitchell's former agenda." Not to mention the injuries, fang marks we never wanted to believe were fang marks.

He frowns. "Think about it yourself, Emily. With all the evidence against lodged me, why in Hades' name would I attack Peterson?"

"Maybe you wanted to scare him into lifting the restrictions, maybe you went blood mad from hunger. I don't know. You don't have an alibi. Even if you didn't do it, your name is smeared all over this," I argue, weariness creeping into my voice. "Mine too now."

Lucian steps closer, his eyes locking onto mine with a mix of intensity and sadness. "Which is why I didn't want you further involved in this investigation, to protect you."

"Protect me?" I bark out a laugh that's more bitter than amused. "You're singing a different tune now. It wasn't even to protect your coven like you claimed, but to protect yourself. Because every time I turn a corner in this case, there's a shadow that looks suspiciously like you." I step closer, searching for the crack in his armor.

He stares down at me. His gray eyes, usually like sharpened steel, now hold a glint of something wild, something frantic.

"Occam's razor," I repeat. "The simplest explanation is often the correct one. You didn't want me poking around alone because it would unravel your pretty little web of lies. You're guilty, and deep down, you're terrified that I'll prove it."

He advances, looming over me. I should step back, but I don't. Instead, I stand rooted, as if he's cast a spell. His hands find my shoulders, grip sure and strong, yet achingly careful.

"Emily, you must believe me," he pleads.

"*Believe* you?" The words come out choked, strangled by the whirlwind of hurt battering inside me.

He doesn't answer with words. Instead, Lucian leans down, and his lips crash against mine with a fervor that steals my next breath. It's rough and desperate, searing through me like a lightning strike, igniting a confusing mix of anger and longing. For a moment, I'm lost in the intensity of the kiss, swaying on the edge of surrender.

But then I remember—anger, betrayal, suspicion. They snap back into focus, and my hands fly up, shoving him away with more force than I know I possess. "You think you can just use your... your masculine wiles to distract me?" I gasp for air, my chest heaving. "I should have let you rot in jail!"

Lucian stumbles back, the regret etched deep into the lines of his face. He runs a hand through his long black hair. "I'll turn myself in," he murmurs, his voice laced with a resignation that almost sounds noble. "For the good of the coven."

"Good of the coven?" I repeat, incredulous. My voice crescendos from a hurt whisper to a shout that echoes off the walls of his bedroom. "What about the good of Emily Lane, huh? Did you ever think about that?"

"Too much," he says bitterly, his anger now matching mine. "Have you even considered what this new claimed crime will do to *my* people?"

"You should have thought of that before you went after Peterson last night," I snap, the frustration and betrayal making my words sharp and harsh. "Jesus Christ, Lucian, if you were thirsty, I was right there!"

"Thinking 'what about Emily' is not the question and never should have been!" he seethes, his eyes blazing with fury. His lips curl into a sneer as he continues, "I let you into my home, into my community. And all you do is take and wonder 'what about me,' 'how is Emily affected?'"

I point a finger at him, my nail practically a dagger aimed at his heart. "After what I—"

"It's not about you," he snarls. His eyes blaze with fury, his lips curled into a sneer. "It's never been about you and what this will do to you. I'm sorry your own sense of morality guilted you into bonding me out. Or maybe it was your own sense of superiority, I've no idea. Regardless, I'm sorry you wrapped your reputation into this, but it was your choice."

Before I can retort, he turns on his heel and strides towards the door to the hall.

As he reaches for the doorknob, I find my voice again, sharp and cutting. "You're sorry?" I scoff, bitterness seeping into every word. "Fine. Go to jail, face the music with no one to bail you out. At least if I'm going down, you're going down harder."

He pauses but doesn't turn around, his voice a whisper that sounds as loud as thunder. "Next time you think you find a cause to champion and abandon, leave the vampires alone. We don't need allies who remain only when convenient."

CHAPTER 23

Under Lawrence's, my boss's boss, scrutinizing gaze, I battle the urge to squirm in my chair, to avert my eyes. His office blends old-world charm with cutting-edge technology, a reflection of the man himself. Meaning if I'm stuck arguing my 'paranormal connection' to someone, he's my best bet.

News broke about the bail form this morning, after Lucian turned himself in. My name and picture, a flattering one at least, flashed over the news as the person who helped him. *Responsible for letting him strike again,* one irritating anchor had surmised. Another claimed I was under Lucian's vampiric spell. Neither speculation bodes well for my career.

Lawrence, a stern-faced man with eyes that have seen many courtroom battles, leans forward, his eyes narrowing. "Do you realize what you've done?" he asks.

The plush leather chair across from his desk might as well be a hot seat. I straighten my back, attempting a posture of confidence rather than repentance. I nod, the weight of my mistake heavy on my shoulders. Lucian's accusations from last night cut through me like a knife. His questioning of my loyalty stings deeper than his betrayal. *Doesn't he realize what I'd been risking for him?* If he were here, I'd throttle him. "Yes, sir," I reply honestly.

He lets out a sigh and leans back in his chair, pinching the bridge of his nose. "You have put our company at risk with your rash decision," he says gravely.

"I understand that, sir," I say, trying to keep any hint of defensiveness out of my voice.

He looks at me for a few moments before speaking again. "The board is furious," he says with a shake of his head. "They want to know how someone like you could make such a careless decision."

I gulp, trying to steady myself. "It was strategic," I begin, a mask of calm hiding the whirlwind of nerves raging inside. "Agreeing to bail out L—the vampire, it was meant to draw in new clientele, broaden our horizons."

"And you think representing paranormals is how we expand?" His skepticism hangs heavy in the air, but I'm ready for this.

"Yes, at some point." I lean forward, trying to impress my sincerity on him. "*Montgomery* was interested in me because of our wavering stance on paranormals. He has connections and influence that could benefit us greatly." My lie about Montgomery feels sour on my tongue. But Lucian and his damned criminal spree have left me no choice. The memory of our last encounter stings, a wound that refuses to heal.

Lawrence raises a bushy eyebrow, one flecked with gray. "And you chose to entice Montgomery at the expense of Mrs. Mitchell? Our *current* client who entrusted her case to you, by bonding out the very paranormal she intended to sue?"

"It was a calculated risk." My voice is unwavering even as my mind races to come up with a plausible explanation that didn't get me disbarred, or worse, fired. "I hadn't filed anything so could wall myself off from the case. Lucian isn't human and I wasn't representing him in his criminal case, so he wasn't a client. Meaning there was no conflict or ethical issue."

It's a technicality I thought up in the early hours this morning, but that's the law sometimes.

Lawrence's expression remains inscrutable, his silence stretching between us like a taut wire. Finally, he leans back in his chair, steepling his fingers in front of him. "You've always been one to push boundaries, Emily," he says. "But remember, every action has consequences."

I nod, acknowledging his words even as a sharp pang of unease twists in my gut. "And my partnership prospects?"

"We'll still have your interview tomorrow," he says, his tone flat. "Too many of us have sacrificed billable hours for it for us to cancel it now."

I hold his gaze, refusing to flinch under his scrutiny. "And perhaps I can present my ideas for further revenue building by courting the paranormal-sympathetic community. I've developed significant contacts there. Actually, last weekend I was invited to a gala fundraiser with people whose names are on a half dozen of the buildings downtown."

I watch as my words sink in, planting seeds of opportunity in Lawrence's calculating mind. It's a gambit, but I've always been good at those. "Think about it," I press on. "The laws are changing, society's views shift as often as the weather. We get ahead of the curve, we lead, no matter which way the wind blows."

"Lead," he muses, as if tasting the word, testing its flavor. "Alright, Lane. I'll consider it. But don't let this... enthusiasm for innovation land us in hot water again."

"Understood." Relief washes through me, though I mask it with a nod of professional gratitude. I rise, smoothing down my pencil skirt.

"Good," he says, dismissing me with a wave, already buried in another file.

I slip out of his office and back down the hall to my own, my mind racing with the implications of what I've set into motion.

As I turn towards my own office, I catch snippets of conversation from John and Susan's cubicles.

"She dropped out," John says, gleeful. "After the second paranormal crime, there was no *way* she was going to primary Peterson."

My steps falter for a moment as I process this information. They must be talking about Stephanie.

"Stephanie dropped out of the mayoral race?" I ask.

John and Susan both look at me with surprise written across their faces. "Yeah," John responds cautiously. "I guess you knew her?"

"Why would you say that?"

"John, hush," Liz hisses, appearing from behind a stack of paperwork. She turns to me with an apologetic smile. "We weren't going to bring up the bail thing."

"I wasn't," John says peevishly. "Stephanie Evans is an entirely different person than the vampire."

"Who you assumed Emily *knew* because she blew a wad of cash on a paranormal," says Liz. She looks back at me, pity in her eyes. "That vampire really was hot. I'd be taken in by him too, I'm sure."

"I wouldn't," Josh says under his breath.

I let out a frustrated sigh through clenched teeth. "Right... Look, can I please get into my office now?"

"Of course," Liz says, the pity in her expression only growing as she steps aside to let me pass.

Before I can enter the room, my phone buzzes. It's a number I don't recognize. With a sigh, I answer, hoping it's not another complication to untangle.

"Ms. Lane? This is Officer Walsh, calling from the Cook County Department of Corrections. One of our Officers has requested your presence here. It's urgent," a clipped voice says.

"Urgent?" I echo, my mind racing. *What now?* Another consequence from the bail form? Lucian demanding a visitor?

"Can it wait?" I ask, even though I know the answer before the question leaves my lips.

"Ma'am, I wouldn't call if it could."

"Right." My heart thumps a warning beat. Either way, it must be Lucian-related. "Fine, I'll be there shortly."

I hang up, the taste of intrigue bitter on my tongue. Whatever is waiting for me, I can't ignore the pull. It's like a thread tugging me forward, and I'm a puppet to its insistence.

"Everything okay?" Liz inquires, head cocked like an inquisitive sparrow.

"Never better," I lie smoothly. "Back soon," I call out, leaving them to their speculations. As I exit, I brace for whatever awaits.

Thanks, Lucian, I think bitterly, allowing myself a moment's spiteful irritation before barricading that particular emotional door once again. I've danced with the devil—or vampire, same difference—and now, it's time to face whatever music comes next.

The jail looms ahead, its cold exterior a stark contrast to the bustling life of the streets. Inside, the air is thick with tension, the scent of antiseptic failing to mask the underlying despair clinging to the walls. Midday brings fewer occupants than my last visit, amplifying the bleakness. A stern-faced officer stands guard at the front desk, his presence less 'welcome committee' and more 'abandon hope, all ye who enter here.'

"Emily Lane," I announce with forced confidence. "I received a call."

"Follow me," he instructs, voice devoid of warmth. His gaze doesn't linger on me, but I still feel weighed and measured. I'd joke about whether I've been found wanting, but my throat's too tight for banter just yet.

He leads me down a corridor, our footsteps echoing ominously. I'd hoped this was about the bail form, but the firm set of the officer's jaw suggests otherwise. Each step we take ratchets up the tension in my chest, coils it tight until I can hear my pulse in my ears.

"Here." He pauses before a nondescript door.

"Is this about the form?" I ask because I can't stand not knowing. The silence stretches out, and I brace myself for a reprimand, a lecture, my own arrest, anything.

"Officer Greene will see you shortly," is all he says before turning on his heel and leaving me to stare at the door, my heart doing an awkward two-step.

With a deep breath meant to steady nerves that refuse to be steadied, I push the door open and step inside.

The room is a box of shadows, each corner shrouded in half-darkness. The fluorescence from the single bulb overhead is more interrogation than illumination, casting stark light that turns the bare walls into cold specters of gray. A solitary chair sits in the center, an island in a sea of nothingness. I swallow, taking in the emptiness with a sense of foreboding.

"Could've at least sprung for a potted plant," I mutter to myself, but the joke falls flat in the oppressive silence. Perched on the edge of the chair, I try to project calm, though I'm anything but. They say waiting is the hardest part; whoever 'they' are, they're not wrong.

Time stretches like an overextended rubber band, and I'm about to start humming to fill the void when the door creaks open. Officer Greene steps through, her face a mask of seriousness that's new since our last encounter. The memory of her kind demeanor outside Lucian's cell clashes with the stoicism she now wears like armor.

"Ms. Lane," she says, her voice low, "thank you for coming."

"Seems I didn't have much choice," I say, my tone lighter than my mood. "What did I do to be taken to this... cozy setup?"

She doesn't bite on the bait of levity. Instead, she fixes me with a gaze that feels like it can peel back layers, revealing secrets. "There's a lot I'd like to discuss with you."

"Color me intrigued." I lean back, trying to appear nonchalant. "But jailhouse chats aren't really my scene. I prefer coffee shops, parks... anywhere but here, basically." Anything to lessen the likelihood that I could end up in one of the cells I've heard so much about.

"Understandable," she concedes. "Which is why I'm asking you to come to my home instead. This conversation requires privacy beyond these walls."

"Your home?" I raise an eyebrow. "Must be some conversation."

"It is." Her eyes hold mine, unblinking. "It's about Lucian."

My internal alarms blare a warning. "We've ceased our... acquaintanceship after he tried to murder the mayor."

"Emily, please. It's not what you think," Officer Greene insists, her gaze unwavering. "I can assure you, it's worth your while."

Curiosity, that ever-present traitor, whispers in my ear, urging me to hear her out. "Fine," I relent, a reluctant nod betraying my interest. "Lead the way, Officer."

"Call me Danielle," she says, and there's a flicker—just a moment—of something vulnerable in her rigid stance. "And thank you."

"Sure thing, Danielle." My response is automatic, but as I stand and follow her out, I'm acutely aware that my day just took a sharp turn into uncharted territory.

Again.

CHAPTER 24

"So, we're going to play hooky then?" I ask, basking in the sunlight as I stride beside Danielle.

"Emily, when was the last time you took a day off? Deliberately, I mean." Greene's—I mean—Danielle's teasing tone rolls off her tongue as effortlessly as the wind carries leaves along the sidewalk. She'd changed out of her uniform and was wearing a rainbow romper and a bold glittery headband, making her look nothing like the sharp—but still friendly—beat cop I'd met.

"Deliberate days off are for people without ambition," I say, but the smile tugging at the corners of my mouth betrays my appreciation for the unexpected freedom. Things are already looking up: I get some outside time, I wasn't arrested at the jail, and I convinced the partners my lapse in judgment was strategic. Sure, my 'outside time' is in route to what will probably be uncomfortable conversation about Lucian, but overall, things are a positive.

We amble toward her place, passing a small bakery and a park. The park is an autumn canvas, dotted with vibrant flowers and a kaleidoscope of colored leaves, a world apart from the park in the vampire quarter. Children's laughter fills the air as they play, while trees sway gently, leaves shimmering in sunlight. I breathe in the joy of the area, the carefree atmosphere something missing in my life.

"Speaking of ambition, I had a chat with a friend recently," Danielle begins, her voice dropping as if she's about to divulge state secrets. "He thinks you'd make a heck of an advocate for paranormals, given your passion and your... unique experiences."

"An advocate?" My eyebrows shoot up, skepticism lacing my words. "I'm a lawyer, Danielle."

"Is there really such a difference?" She grins, pushing open the iron gate to her quaint front yard. "You've got connections on both sides now. You can get paranormals' names out there as something other than boogeymen. You're practically a bridge between worlds. And, hell, paranormals need lawyers too."

"Connections don't make a career," I mutter, but even to my own ears, it sounds like I'm trying to convince myself more than her.

The aroma of home-cooked comfort greets us as we enter. Danielle's home, unlike my sterile apartment, exudes nostalgic charm, with kitschy knick-knacks and a kitchen table that's seen decades of use. I'm immediately at ease, enveloped in a warmth that should have reminded me of childhood, but doesn't.

"Maybe not," she concedes, directing me into what must be the family room, full of worn furniture with patterns that scream '80s aesthetics. "But Emily, think about the impact those connections have had on you—on your life and your career in the past two weeks. And, for a practical point, you've got a built-in set of clients and no competition."

I sink into the cozy couch, taking in the framed photos on the walls and the mismatched throw pillows. "Sure, there's been an impact," I acknowledge, fiddling with the tape recorder in my pocket. "But being drawn into a world I barely knew existed doesn't automatically qualify me as their champion."

"That's not what I'm suggesting," she says, her gaze gentle but firm. "We don't need a champion. But we need someone who is willing to try, to support us. Someone who will fight for opportunities we're missing. Someone who will show up, even when it's uncomfortable and failure's inevitable. Until we're at the table, use your seat on our behalf. It's about being an ally when we need one, not only when it's convenient for you."

Lucian's words batter around my brain: *"Next time you think you find a cause to champion and abandon, leave the vampires alone. We don't need allies who remain only when convenient."* Guilt tries to rise, but I shove it down.

"Tried that already, bought the t-shirt, and got kicked out at closing," I quip, though it sounds more petulant than I'd like. "I've been advised to take my ball and go home."

She sighs, her disappointment palpable. "And so, you gave up on us?"

I throw my hands up in frustration. "I did my best, more than anyone else was willing to do. It's not my fault Lucian screwed the community over by going after Peterson," I snap back, but her words linger in the air between us like a heavy fog. "...Did you say 'us'?"

"I did." She gives me a look that's all too enigmatic, a smile playing at the corners of her mouth like she's privy to some cosmic joke. "Because, Emily," Danielle begins, stepping closer, "I'm one of them."

My heart stutters, a beat out of sync. "One of who?"

"A paranormal." Her voice is steady, resonant in a way that suddenly feels less human and more... otherworldly.

"Come on, Danielle. This isn't the time for jokes." I aim for levity, but there's an edge of warning to my words. The room seems to close in around us, shadows stretching with the fading daylight.

"Jokes?" She tilts her head, hair catching the light in a way that now seems less than natural. A shimmer ripples through her form, and where the personable officer once stood, now something wilder peers back at me—features sharp and canid, eyes glowing with an amber fire that seems to reflect off her cropped brunette hair. She still looks human. But also... more. Like the intensity and hue has been turned up. But instead of a vibrant landscape scene on my camera, it's a paranormal. Unlike the full transformation Alistair made into a panther, Danielle looks half-human and half-wolf.

"Jesus, Greene..." The word catches in my throat. Every rational instinct denies it, but the evidence stands before me, breathing and smirking like it knows just how much my world has tilted. "Danielle," I correct myself, or whatever name applies to the paranormal wearing her face.

"Actually, it's both," she says, her voice oddly comforting despite the transformation. "And I'm a werewolf, if the term hasn't shown up in any of your legal books."

It hasn't. That's kind of the point, I'm guessing.

"Right. Werewolf." I swallow hard, trying to ground myself. It's one thing to traipse through the underground with a supernatural guide, it's another to have joined a half-transformed werewolf for midafternoon tea. "So that 'full moon' thing is also a lie?"

"Not quite. I heard you have a pair of truthviews," she says. "Those glasses of yours."

My hand reaches into my jacket pocket, brushing past the tape recorder to find the glasses Stardust insisted I keep on me until Ray needs them back.

"Put them on," Danielle prompts, nodding toward my pocket.

With a reluctant sigh, I obey, slipping them over my ears and settling them into place. The room shifts again, colors bleeding into sharper contrast. There, lounging nonchalantly on her secondhand sofa is Greene—no longer half and half but a sinuous werewolf in full, furry glory—and beside her, what must be a hobgoblin. Unlike Wilkin's smooth scales, their skin looks like the texture of a crocodile. They're hunched and grizzled, like something that crawled out of a child's nightmare to raid the fridge.

"Sweet mother of—" My voice breaks as I reel back, nearly tripping over my own feet. "Who the hell is that?"

"Relax, Emily. That's Gregoria," she says, gesturing toward the paranormal with a dismissive wave. "She's lived here longer than my family."

"Gregoria?" My laugh is short, manic. "Of course. Why wouldn't she be here?"

"Take a breath," Danielle says. "You're not alone in this. And trust me, there's more to the story than you realize."

"More to—" I start, then shake my head, disbelieving. "No, let's stick with the current chapter, shall we? One existential crisis at a time."

"Fair enough," Danielle concedes with a wolfish grin that's all teeth and no humor.

"Great," I reply, forcing steadiness into my voice as I remove the glasses and tuck them away. "Now, if Gregoria could give us some privacy."

"Of course," Danielle says, the smile never leaving her face. "She says she'll go visit Herle."

"Fantastic," I retort dryly.

"Listen, Emily," Danielle says, humor gone and her voice carrying a gravity that roots me to the spot. "I know you're set on Lucian being behind all this, but paranormals didn't kill Mitchell *or* take a shot at Peterson."

"Didn't they?" My words come out sharper than I intend. It's easier to be angry than admit I'm floundering in waters too deep for me. "And I suppose Lucian has an alibi gift-wrapped with a bow?"

She doesn't flinch at my tone. "That was you remember? Lucian's many things, but he's no murderer. The evidence piling up against him—it's convenient, isn't it? Too convenient."

"Convenient like me as his first alibi," I say, but there's a crack in my armor, a slither of doubt that worms its way through. "But all signs point to Lucian. He had the motive, the opportunity—"

"Or someone's making sure it looks that way." Her gaze locks onto mine, unwavering. "Think about it, Emily. Who stands to gain from all this chaos? From framing Lucian? From getting Mitchell out of the way?"

"Nobody sane." The thought is like a pebble in my shoe, irritating, persistent.

"Sanity's overrated," she quips, but her eyes are serious. "You need to ask yourself this, Emily: are you so gung-ho against Lucian now because you truly believe he's guilty, or because you let yourself trust him and feel like you got burned?"

I wince at Danielle's words, her blunt assessment cutting through my conflicted emotions.

"I looked you up, you know," she continues. "When this all started and you showed up at the jail. No known associates, only family across the country. A few people not quite friends, no long-term relationships. Your longest consistent association in Chicago was with the vampires, which keeps going hot and cold."

"And?"

"You need connections, Emily. Something real, something that matters, something other than your nine-to-five. And the paranormals, as different as they are from you, need someone like that in the human world. Someone who can bridge the gap between their world and yours that isn't politician with an agenda. Not a champion, not a savior," Danielle says, her tone turning earnest. "But an ally. A voice that speaks for understanding and peace. Don't let a little fear have you toss out an opportunity for doing good."

"Opportunities I relish. Lucian getting set up for a second crime? Paranormals suddenly wanting to be bound by human laws?" I throw my hands up. "That's a whole new level. One that will destroy my credibility at work."

"Do you want to work for someone that demands that?" she asks, not unkindly.

Irritation prickles at my skin. "So says the werewolf in hiding."

She flashes her teeth at me, fast and feral. "I may be hiding from the bigots in the police force, but at least I'm not hiding from myself," Danielle retorts, her gaze piercing through me.

"That's the thing about paranormals, Emily. We own who we are, shadows and all. Can you say the same?"

"Maybe." I cross my arms, a stubborn shield against the onslaught of doubt. "But what if I like the mold I'm stuck in?"

"Don't mistake security for fulfillment," she advises gently, her eyes a blend of understanding and challenge. "Sometimes stepping into the unknown is where we truly find ourselves."

"Even if I did... risk it all to help," I say, more to myself than to Danielle, "what guarantee do I have that it'll make a difference? That it's not all for nothing?"

"Guarantees are for appliances, not life," she says, crossing her arms. "You won't know until you try."

"Ah, so in the grand cosmic kitchen, I'm the blender that might explode mid-smoothie." My attempt at humor does little to lift the weight from my chest. "But what flavor of disaster am I blending here? Ethical quandary with a sprinkle of professional suicide?"

"Could be a dash of empowerment instead," she counters.

Finally, I release a heavy sigh. "Fine," I concede, meeting Danielle's unwavering gaze. "I'll consider what you've said."

A flicker of satisfaction gleams in her eyes before she nods, a silent acknowledgment of my small step towards something greater than myself. "Good," she says before a mischievous glint dances in her gaze. "Now, about Lucian..."

I raise a hand, halting her. "Drop it, Danielle. For now, Lucian made his bed and I'm not helping him out of it. Let's leave it at that."

"Alright," she concedes, but there's a promise in her tone, a certainty that this isn't over.

CHAPTER 25

After a night spent tossing and turning, my morning finds me pacing circles in my apartment, the familiar creak of the third floorboard by the fireplace counting each lap. The sun is already wrestling with the horizon, casting a soft glow through the battewindow that does nothing to ease the turmoil brewing within me. Today is the day of my partnership meeting, and the weight of the decision I have to make sits heavy on my shoulders, dragging me down with each step.

The news streaming on my computer breaks through the silence. "We're joined this hour by Mayor Peterson and District Attorney Ava Sinclair to discuss updates on the Lucian Belmont case. Listeners will remember Belmont was rearrested earlier this week on attempted murder charges—"

I slam the laptop shut, shutting off the sound before it can further unsettle me.

"Security or connection, Emily," I mutter to myself as I run a hand through my dark hair, now freed from its usual restraints. "Which one will it be?"

People leave. I got that memo too young, when my parents decided that their daughter wasn't enough of a reason to stay around and stay sober. Friends drifted away over time, disappearing into their own orbits. So, I built walls high and mighty, making sure I'd be the one doing the leaving if it ever came to that. It was easier, safer.

Greene's claim that my longest connection in Chicago being the vamps is laughable. "Found family in a coven, huh?" I scoff, remembering the dead ends that materialized. No answers there, no secret recipe for belonging.

The buzz of my phone snaps me out of my reverie. It's Matty, again, persistent as ever. The screen lights up with messages not just from him but from my law school crew as well. They're still here, somehow, despite my best efforts to keep them at arm's length, wishing me luck on the interview.

"Can I really give up the partner track? The prestige, the paycheck, the proof that I've made it? For a chance?" I ask the silent room. Becoming a partner has been my goal since I stepped into law school, my armor against instability. My dedication to the firm isn't just a bullet point on my resume; it's written in the late nights, the early mornings, and the weekends sacrificed at the altar of casework. Yet, here I am, considering trading it all for something as unpredictable as relationships and allying with the supernatural.

"Decisions, decisions," I say to no one in particular, my voice laced with the sarcasm that often serves as my shield. But beneath the sardonic tone, there's a question that's growing harder to ignore: Is the risk of opening up worth the reward of not having to face everything alone?

With a sigh, I glance at the clock. Time is ticking, relentless and indifferent to my internal battle. In less than an hour, I'll sit before the partners, and I'll need to know which path I'm choosing.

"Emily Lane, attorney at large, defender of the supernat ural... or Emily Lane, partner," I rehearse, trying each title on for size. Neither feels quite right... yet.

In need of guidance from someone other than myself, I snatch Stardust's glasses off my cluttered dresser. They're ridiculous really, with their oversized frames dusted in a fine sprinkle of glitter.

"Alright, Herle," I say to the room, "time to come out and play philosopher." The glasses perch precariously on my nose as I survey the room. The early morning light filters through the glasses' tinted lenses, casting a prismatic glow over my thrift-shop chic decor. But there's no sign of Herle. No magical aura, no flitting shadow, nothing.

"Typical," I say, flicking the frames off in annoyance. "Even the supernatural has better things to do than deal with my existential crisis."

The clock on my wall ticks mockingly, echoing the pounding rhythm of my heart. I straighten my blazer with a jerk, rolling my shoulders back to shake off the disappointment. It's a familiar routine—the armor of professionalism slipping into place as easily as the knock-off heels I step into.

"Emily Lane, you can't dawdle over invisible, possibly made-up, hobgoblins," I scold myself, grabbing my purse and stepping towards the door. "Not when you've got veritable dragons to slay—or rather, partners to impress. Probably."

Partnership is a title I've clawed toward, a shiny badge to pin to my chest that screams success. But success at what cost? If I take it, I lock in my future—a future potentially void of connections that might finally stick.

"Stop it," I tell my traitorous thoughts. My hand pauses on the doorknob. "No second guessing, not now. Not until later."

And so, with a deep breath that feels like it's filling my lungs with courage—or maybe just good old-fashioned stubbornness—I open the door, turning on my heel with a click that sounds like a starting pistol.

Instead of freaking out in my office, I'm stuck waiting in reception. The glass windows reveal a woman staring back with ironed lines and tailored edges. My hands fidget with the lapel of my suit jacket, smoothing out imaginary wrinkles.

"Get it together, Emily. Get partnership and *then* panic about what to do, how to help," I mutter to myself. The window throws back an image of determination framed by dark hair and piercing blue eyes that seem to say, 'You've got this.'

God, I hope so.

I take a deep breath, feeling the fabric of my suit cling to me like a second skin—a suit of armor for the modern gladiatrix.

The conference room door swings open with a confidence I wish I felt. *No backing down now, Lane.* Striding into the lion's den, I flash the assembled partners a grin that's part charm, part challenge. They glance up from their leather thrones, expressions ranging from mildly interested to stone-cold stoicism.

"Good morning," I begin, my voice steady as I lay out the case for myself—because that's what this is, isn't it? A trial where I'm both lawyer and defendant. "I want to thank you all for considering me for partnership."

Second guessing or not, I walk them through my track record, citing the successful cases I've spearheaded, victories won not simply through legal acumen but through sheer, bloody-minded tenacity.

"It's not just about knowing the law," I tell them, pacing slowly before the long mahogany table like a general surveying her troops. "It's about understanding people, finding the heart of the matter, and never, ever giving up until justice is served."

Lucian's face flashes through my mind and I swallow the insincerity his existence brings to my speech.

I can see a few nods, a scribble of a pen on a notepad—small victories, but they fuel the fire. Then again, maybe they're doodling. Hard to tell with these poker faces.

"And if there's any doubt," I finish, locking eyes with every single partner in turn, "let me be clear: I'm in this for the long haul." I pause, forcing out the words that might be a lie. "You're not just investing in a lawyer; you're investing in someone who will carry the firm's legacy forward."

I take my seat. Battle lines drawn, arguments made—I've thrown down the gauntlet. Now it's their move.

The silence hangs in the air, almost tangible. Then, like a crack of lightning that breaks the quiet before the storm, Mr. leans forward. His spectacles slide down the bridge of his nose as he peers at me over the rim.

"Ms. Lane," he begins, voice dripping with gravity that instantly tenses every muscle in my body, "your record is impressive. No one here doubts your dedication or ability. However, we must address the... recent emphasis on a certain subset of the community."

There it is, being brought into the open. The elephant in the room that I've been dreading since my face was plastered all over the news.

"Are you referring to my... relationships with the non-human population?" I ask, ensuring my tone remains neutral, though a part of me wants to roll my eyes. There's no need to be coy, especially since my face is still on the tv.

"Exactly," he says, tapping his pen against the mahogany table in a slow, deliberate rhythm. "There are concerns about the... nature of these relationships. Can you maintain professional boundaries? We understand the business opportunity in maintaining relationships with paranormal sympathizers. Mr. Montgomery alone triples your book of business. But representing paranormal sympathizers is a far cry away from *befriending* paranormals, bonding them out from their crimes. Your personal involvement with these beings influences our firm's image and reputation. We pride ourselves on being an establishment of integrity and credibility."

I resist the urge to scoff at the hypocrisy dripping from his words. Integrity and credibility, sure—unless it involves paranormals. No wonder Greene keeps herself hidden and the rest of the Underground never surface for fresh air. My jaw clenches, but I keep my expression composed.

"Mr. Haskins," I interject, injecting a dose of confidence into my voice. "Any of those relationships don't impede my work or dedication to this firm."

"But *paranormal* sympathizers," one of the partners attending via video interjects with a disapproving wrinkle of her nose.

A few others echo her distaste.

They talk about 'paranormal sympathizers' like it's a dirty word, a stain on an otherwise perfect reputation. The unspoken accusation that my connections to beings outside human comprehension somehow diminish my worth as a lawyer. It's infuriating and disheartening at the same time. And then it hits me suddenly: I'd implied the same, each time I told Lucian or the paranormals that I wasn't publicly standing with them.

Before I can decide how to react to that uncomfortable realization, Davenport leans forward, elbows on the gleaming mahogany table.

"Emily, let's cut to the chase," he says, voice rich with that hint of amusement that has always unsettled me. "We're all aware that green is the only color that truly matters in our line of work. Money doesn't care where it comes from. We'll accept a little discomfort in your clientele's politics for the business they'll bring."

Davenport's words echo in my mind, taunting me with their callous pragmatism. *Can I truly turn a blind eye to the discrimination just because it comes wrapped in dollar bills and security?* A bitter taste settles on my tongue as I realize that maybe I've been too focused on climbing the career ladder that I failed to see the rot festering within the rungs. My hands grip the armrests of my chair, nails biting into the polished wood as conflicting emotions churn within me.

"Distasteful clientele or not," Davenport continues, leaning back with a satisfied grin, "as long as those billable hours keep ticking, who are we to discriminate? After all, diversity is quite profitable these days."

"Good point," another partner chimes in, her gaze sharp and greedy.

"This really is all a formality, Emily," Davenport says. "Congratulations. You've made partner."

The words hit me like a wave, and I'm momentarily submerged in disbelief. Adrenaline and shock mingle in my veins. They're offering me the keys to the kingdom, the very thing I've hungered for more than anything. I take a deep breath, trying to push back the flood of conflicting emotions threatening to overwhelm me.

"Thank you," I breathe out, unsure what else to say while my mind rocks.

As if to seal the deal, a box holding a fancy pen is slid across the table toward me—a symbol, sleek and silver, promising power and responsibility. I open it, picking it up and turning it over in my fingers, the cool metal grounding me. I now know exactly what Stephanie meant when she flaunted Peterson's gift.

"Welcome to the other side of the table, Lane," one partner murmurs as the room clears.

I tuck the pen away, a talisman of success, but—I ask myself again—*at what cost?*

The door to the meeting room closes with a soft click behind me, sealing away the chorus of congratulations still humming in the air.

Drawing my phone from the pocket of my suit jacket, I thumb open the messaging app and hover over the 'New Message' icon. My fingers dance across the screen—a flurry of letters that spell out a proposition for Friday night revelry.

"Fancy a drink?" I type and hit send before nerves can make me second guess the choice of recipient. The message zips off into the digital void, its destination a secret tucked between me and the illuminated pixels.

I slip my phone back into my pocket, a smirk curling my lips as I imagine the look on their face when they read my message. My evening plans are set: a little heart-to-heart with someone who may or may not have *my* best interests at heart.

The mortuary is a world away from the lavishness of my firm, a somber place where silence reigns over cold rooms filled with solemn tributes to lives that used to be full of energy. The building reminds me of its owner: stark and gray, devoid of decorations. A barred window is next to the heavy door and my distorted reflection stares back at me.

"Actions matter," I whisper into the glass, hoping to convince myself. "They have to."

Pushing open the heavy door, I'm met with the sharp scent of embalming fluid. Sara awaits me near a row of gleaming steel tables, her hazel eyes meeting mine with an inscrutable gaze.

"Emily," she greets me with a cool nod, her voice cutting through the hushed ambiance like a scalpel through flesh. "You mentioned a drink?"

I take a moment to compose myself, steeling my nerves against the icy demeanor that never wavers from Sara, and brandish a bottle I picked up on the way. "I... I needed to talk," I begin tentatively, unsure of how to breach the invisible barrier between us.

Sara arches an eyebrow, a silent invitation for me to continue.

I swallow the lump in my throat, trying to find the right words. "I made partner today," I blurt out.

"Congratulations," she finally replies, her voice neutral.

"I know you might not be my biggest fan," I press on. "But when a *cop* suggests your next career move might involve advocating for paranormals that go bump in the night, you start to question if you accidentally signed up for a hidden camera show. So, I figured, go big and go to Sara for advice." I aim for a joke, but it falls flat.

Silence hangs in the air, thick enough to slice with my law school letter opener—which, incidentally, is probably hiding under a stack of briefs back at my apartment. This whole scenario is ludicrous, and yet here I am, spilling my guts to someone who might prefer I be on one of her slabs.

"Go on." Her voice is laced with annoyance and maybe a touch of curiosity—the good kind, not the 'killed-the-cat' variety.

Taking a deep breath, I lean against the cold metal table behind me and try to steady my shaking legs. "I had a bad childhood," I admit, feeling exposed. "A lot of us did, I know. I'm not special in that regard. But I pushed through, driven by the promise of security. I chased that brass ring with everything I had, believing it would protect me from ever feeling powerless again."

"Okay," Sara says but there's no bite in her words. Annoyance, sure, but something else... recognition, maybe.

"I thought making partner was all I wanted," I confess, my voice barely above a whisper. "Greene, the cop I mentioned, said that maybe... maybe it matters who we are to others," I continue, my voice hesitant yet resolute. "Not just what we do or how successful we are, but the connections we forge along the way. That *that's* the security that matters. I've never thought of it that way. And then when I think about how my firm treats paranormals? How *I* treat them, in exchange for security..."

Sara's gaze softens almost imperceptibly as she listens to my words, the tension in the room easing slightly. "Success isn't just about climbing the ladder," she says, her voice carrying a wisdom beyond her years. "It's about who stands by you and looks up to you for who you are, not only what you've done." She sets aside the tool she was holding, stepping closer until only a few feet separate us.

"I get it," she continues, her tone understanding. "We all strive for something—acknowledgement, power, security. But what are you willing to sacrifice for that corner office, Emily?" She raises her brows. "Lucian? Stardust? Tina? *That's* what you're choosing between. How'd you feel if someone had you on one side of that scale, and found you wanting?"

They had. Mom and Dad, giving me the trauma that created my high walls and sharp personality. And a sudden wave of clarity washes over me, stripping away the layers of ambition and insecurity that have clouded my judgment for so long. I'd been doing the same. Sure, I'd convinced myself otherwise by stepping up, putting in the minimum. I was investigating Mitchell's murder, better than people who wrote Lucian off entirely. But only just.

"It's not too late, Emily," Sara adds softly, her words carrying a glimmer of hope. "Show up and step up, every day, even when it's hard. Just try again tomorrow."

"Greene also suggested representing them. Not the champion but working for change to help uplift the cause. Less othering. Wouldn't that be something to see," I muse.

Sara leans against the table beside me, her arms crossed. "And where does Lucian fit into that?"

My lips press into a thin line. "He's a different story." It feels like I'm pulling teeth.

"Why? Because he pissed you off?" she asks, her voice tight, as if she's trying to strangle the words before they betray too much.

"No," I snap. "Because he has no alibi for the Peterson plot and dragged me down with him. Betrayal tends to break trust. And right now, trust is thinner than the veil between worlds," I say bitterly, feeling a pang in my chest.

"Emily, you know how little I think of you and even I know you're not that naïve." Her eyes flicker with something akin to exasperation—or is it pity?

I stand abruptly, grabbing the wine bottle. "Well, this has been enlightening. Thanks for the advice. I'll see you at the next sympathizer mixer."

But she steps in front of me, blocking my way. "This is part of it. It's not about you or your feelings."

I want to stomp my feet or scream into a pillow. "Fine. So don't take any of it personal, even when it hurts, got it."

"Or don't let it shut you down," she counters with a shrug. "And anyway, it wasn't a betrayal. Not towards you."

My frustration bubbles at her calm demeanor. "Then what do you call it?" I challenge, my voice sharper than intended.

Sara's gaze flickers, her hazel eyes hiding more than she reveals. "Lucian has his reasons for keeping certain truths close to his chest," she begins carefully, as if choosing her words with precision. "You're not the only human he's looking after. Or even the first."

There's an implication in her tone, a subtle nudge towards something I should have remembered. It reminds me of the camaraderie between her and Lucian when we went over the autopsy report. Sure, he came home to me, but only because I convinced him I was a safer bet than Sara.

The thought settles heavily in my stomach. Hurt mingles with disappointment, and a tinge of jealousy colors my thoughts. I had allowed myself to entertain the idea that Lucian and I were moving towards something real, something beyond the boundaries of our current interactions, something I was... maybe... finally ready for. But it seemed our connection wasn't as unique or significant as I'd thought.

A bitter taste lingers in my mouth as I try to push aside my hurt and resentment. It wasn't Lucian's fault for maintaining his secrets, for prioritizing others over me. We'd only known each other for a week, after all. And that kiss... it isn't like it had a promise attached. Especially when I still have Matty on my mind.

Shoving aside the flutter of hurt and rejection, I straighten my posture, forcing a small, wry smile on my face. "Okay," I finally say, "what do we do?"

CHAPTER 26

More papers and files clutter every surface of my desk-slash-dining table, evidence of my recent truce-turned-partnership with Sara to help Lucian—with no strings attached this time. But as I wait for her arrival, I'm determined to find my housemate. If I'm 'connecting' with the paranormal sect, might as well start at home.

"Okay, Herle," I mutter to myself, "let's see if you're brave enough to insult my hair to my face."

I turn slowly, scanning the room through the tinted lenses. The living room looks no less mundane than it did a moment ago—no hidden specters, no secret messages scrawled on the walls. Disappointment is an understatement; it's like expecting a guitar solo and getting a kazoo.

"Come on, Herle. Don't be shy," I coax the empty air, feeling the ridiculousness of the situation seep into my bones. But there's nothing. With a resigned sigh, I remove the glasses and toss them onto the table with a clatter, where they join my notes and crime scene photos. Trying to channel my inner Scooby-Doo has failed me again.

"I'm seriously thinking they made you up," I grumble to the silence.

A sudden knock at my door interrupts my thoughts, and I stomp over to open it, revealing Sara standing in my hallway.

Her platinum hair is pulled back into a tight braid, and those piercing hazel eyes survey the disarray in front of her with a hint of amusement.

"Stardust let you keep those?" Sara asks, stepping inside, her tone tinged with curiosity.

"Until Ray needs them," I say with a shrug. That I'd not looked for him since my fight with Lucian I keep to myself.

"You know that Stardust takes Ray to the Underground every night," she says idly as she takes in the chaos of papers and files surrounding us. "I'm surprised he hasn't taken the tunnels to take them back. There's an entrance down the street from here."

Warmth pools in my stomach. Maybe my friendship with the paranormals wasn't as one-sided as I'd thought.

We settle at our designated table, our makeshift command center amidst a sea of scattered paperwork. As I begin to organize the jumble of files, aligning them into neat stacks, Sara watches with a raised eyebrow, silently challenging me. It feels like a game of domestic chess as we both try not to be the first one to topple. "Alright, Harper," I finally say, "let's make sense of this jigsaw puzzle."

We sift through the evidence, comparing notes and time-lines. My tape recorder sits nearby, a silent sentinel recording every hypothesis and hunch with its blinking silence. I lay out what I know, watching Sara process the information like she's fitting together the fragments of a particularly tricky autopsy.

"It doesn't add up," she muses, tapping a photograph that she had copied from one of the autopsy files.

"Nothing about this case adds up," I agree, tracing a line in my own notes. "Except for one thing, that it all points straight to Lucian. Add in Peterson's accusations..."

"But anyone could have been responsible for those attacks," Sara disagrees. "Lucian's alternative form is a closely guarded secret; *no* one knows what it is. Even if Peterson did witness a vampire transformation, there's no way of proving it was Lucian."

My brows raise in surprise. Lucian had revealed his ability to transform into a raven to me, but if no one else knew, except his departed sister, then how did Peterson guess? "I don't know, it seems too convenient—"

"I still think there's something about the murder weapon," she interrupts, staring at the picture of Mitchell's mangled neck. "I know there was no lead or ink in the wounds, but besides someone carrying around a steel rod, it's got to be—"

My phone vibrates on the table, cutting her off. I glance at the screen, and an unintentional smile tugs at the corner of my mouth—Matty's name flashes, followed by a string of words that hint at brunch and unmistakable flirtation. I dismiss it with a click.

"Don't worry," I assure her. "No distractions. We're figuring this out or we'll die trying."

Sara's hazel eyes narrow at my dismissive tone towards the text, and she raises an eyebrow. "Good to know you finally have your priorities straight," she says with a chuckle.

Her laugh fades into a gentle silence, and I sense the shift before she even speaks. "So, about last night," she says. "You mentioned your childhood—how you always wanted to prove yourself. Is that why you're so driven now?"

I hesitate, my usual sarcasm retreating in the face of genuine curiosity. "Something like that," I concede. "Growing up, I learned that if you want something done, you do it yourself. And making partner at the firm... it's validation, you know?"

"Validation," she repeats softly, pondering the word as though it's a relic from a foreign land. "I suppose we all seek it in some form. For me, it was Lucian's coven that gave me a place when I had none." Her voice is steady, but there's a tremor of old pain lurking beneath the surface.

"Can't be easy, aligning with paranormals in public," I muse aloud, thinking of the professional masks we both wear. I can see the depth of her loyalty to Lucian. Jealousy or otherwise, it makes me appreciate her even more, admire her strength in staying true to herself despite the risks.

"It's not great for business," she admits. "But standing with them feels more honest than hiding everything." She meets my gaze, and there's steel in her voice. "You know that, right?"

"I do," I agree, leaning back in my chair as I weigh her words against my restless ambition. My decision wasn't made lightly but I haven't figured out the balance. With partnership in my back pocket, I'm hoping I can manage both.

Just as we start to delve back into Lucian's case, the phone rings, interrupting our discussion. I let out an exasperated sigh and answer it, pinching the bridge of my nose as if that could stave off the headache brewing.

"Now is really not a good time," I mutter into the phone, trying to focus on the case at hand.

"Emily, listen to me," Montgomery's voice crackles with urgency through the speaker, "It's imperative that you're seen at Peterson's fundraiser tonight."

My hand falls to the table with a heavy thump. "Seriously?" I snap. "You realize he's likely got a bone to pick with me. He might be *on* the news a lot, but I'm certain he watches it and will have caught the 6 o'clock specials showing my photo as the reason Lucian was out of jail when he was attacked."

Sara raises her head from her work and mouths a question. I wave her off impatiently.

Montgomery's voice holds a note of insistence, cutting through my skepticism. "It's important for appearances. Your presence there will speak volumes."

"I'm an attorney, not a lobbyist," I continue, crossing my arms in defiance. The thought of attending another political fundraiser, especially one thrown by Mayor Peterson, is enough to make my skin crawl.

But Montgomery is insistent, his voice carrying a weight that brooks no argument. "This isn't about politics. There's something brewing at that fundraiser. I want eyes on the inside until I can arrive."

I narrow my eyes at the phone, suspicions rising like a stubborn tide. "What do you mean, Montgomery? What's really going on?"

But all I get in response is a cryptic directive: "Just be there." And he ends the call.

"When do I actually do *legal* work for this guy?" I mutter to the room with a frustrated huff, sliding the phone across the table like it's a plague carrier and not just a normal extension of my body.

Sara raises an eyebrow, another silent question. I push myself away from the table slightly, fingers drumming a staccato rhythm on the wooden surface.

"Well," I start, the word hanging in the air between us, "Looks like this partnership will need to reconvene tomorrow. My evening got booked."

Sara frowns. "By whom?"

"New client," I respond vaguely. "I can't reveal his identity but..." I give her a quick once over. "You'd probably get along with him. Blunt, direct, and sympathetic towards supernatural beings." I pause, my brow furrowing. "Or so I assumed. Until this latest assignment."

What's next? Me rubbing elbows with Tom and his anti-paranormal ilk?

"What's he want you to do?" Sara asks.

"Attend Mayor Peterson's fundraiser."

She scrunches up her nose in disgust. "You can't be serious."

"Odds they'll let me in the door when they see my face?" I ask dryly.

Sara shakes her head incredulously. "But why? What does this new client want from you?"

"I have no idea," I admit, frustration seeping into my tone. "But... I wonder if it has something to do with Lucian."

Montgomery is a wildcard. Send me to Stephanie, to be seen among the sympathizers as his agent, okay. But why hire me to represent his interests, and then throw me in front of the politician who has the best reasons to distrust me *because* of Lucian?

I sigh heavily. "Shall we continue our search tomorrow?"

Sara stands, gathering the scattered papers and evidence. "Do you mind if I keep working on it?"

I shake my head. "Go for it. Maybe you'll figure it out before Lucian gets *allegedly* framed for another crime."

She frowns at me slightly but apparently thinks better of reprimanding me. And really, what can she say? I'm not taking it personally, but it doesn't mean I don't have feelings. And Lucian stabbed them in the neck... in the not-fun way.

"Don't take that," I say, snatching my tape recorder from the pile of evidence. "I might need it."

Just in case.

CHAPTER 27

The clink of fine crystal and the low hum of small talk envelop me as I push through the heavy doors into Peterson's foyer. A chandelier winks overhead, casting rainbows on the polished floor. I slip past the groups of laughing donors, their jewels glittering almost as much as their eyes when they spot someone worth impressing. I know that my recent stint on the news—thanks to bailing out Lucian—has branded me as some sort of renegade, a possible co-conspirator in Peterson's near-miss with mortality. I'm an exposed nerve, each glance that skitters in my direction sends a jolt down my spine—am I recognized? Pitied? Blamed? The thought alone is enough to make me wish for invisibility. My hand tightens around the slim recorder in my pocket, a lifeline in this sea of finery and fakery.

Amidst the sea of flawless faces and glitzy guests, I spot a familiar figure standing near the grand staircase and weave through the clusters of people towards him. Matty's calm composure shifts to surprise as he sees me approaching.

His expression turns guarded as I reach him, the ever-present facade of professionalism firmly in place but there's concern swirling in his brown eyes.

"Emily," he greets quietly. "What are you doing here?"

"One of those spontaneous things," I say, my tone light. "Not happy to see me?"

Matty's gaze flickers over my shoulder briefly before returning to me and his expression softens. "Absolutely. Just surprised. Sinclair insisted the entire DA's office show up to support Mayor Peterson, which is why *I'm* rubbing elbows with the elite tonight." He trails off, raising his brows expectantly.

But I don't take the bait. "It's quite the spectacle. Peterson certainly knows how to throw a fundraiser."

Matty smiles, but there's a nervous tension lingering beneath his facade. "That he does. But... I can't help but wonder if there's more to your presence here than only spontaneity. Not that I'm complaining," he adds with a crooked grin, the worry in his eyes now tinged with a glimmer of hope.

I chuckle, shifting slightly on my heels. "Can't a girl spend a night hobnobbing and enjoying free canapes?"

"Not when that girl is you," he replies. His eyes dart towards the crowd, scanning for any prying ears. "You're lucky they let you in the room after this week's breaking news. Please tell me you've given up on your vigilante crusade."

"Not entirely, but I can promise you there will be no masked heroics tonight," I say with a sly grin. "I'm here for legitimate legal work."

"Speaking of, I wanted to take you out to celebrate your partnership." He leans in close. "Just us this time. But don't be surprised if Megan has something planned for next Tuesday."

"Emily Lane," a voice purrs, smooth as silk sliding across my skin. I halt, turning to find Mayor Peterson detaching himself from a gaggle of admirers, his confident stride bringing him closer. For a fleeting second, something flickers in those warm green eyes of his—a hesitation? Fear? It's gone before I can decipher it, replaced by that trademark charm that's rumored to have swayed even the most paranormal-averse voter.

Before Mitchell joined the race, that is.

"Mayor Peterson," I say, keeping my tone even, although I'm internally bracing for... well, anything. He's close now, the faint scent of his cologne mingling with the ambient aroma of wealth that permeates the room.

"May I steal you away for a moment? My office is just through there." He gestures vaguely with a nod of his head, his smile all politeness edged with something darker. Intrigue? Desperation? "I think it would benefit us both to have a private chat."

"Lead the way," I say, my voice betraying none of the curiosity clawing at my insides. At the very least, I'll have something to report to Montgomery.

"Excellent," he murmurs, and there's an undercurrent of satisfaction in his voice that rings alarm bells somewhere deep within me.

Matty shifts uncomfortably, his eyes darting around the room as if searching for an escape route. A nervous twitch tugs at the corner of his lips, betraying the composed facade he wears like a mask.

I touch his arm. "Catch you later?"

He nods, offering a strained smile that doesn't quite reach his eyes. "I'll find you," he promises.

I follow Peterson through the throngs of people, their conversations fading into a background buzz. His house is as labyrinthine as Lucian's, though I won't mention the comparison. We turn down more hallways than I can count on one hand until we finally arrive at his home office.

The office door clicks shut behind us, sealing away the distant murmur of the fundraiser like a whisper lost in the wind. I let my gaze roam over Peterson's sanctuary, a luxurious spread of mahogany and leather that screams power with a capital 'P.' As surreptitiously as I can, I click my tape recorder on.

Peterson takes off his suit jacket, hanging it on a coatrack. "Make yourself comfortable," he says, gesturing to an armchair.

As I sink into the plush velvet, my gaze is drawn to the dozen framed photos on the desk, showcasing Peterson throughout his life. Two photos look out of place as they aren't a shrine to Peterson. The first, a black and white in a silver frame, is of a young couple. Beside it, a hazily colored photo of that same couple holding a young girl.

"Brandy?" Peterson asks, already halfway to pouring a couple of glasses without waiting for my answer. His movements are practiced, the roll of his sleeves to his wrists deliberate.

"Sure," I say, my gaze sharp. Let's see where this little tête-à-tête takes us.

"My favorite brand," he declares, handing me a glass.

I swirl the drink, watching it cling to the sides before settling back down—a slow dance of amber temptation. "It looks lovely. Thank you."

Peterson leans back against his desk, glass in hand. "You know, Emily," he begins, and I steel myself for the pitch, the persuasion, the play.

He takes a slow sip of his drink, eyes narrowing ever so slightly as if weighing how much to reveal—or perhaps, what line of attack to take. "My stance on paranormals has... evolved. There's history there, you see."

"Is that right?" I lift an eyebrow, the drink untouched on my lips. "Change is the only constant, as they say."

"Indeed." He rolls up his sleeves further, revealing pale skin marred with angry red scratches. "You've heard about my little run-in with Lucian, I presume?"

"Hard to miss when it's splashed across every news outlet," I say, finally taking a cautious sip. The brandy is smooth, with a bite that lingers, much like the subject at hand.

"Lucian did this because of my changed stance of paranormals. Ironic, given the initial restrictions were due to his own actions," Peterson says, almost casually, rotating his forearm to show off the evidence of his altercation.

"Looks painful," I comment, leaning in for a closer look. It doesn't escape me that the scratches seem perfectly spaced, as if one's *own* fingers could also be the culprit. *A self-inflicted wound to garner sympathy or something more sinister?*

"I consider myself lucky to have fought him off and kept my life," Peterson says, flexing his fingers which appear conspicuously free of any defensive wounds.

His eyes flicker with a hint of nostalgia. "Paranormal *sympathists*," he muses, tracing the rim of his glass with a thoughtful finger. "That's what my family was. My great grandparents down to my folks, ending with me." He chuckles, a dry, hollow sound. "But imagine, during prohibition, when hiding a bottle of gin was scandal enough, my great grandad stumbled upon a whole other world needing refuge."

I quirk an eyebrow, intrigued despite myself. "And he opened his doors to them?"

"More than that," Peterson says, his voice dipping into reverence. "He advocated for them, saw them as equals, always had. And Eleanor," he gestures to the antique frame on his desk with the photo of the young couple and their daughter, "my grandmother, she literally gave them room and board."

"Sounds like formidable people," I admit, sipping the brandy, its warmth spreading a false sense of relaxation through my limbs.

"Michael Carter was his name," he continues, pride swelling in his tone. "Guess it was inevitable that some of that... sympathetic blood trickled down to me."

"And yet here you are, shifting stances faster than a chameleon." The words slip out before I can catch them, but then, why bother? We're beyond pretenses.

Peterson's smile doesn't waver, but something sharpens in his eyes. "Times change, Emily. So do truths. Lucian—the paranormals—they aren't who my family thought."

"Because of one?" I challenge, unable to mask the skepticism lacing my voice.

"Sometimes, one is all it takes," he states firmly.

An uncomfortable silence stretches between us. My gaze drifts to the photograph he'd gestured towards earlier, the sepia tones whispering of a time long past. The faces of his great grandparents stare back at me, noble and kind, if a tad austere. But it's the photo beside them, of the couple in their prime, that draws a second, longer look. His features seem oddly familiar...

"Doesn't he look like..." My voice trails off as recognition dawns, chilling and undeniable. An older Lucian could be superimposed on his great grandfather's visage, and no one would bat an eye.

"Me?" Peterson quirks a brow, but there's something dark behind his gaze.

I flit my gaze to his face, and the similarities to his ancestor—to Lucian—suddenly align. They could be cousins. *Uncle* and *nephew*, with Peterson the elder in appearance.

"Yeah," I murmur, setting down my glass, the brandy now tasting more of iron than oak. "In the right light."

The laughter of a child, high and unburdened, slices through the thick air of tension in Peterson's office. I swivel toward the sound, grateful for the interruption. A boy barrels into the room, flanked by an anxious parent and an aide whose smile doesn't quite reach her eyes.

"Mr. Mayor!" The kid's voice is a burst of enthusiasm in the stiff formality of the fundraiser. "Can I have your autograph?"

"Of course, young man." Peterson's face softens, the hardened lines of politics smoothing into benign warmth. He bends down to the boy's level, his previously rolled-up sleeves now a facade of casual approachability.

"Wow, you have a lot of pens!" The kid's gaze fixates on the set of fancy pens Peterson pulls from the top drawer of his desk. The tips glint in the lamplight, sharp as needles.

"Ah, these old things?" Peterson chuckles, winking at the child. "Just part of the job. You see, I'm an ordinary person—"

"Who pulls the strings of the city's political puppet show," I murmur under my breath, my words lost in the shuffle of amused adults. Something about those pens nags at me, a splinter of thought that refuses to be ignored.

"Here you go." Peterson caps a sleek fountain pen, his signature glistening on the scrap of paper the aide had provided. "Remember, anyone can make a difference. Even with something as simple as a pen."

A pen. My heart hammers a warning, adrenaline surging as fragments of memory coalesce into a sharp point. He'd given Tom and Stephanie a set of pens, similar in their opulence. Pens with pointed steel nibs that remained *empty* until the ink cartridge is installed.

"Thank you, Mr. Mayor!" The boy beams, clutching the paper like a treasure as he's ushered out by the parent and aide, leaving behind a lingering echo of innocence.

"Kids, they're the future, aren't they?" Peterson straightens up, slipping the remaining pens back into his desk, unaware of the storm he's ignited in my mind.

"Very true," I agree, though my thoughts are light-years ahead, piecing together puzzle pieces I hadn't even realized were scattered.

Peterson had given the candidates a set of steel-tipped pens. It was likely he'd given Mitchell one too. And Mitchell's desk—it had that empty space, where I thought maybe a cufflink box was taken. But it was the perfect size for a pen box, like Stephanie's and Tom's. Wilkin said the murderer had taken a box with him, the human who looked like an older Lucian, who'd drank brandy with Mitchell before his death.

"Emily? Are you alright?" Peterson's voice cuts through my rapid thoughts, his brows knitting together in faux concern.

"Never better," I say, the words a little sharper than intended. I force my attention back to the room, back to the man sitting before me. Michael Peterson—the epitome of tailored suits and political smiles. Could this poised figure really be a murderer? The idea prickles at me, refusing to be smoothed away.

"Forgive me if I'm being forward, but you seem... preoccupied," he says, eyes searching mine for a clue.

"Your story about your family—it's quite captivating." I deflect, hoping my face doesn't betray the frantic detective work unfolding behind my eyes. "It's given me a lot to think about."

"Ah, yes, well, history has its way of shaping us," Peterson replies, a touch of pride creeping into his voice.

"Indeed," I say absently, my gaze drifting to Peterson's desk where the pens disappeared moments ago. The cufflink found at the crime scene—that had been too convenient, hadn't it? Almost like someone wanted to leave a trail leading straight to Lucian. Someone who looks like Lucian in the right light, and whose ancestor's name is on Lucian's family tree. Whose family stories might pass along Lucian's secondary form.

"Something wrong with my desk?" Peterson asks, following my stare.

"Just remembering the craftsmanship of your pens," I lie smoothly, offering a tight smile. "They're similar to the ones Tom and Stephanie have."

"I like to inject a little ceremony into the race," Peterson explains, hopefully unaware that his casual display may have revealed a deadly secret. "It's a tradition of mine to gift pens. It's a pity Mitchell didn't stay in the race long enough for me to give him a set." The expression he reveals is all teeth.

Mitchell had been in the race for months, and Tom got his pen set on day one, but I don't mention that.

"Forgive my ignorance about politics," I start, trying not to let my suspicions show. "But was there any concern about Mitchell winning?"

Peterson furrows his brow in fake contemplation. "There's no way to know for sure. But he had his supporters."

The air in Peterson's office is thick enough to slice with a gavel, and here I am, doing just that. "Supporters you're now courting," I remind him.

He raises his glass in a mock toast. "Ah, so you do understand politics."

And suddenly, it all clicks. Peterson left with the pen box, leaving no trace of his guilt, and conveniently dropped the cufflink—to frame Lucian, to stir up fear against paranormals so he could jump ship, and gather sympathy from both sides of the aisle, all the while removing his biggest competition.

Perhaps I should give Tom Turner a head's up.

Chapter 28

"So, do you have Mitchell's pen set tucked away for safe-keeping, or is it out making rounds as an accomplice for another crime?" I ask him, the smirk on my lips not quite reaching my eyes.

Peterson leans back in his chair, the leather creaking under the weight of his guilt. Or maybe just his body, I'm not a mind reader. "What are you talking about?"

"I'm talking about you murdering your competitor for politics and profit." My patience is wearing thinner than the veneer of his respectability.

"You're barking up the wrong tree," he deflects with a little too much ease. "Clearly your sympathies with your vampire friends has addled your brain."

"How about I enlighten you, and you tell me if I'm wrong?" My voice is ice, cold enough to freeze the blood in his veins. I lean forward, propping my elbows on his desk. I run him through the facts, from the convenient cufflink Lucian's father would have passed down, the suspiciously missing pen set he'd no doubt given Mitchell with nibs that were likely a perfect match for Mitchell's wounds, his history and relationship with the Belmont family, and capping it off with the self-inflicted wounds on his arms.

There's a flicker of something in Peterson's warm green eyes, a glint of steel I hadn't noticed before. He sighs, a sound heavy with resignation. "Clever," he concedes, and I can tell this is where the curtain rises on his one-man show. "That's a great story. If you ever give up the law, you should consider a career in fiction."

"We just need to make a call, look at Lucian's family tree, see where little Mikey Peterson, named for Lucian's great-great-whatever nephew, Michael Carter, fits in. Add in your inconvenient tradition of handing out steel-tipped mini-daggers to your competition, and I'm sure I can at least get to 'probable cause,'" I say, keeping my tone level despite the way my heart is hammering against my ribcage. This is it—the moment where I either break the case wide open or tumble down a rabbit hole with no end in sight. "And if there weren't a paranormal at the other end of this, the cops would have figured this out and not needed little ol' me to do it."

He shifts uncomfortably, his mask of composure slipping. There's a certain satisfaction in watching the mighty falter, especially when they're fueled by hubris rather than reason.

"Emily, you have to understand, I tried to reason with him, but that mafia scum refused—" Peterson starts, but I cut him off with a wave of my hand, even as vindication floods my veins.

"Understand? What I understand is that rationality took a backseat the moment you decided murder was a viable campaign strategy."

Peterson bristles, and something unsettling crawls over his face. He leans forward, menace seeping into his tone like poison. "You think you're so clever, don't you? Figuring out I killed Mitchell," he hisses. "But if you go public with this,

I'll make sure your reputation is shredded before you can say 'objection.'"

I raise an eyebrow, unimpressed. "Threats, Peterson? Really?" I glance around his opulent office, the walls lined with degrees and accolades—a testament to his once-respected status. "Last I checked, we're not alone in this building. A full house of witnesses isn't the ideal audience for your intimidation act."

His jaw clenches, and I know I've hit a nerve. *Good.*

"Besides," I continue, tapping my finger against the arm of the chair, adopting the cadence of a lawyer delivering her closing argument, "you admitted to murder. That tends to put a damper on one's credibility."

Peterson rises, the chair groaning behind him. His face contorts with fury, and I brace myself, knowing I'm treading dangerous waters—waters infested with sharks like him. His eyes, once the epitome of trustworthiness, now simmer with a toxic blend of desperation and malice. He runs thin fingers over the mottled bruises and scratches that paint his forearms—his so-called evidence of Lucian's brutality.

"See this, Emily?" His voice takes on a sing-song quality, grotesquely out of place in the heavy air between us. "The public already bought the story once. And they'll buy it again."

I snort, despite the tightening coil of danger in my gut. "So, what's your play, Peterson? Ruin my good name or go for round two with your self-defense shtick?"

He smiles, but it's all teeth and no humor. "Whatever it takes to preserve the greater good. You know how the game is played."

"Except," I counter, rising from my seat, "you're not the only one who knows how to spin a narrative."

His grin evaporates like mist under a scorching sun. In a flash, he lunges across the room. Instinctively, I dart to the side, but his hand snags the hem of my blazer, tugging me back toward him. My heart jackhammers against my ribs as I twist free, adrenaline spiking.

"Help!" The word tears from my throat, raw and instinctive, even as I know the thick walls muffle my shout.

Peterson's breath huffs against my neck. I can't let him win—not when Lucian's freedom, not to mention my own life, hangs in the balance. Channeling my younger days, I elbow him squarely in the face, relishing the satisfying crunch.

"Nice try, but you'll need more than brute force to take me down," I hiss, ducking another wild swing.

"Emily, you naïve paranormal-loving fool," he growls, blood trickling from his nose. "You think you can expose me without consequences?"

"Better than letting a murderer run the city," I shoot back, sidestepping another grab as I search for something heavy to hit him with. But my heel catches on the edge of an ornate rug, and I stumble, off-balance.

Peterson sees his chance; I see my mistake. This is it: the moment where either he goes down, or I do.

He charges like a bull, arms outstretched, aiming to crush me against the mahogany bookshelf. But I've read this plot before, and I refuse to be the tragic heroine caught in the last act, springing away at the last second toward the door.

My fingers claw at the handle, slick with sweat and fear. If I can make it through the door, into the throng of potential witnesses...

But Peterson is relentless, driven by whatever twisted ideology fuels his rage. He's close—too close—and there's no time left for clever quips or calculated risks.

"Back off, Peterson!" I warn, breathless. I push against the heavy door, muscles straining, willing it to yield. Freedom is inches away, but so are Peterson's grasping hands. The scent of his cologne mixes with the copper tang of blood from his broken nose, creating a nauseating perfume of imminent danger.

"Never," he hisses, the word punctuated by his hand clamping onto my shoulder, fingers digging in with the ferocity of a cornered animal. The other wraps around my neck.

It's now or never.

"Help!" I screech again, louder this time, my voice bouncing against the mahogany walls. "He's trying to kill me!"

"Emily, you foolish girl," he sneers, his breath hot on my neck. "Did you really think you could expose me so easily?"

"Let go," I gasp, my voice more of a snarl than I intend. But I'm not some damsel—no way I'm going down without clawing back.

His hand tightens around my neck, a vice of desperation and malice. The pain brings clarity; the fight-or-flight instinct that's kept humans alive since the dawn of time kicks in hard. I elbow him in the stomach and twist, trying to wrench free from his grip, but it's like fighting iron shackles.

It's then—the second that hope starts to fade, when the darkness seems ready to swallow me whole—that a blur of motion catches the corner of my eye. Peterson's grip slackens in surprise, and he utters a choked gasp.

A hobgoblin, all sinewy muscle and silent, scaly, grace, is there between us. *Where in Hades did they come from?* The paranormal moves with a speed that defies their squat form, a fluid shadow darting through the light of the room.

"Unhand her," the hobgoblin commands, their voice gravelly but unmistakably firm.

Peterson looks as if he's seen a ghost—or worse, a monster from under his bed made flesh. His eyes bulge with disbelief, his mouth agape in shock. He stumbles backward, but the hobgoblin is relentless, advancing with a predator's focus.

"In my home?" Peterson breathes out, staggering like he's drunk on fear.

Before Peterson can regain his composure, the hobgoblin strikes—a swift, precise blow to the head. It's so efficient, so brutally simple, it almost seems anticlimactic. Peterson crumples to the ground like a stringless marionette, his threat extinguished by a single, well-aimed hit.

"Thanks for the assist," I mutter, despite the adrenaline still pumping through my veins. My heart's racing a mile a minute, but I manage a half-smirk at the hobgoblin. "Nice timing."

The hobgoblin nods once, stoic and unreadable, and then turns to scan the area with eyes that miss nothing. I take a moment to catch my breath, watching Peterson sprawled on the floor.

"Until next time," the hobgoblin says gruffly.

"Tell Herle 'hi' when you see him," I quip, because if you can't joke in the face of danger, what's the point?

The air shivers with the last echoes of magic as the hobgoblin's form winks out of existence, just as Matty, Sinclair, and a gaggle of bewildered police officers pour into the room. I whip out my tape recorder with a flourish, feeling like a magician revealing her final trick, even as my limbs quiver like the magician's skittish rabbit.

"Before you aim those handcuffs in my direction, listen to this," I say, thumbing the play button. Peterson's voice fills the room, his confession and our fight casting a heavy pall over the astonished faces crowding around me.

"Matty said I couldn't get Lucian off the hook unless I bagged a confession on tape," I say, trying to keep the mood light despite the gravity of the evidence unfurling from the speakers. "I do love a good challenge."

You could cut the surprise with a knife—it's that thick. Heads swivel, eyes widen, and there's Sinclair, looking as if she's been force-fed a whole grove of lemons. Her jaw sets in a rigid line as she listens to the beginning of the tape, my summary of the evidence.

"By the way, you might want to look for a pen box with Mitchell's initials on the shafts. They're more than just writing instruments." The implication hangs heavy in the air, and I let myself enjoy a moment of smug satisfaction.

Matty's eyes widen as I finish, and he rushes towards me, propelled like a wound-up toy finally unleashed. "Are you okay?" he asks anxiously, his hands hovering over my body as if he's afraid any touch might hurt.

I flash him a confident grin, but the wince that follows betrays me. "Better than ever. You should see the other guy."

"I can," Matty replies, his gaze flicking over to where an unconscious Peterson is being pulled into a seated position by officers. "And you look about the same."

"A paranormal did it," I announce to the room. "They saved me and took down Peterson before he could add an attempted murder charge to his rap sheet."

The others in the room who *hadn't* been stunned by Peterson's taped confession now wear looks of even bigger shock and disbelief at my revelation.

"They will remain anonymous, but they deserve all the credit," I state boldly, my eyes locking onto Sinclair's with a pointed gaze. My tone turns demanding as I continue, "So, about dropping the cases against Lucian? Both of them?"

"Fine," Sinclair concedes through gritted teeth. "I'll look into it."

"I'm hoping there'll be an official statement and release this evening," I ask, my tone acidic. "Given how quickly you moved to arrest Lucian the first time, I can't *imagine* there'll be a delay in any decisions now."

Sinclair sighs heavily, her gaze flickering towards Peterson. "We'll need to spin this so it doesn't reflect poorly on the department," she says, more to herself than to anyone else in the room. "But yes, you can expect a statement at the 11 o'clock news."

Matty lets out a good-natured sigh and holds up his phone. "I'll call the judge."

The tension dissipates ever so slightly, but victory doesn't quite settle comfortably on my shoulders—not yet.

Once Sinclair left to take the steps needed to release Lucian, Matty chatted up an EMT outside, convincing them to take a peek at the angry bruise encircling my neck—a memento from my scuffle.

"Emily, you said tonight was about billable hours, not vigilante work," Matty chides once the EMTs are done with me, but there's a twinkle of admiration in his eye.

"You've got to admit, it was one hell of a takedown, even if I wasn't the one throwing punches," I say, rubbing my sore neck. Peterson is being escorted into a cop car, looking less mayoral by the second.

"I'll give you credit for finding trouble," Matty mutters, leaning against the ambulance.

"One does need hobbies." I feign innocence, patting my hair as though I've stepped out of a salon rather than a supernatural skirmish.

He rolls his eyes but can't hide the small smile tugging at the corners of his mouth.

Before we can continue our banter, Montgomery exits a car across the street and stalks up the driveway, his impeccable suit looking like he should have attended this soiree instead of me. I narrow my eyes at him, my arms folded as if they could shield me from any more unexpected twists.

"Quite the spectacle, Emily," he begins, voice smooth as silk and just as slippery. Montgomery's eyes slide over to Matty, who nods stiffly in response.

"Was this why my attendance was so crucial?" I demand, scowling. "You could've saved us both some trouble with a simple text: 'Peterson's the culprit. LOL, G2G, TTYL, BYE.'" I wave a hand theatrically. "Put your personal flair on it."

He gives me an inscrutable look, a smirk tugging at the corner of his mouth. "No, I certainly didn't plan for this. But it's quite convenient for me. Now, I must unruffle a few feathers. Keep up the good work."

"Convenient?" I muse aloud after he walks away. "If by 'convenient' you mean utterly unexpected and bizarrely contrived, then sure, we're practically in a Hallmark movie."

Matty shakes his head before leaning in to buss a kiss on my cheek. "I doubt dinner will be as eventful as this but let me know. Monday night?" He offers a soft smile. "I figure you might need tomorrow off to decompress."

"Or to find more trouble," I say, tilting my head, which aggravates my neck and earns a grimace.

He plants another kiss, this time on my lips. "That wouldn't surprise me. I've got paperwork to handle thanks to your escapade, especially with an 11 p.m. deadline looming. Will you be safe getting home?"

I nod. "I'll text you tomorrow."

As Matty walks away, I lean against a car in the driveway, relishing the coolness seeping into my skin. Peterson's actions will send ripples through the murky waters of our city, and I wonder what paranormal surprises will surface next.

Chapter 29

On Monday night, I march down the street, my heels clicking a staccato rhythm against the pavement that could give the local jazz band a run for their money. Even the rundown vampire quarter park is a welcome sight after a day of artificial light and the scent of recycled air in the office. I breathe in deeply, and the chill of the evening is like a slap from Mother Nature herself—bracing, with a hint of 'wake up, honey, you're not in Kansas anymore.' And my mind whirls like a tornado, much like the leaves swirling across my path.

"Emily Lane, attorney by day, paranormal confidante by night," I mutter to myself, wrapping my coat tighter around me as if to ward off the absurdity of my life. I'm half-tempted to add 'vampire liaison' to my business cards. It'd certainly make for a conversation starter, or ender, depending on the company. I've got more supernatural contacts now than a graveyard has ghosts, and let's not even start on the office politics.

Thanks to my relentless determination and an otherworldly ally, Peterson is now behind bars waiting his own trial. The interim mayor has lifted all the temporary restrictions on paranormals, and suddenly, they're not the 'monsters' the media painted them as for weeks. They're hailed as heroes, including my anonymous benefactor. The press labeled me a hero too, but all I feel is a heavy weight of guilt and exhaustion.

The local news begged for an interview, and I'd taken the opportunity, better to get ahead of the hailstorm that might come for me.

On Sunday morning, I sat across from the news anchor in a cramped studio, my ponytail back in place, displaying the necklace of bruises Peterson gave me.

"You mentioned that you had help in taking down former-mayor Peterson. What kind of help?" the news anchor, Maggie Hart, had asked. She was a younger journalist, more used to reading from a teleprompter, or so Liz told me when the interview had aired.

"I discovered the mayor's guilt, but I would have been nothing more than a stain on his carpet if a paranormal being hadn't intervened and saved me," I said, looking directly into the camera instead of at my host. "Despite the widespread prejudice against their kind, this being revealed itself and risked its own safety to protect me."

Maggie looked rapt. "How did the authorities respond when you told them about the creature's actions?"

"Initially, there was skepticism," I admitted. "But the evidence I provided, along with the eyewitness account, left no doubt. Sinclair and the police have acknowledged the paranormal's heroism, and they are now considering how to officially recognize his actions while maintaining his desired anonymity."

Maggie leaned forward, the cameras panned in. "Emily, coming forward like this, especially in such a charged atmosphere, takes a lot of courage. How do you feel about publicly supporting the paranormal community now?"

"I was worried at first. The stigma and potential backlash were daunting." I dialed up the support that Danielle and Sara said I had the power to provoke, using a little white lie about my motives to spin the public's favor. "But after seeing the bravery and humanity of the paranormal who saved me, I realized that standing up for what's right is more important than fear. Paranormal beings deserve the same rights and protections as anyone else. They are part of our community, and they deserve justice and equality."

The interview ended with Maggie turning to the camera with a serious expression. "Emily's story is a powerful reminder of the importance of truth and courage. For Metro News 7, I'm Maggie Hart. Stay with us as we continue to bring you the latest updates on this case."

The memory fades as I reach the cobblestone steps leading into the residential area just before the park.

Even with the interview, and positive spin from the press, the firm isn't sure what to think. They're, of course, grappling with my newfound fame, and truthfully, so am I. *Outwardly*, the firm is nodding along with the rest of the city, or at least that of its non-sociopathic inhabitants, bless their conflicted souls. There's a collective guilt festering in their hearts for how easily they fell for Peterson's machinations. And it only adds to my own guilt for not seeing through it sooner and for abandoning those I was trying to befriend.

Johnson & Marcus will watch which way the wind blows. If it blows away from the paranormals, I'll be left high and dry. But as much as I'd love to break free from Johnson & Marcus's toxic politics, I'm stuck to them financially. And deep down, despite everything, a part of me still craves that 'partnership' approval.

"Thinking of taking up another new vice?" Lucian's voice cuts through the air, smooth as the edge of a legal brief.

I turn, finding him leaning against an ancient oak, the bark nearly as textured as the history etched in his gray eyes. There's a casual grace to his stance that makes my own posture feel stilted in comparison, especially given his latest stint behind bars.

"Thought I'd try birdwatching," I quip, crossing my arms. Despite my defensive posture, I can't deny the electric charge that zips through the air, crackling with the unsaid and the unfinished. "But I'm more interested in nocturnal species lately."

"A fascination with creatures of the night. How fitting." He pushes away from the tree and steps closer. It's deliberate, as if testing the space between us. "I assumed you'd heard I lifted the restrictions on the park."

"No. I took a gamble, hoping to catch Stardust here," I confess, gesturing to the glasses nestled like a necklace along my collar, a reminder of an errand to fulfill.

"Emily," Lucian begins, his voice dropping a notch from our earlier light-hearted chatter. "I must thank you for what you did. But I'm sure you understand this is only the beginning. What Mitchell wanted, what Peterson tried, my coven remains at risk."

"Catching a murderer does tend to shake things up," I say with a dark chuckle, the taste of the word bitter on my tongue. "Distant relative or not."

He nods, his expression unreadable. "The upcoming mayoral election, the shifting tides of public opinion—it all adds to the storm we will always face. The existing regime's softening towards us is certainly precarious and time limited. You understand that, don't you?"

"I get it," I reply, meeting his gaze head-on. "The city might be catching its breath for now, but the storm's far from over, to stick with your analogy. Mitchell's death has stirred the waters, and there are ripples yet to come."

The tension between us crackles like the storm he's just warned about. "I spoke with Sara," he adds. "She told me of your conversation. Officer Greene echoed it. They played me the interview on one of their phones."

"No secrets with the paranormals, I guess," I say dryly.

He gives a small smile. "Very few. But you're privy to more than most. You've become a part of this world in a way few humans ever do." His eyes scan over me thoughtfully before adding, "You have influence here, power even."

I let out a surprised chuckle. "Power? Right. My ability to subpoena is really going to impress the supernatural crowd."

"Never underestimate the power of a voice," he says, a smirk playing on his lips. "Or the lawyer who wields it."

"Is this where you tell me 'with great power comes great responsibility?'"

"Something like that," he says, but there's a seriousness in his tone that suggests he's not joking. "You've chosen us and we're relying on you now. Don't disappoint us."

"Great," I sigh, turning back towards the playground where Stardust usually loiters. "No pressure." One foot in the office, the other in the crypt. Talk about work-life balance.

"None at all," Lucian confirms, falling into step beside me. "Just know you've merely scratched the surface, and there are deeper currents ready to drag you under if you're not careful, perhaps taking us with you."

"Thanks for the pep talk, Dracula." I roll my eyes, but I can feel the gravity of our conversation anchoring me. This is real; the stakes are high, and somehow, amid all the chaos, I find myself craving the clarity this strange new role offers.

"Anytime," he says warmly.

As we approach the swings, I catch a glimpse of Stardust, his glittery ensemble outshining the moon. He's standing next to Ray by his favorite bench.

"Emily!" Stardust calls out, waving a hand that glimmers like a disco ball in the twilight.

"Hey, Stardust," I call back, brandishing the glasses I brought for him. "You're the vamp I was looking for. But it looks like I'm too late."

I glance at Ray, taking in his transformed appearance. He looks better than he has in months. His dark hair is styled in a jagged, edgy cut that frames his tan face instead of his usual bedhead. And instead of a stained track suit, he's clad in a leather jacket over a band tee and artfully ripped jeans. But the pièce de résistance is the pink sparkly glasses perched on his nose, identical to the ones in my hand.

"Like the specs, Ray," I tell him. "You'll give the stars a run for their money."

Ray beams, adjusting the glasses with a flair that suggests he's well aware of how dazzling he looks. "Only the best for the Underground," he says, winking as if we share some secret. And maybe we do, now that I think about it.

"You're looking great," I offer genuinely. "How are things?"

As Ray gives me a rundown of what he's been up to and his own personal adventures while I'd been playing detective, Stardust hooks an arm around his waist and rests his chin on Ray's shoulder. He gives me an intense look that makes me wonder what's going through his mind.

"And so, once I was released, I realized I needed a better support system," Ray explains with a hint of determination in his voice. "I got out of there as fast as I could. Right now, I'm staying at a hotel, but once I find a job, I'll be looking for a place of my own."

Stardust playfully chimes in, "We keep telling him he's welcome to stay in the quarter, but he's too good for that now."

"I might know of a job opportunity," I offer, recalling the sign I spotted at Elegance in Metals. "It's early morning hours, so it'll leave you plenty of time to embrace your nocturnal side."

After our conversation ends, I hold out the glasses to Stardust.

"Keep them, Miss Missy," Stardust offers, an enigmatic smile blooming on his full lips. "A souvenir from your adventures—or an invitation for more."

"Because every lawyer needs a pair of blindingly bedazzled eyewear," I retort, but I pocket them anyway. A girl never knows when she'll need to traverse the monster underworld, right? Warmth pools in my gut that I've earned a place in their world.

"See you around," Stardust says, slipping his arm around Ray's shoulders as they saunter away, leaving a trail of whispers and second glances in their wake.

"Count on it, rock star," I reply, though they're already mixing into the crowd.

With my errand complete, I check the time on my phone and realize I have only thirty minutes before meeting Matty for dinner. I can't afford to dawdle in the vampire quarter. A gust of wind sends a strand of hair flying out of my bun as

I turn towards the entrance, with Lucian following closely behind.

"Watch your step," he murmurs, his hand lightly touching the small of my back as we navigate the uneven sidewalk. It's a casual gesture, but it sends an unexpected shiver down my spine.

"Always do," I quip, stepping over a crack with exaggerated care. The touch lingers a second too long to be entirely innocent, and I'm acutely aware of the tension that hums between us, a live wire of unspoken questions and possibilities.

"Emily," he starts, and there's a hesitance in his voice that piques my curiosity, especially knowing his connection to Sara. "You're welcome to stay tonight. We could finish what we began a few mornings prior."

I'd been burned by both men, though to some extent that was mutual. I'd felt betrayed by both and *maybe* done a little betraying of my own. But I'm taking it slow, dipping my toes into the waters of 'real relationships,' starting with legitimate friendships and seeing where things lead after that.

"No... I should get going," I say, sliding my hands into the pockets of my coat. "I've got a dinner date."

"A lucky fellow," he says, his gaze holding mine a beat too long. "Take care, Emily. Until next time."

"Until next time," I echo, watching as he disappears into the night.

I stand there, alone under the streetlamp, letting the anticipation coil in my gut. This game we're playing has more layers than I thought, and I'm not just talking about the legal ones. There's something exhilarating about standing on the precipice of the unknown, about being a player in a world where the rules are constantly rewritten.

With a determined nod to no one in particular, I turn on my heel and make my way towards my evening plans. One thing's for sure: I'm not only a lawyer. I'm a mediator, an ally, maybe even a catalyst. And as I consider the world waiting for me, I can't help but feel that I'm on the brink of something monumental.

"Let the games begin… again," I whisper to myself, a half-smile playing on my lips as the city swallows me whole.

AUTHOR'S NOTE

Thank you for reading FANGS AND FELONIES, the first in my Emily Lane Paranormal Mysteries series.

If you're interested in more of my writing, check out my website (**kmalady.com**). You can find other fun information there about my other projects, like *The Ascend Trials* (a romantic YA portal fantasy all about subverting tropes), *Threads of Fate* (an NA romantic fantasy series adapted from greek myths), and more!

Sneak Peek of Book 2

"Are you Emily Lane?" The voice comes from a guy slouched in a corner booth, his hood pulled low over his eyes, which are fixed on me with an intensity that suggests he's not here for the free Wi-Fi.

"Depends who's asking," I say with a biting smile. I meander beside his booth, my professional curiosity piqued despite the alarm bells chiming in my brain. At least this might give me a chance to test out my newly earned self-defense moves.

He pulls down his hood, revealing tan skin and chiseled features capped by wavy brown hair. He's built like an unsinkable battleship, with broad shoulders and a powerful frame. A faint scar cuts across his left cheek, while a dark tattoo peeks from beneath his collar.

"Rhett Baxter," he says, thrusting out a hand that looks strong enough to crush walnuts... or skulls. "Dani—Danielle Greene sent me. She said you might be able to help... someone like me."

I take a bracing sip of my latte. "Officer Greene?"

My ally who hides her lupine identity from most, but cheers loudest for my advocacy in the paranormal world.

The surprise must be written all over my face because he nods, a hint of a smile dancing across his rugged features. "Yes, she believed you could help with a... situation."

I swiftly fish out the rose-tinted glasses from my bag, a gift from a vampire to pierce through certain glamours and unearth the secrets paranormals wish to keep hidden. Think 3D glasses, but instead of another dimension, they reveal another layer of our own. Through the lenses, I don't just see Rhett Baxter, I see him in his paranormal form. His appearance morphs and twists into something primal and fierce—a creature with the body of a wolf but the visage of a half-human beast, sporting an elongated snout and baring gleaming teeth. Thick fur blankets his form, a tapestry of grays and blacks. His once-piercing blue eyes now glow a fiery yellow. The glasses reveal his true form: a werewolf.

PICK UP A COPY OF COVENS AND CURSES TO READ ON.

www.ingramcontent.com/pod-product-compliance
Lightning Source LLC
Chambersburg PA
CBHW061649190726
48289CB00006B/1804